PENGUIN BOOKS
THE CHILDREN OF DESTRUCTION

Kuber Kaushik was raised on a steady diet of Asimov, Tolkien and Pratchett, and his love for the written word has only grown stronger over time. In the last decade and a half, he has been a blogger, copywriter, content writer, script writer, screenwriter and novelist.

The first feature film written by him, *Shadows Fall*, was produced in 2016, and was both screened and has won awards at film festivals in Los Angeles, Panama and Europe. His other works include a number of short films, short stories and even a comic strip chronicling the history of healthcare from 6500 BCE onwards and the insanity therein.

Nowadays, his time is spent tinkering with three other novels, exploring and building new worlds with each story. He currently lives in Delhi and can be found on Twitter @thegingap.

THE
Children OF
Destruction

~

KUBER
KAUSHIK

PENGUIN BOOKS

An imprint of Penguin Random House

PENGUIN BOOKS

USA | Canada | UK | Ireland | Australia
New Zealand | India | South Africa | China | Singapore

Penguin Books is part of the Penguin Random House group of companies
whose addresses can be found at global.penguinrandomhouse.com

Published by Penguin Random House India Pvt. Ltd
4th Floor, Capital Tower 1, MG Road,
Gurugram 122 002, Haryana, India

First published in Penguin Books by Penguin Random House India 2019

ISBN 9780143441151

Typeset in Aldine401 BT by Manipal Digital Systems, Manipal
Printed at Manipal Technologies Limited, India

www.penguin.co.in

This is a legitimate digitally printed version of the book and therefore might not
have certain extra finishing on the cover.

To my sister, Aleya—my first fan, editor and hero.
My eternal gratitude for introducing me to the Discworld.

In the beginning there was the story,
Because the story
Is how we know there was a beginning.
In the end there is a saying,
Because in the end
Sayings are all that are left.
The world that we live in has many roads,
As many as there are stories,
As many as there are stars.
On one such road, both beginning and end
Are a single story,
Starting with a single saying.
It goes:
'There once was a war between Man and God . . .
. . . and God lost.'

—Excerpt from Lillian White's *The World I Left Behind*

Prologue: Rain

A rickety wooden gate shook gently in the breeze, dividing the world neatly into what lay beyond and what lay behind.

It was a grey sort of day, the clouds drizzling intermittently while lazily blocking out the sun. Beyond the rickety wooden gate, the rice fields sounded musically as the rain fell, the water of the skies blending with the water of the earth.

Across the rippling puddles, mortal creatures leapt and danced, croaking, hissing or simply sinking without a word. The water spirits were also awake, dancing between raindrops as they played a thousand different games all at once. They spun around, invisible to mortal eyes, laughing gleefully and maliciously as was their wont.

And behind the rickety wooden gate was a garden.

It was a simple garden. The grass was green and trimmed. The bushes were only slightly overgrown. Other than the occasional wildflower, there was only a single tall willow, tucked away in one corner.

The house behind the garden was similar. Unadorned and unpolished, built of an amalgam of wood, plaster, clay tiles and other materials long obsolete. It was the sort of house as might be inhabited by a man of simple tastes.

There was one exception, though, and that was where the house met the garden. A platform—only a few square metres in size—extended from the house, rising above the grass on short stilts. A neatly tiled roof protected it from the rain, and the edges of the platform were lined with a short, elaborately carved wooden rail. On one side of the platform, a circular stone pit was built into the wood with a metal grille on top. Beneath it was the soft glow of a small fire; on top of the grille rested an ornate kettle.

It wasn't whistling yet, but the man seated next to it was.

He faced the rain-swept garden and, while his whistling resonated with the gentle drizzle, he seemed more absorbed in the surface of the table in front of him. On it was placed a chequered *shogi* board, nine squares by nine squares, with numerous intricately engraved playing tiles placed across it. A game seemed to be in progress, and it was undoubtedly one of those games in which progress could only be measured in decades. The man tapped his fingers on the board, the hollow sound providing a beat to his whistle.

In describing the man, the word 'secretive' would almost certainly be required. There was something shrouded about those sharp, angular features. The way the head tilted forward—always casting a shadow over the eyes—as the loosely flowing dark hair carelessly draped downward, a curious sandiness at the roots betraying the dye. He wore simple clothes. A threadbare sleeveless jacket over a plain bottle-green shirt. The khaki-coloured pants stopped inches short of his ankles, and a closer examination would have revealed the odd thread trailing off at the hem.

Even with the light patter of the rain, and the sound of his whistling, the click of the gate being opened was all too audible. The man raised his eyes from the shogi board and smiled.

The spirit at the gate didn't dance between the raindrops, instead letting them drop merrily on to her conical bamboo *sugegasa*, the 'rice hat' of both elder days and modern fashion.

She was dressed in a reddish kimono printed with white leaves and wore thick wooden slippers. Oddly enough, rather than being marked with mud and grime, they appeared to be quite clean.

'Wrong era for that dress,' commented the man.

She tilted her head to the side, revealing inhumanly green eyes, as a thin rivulet of water poured off the hat. 'My country,' she said, 'I can dress however I want to. Besides, you're one to talk about the wrong era.'

The man looked around at his rustic surroundings in feigned confusion. 'Whatever do you mean?'

'People have expectations, you know,' she said conversationally. 'New York, I believe, would provide the most appropriate venue. Perhaps in a tall penthouse; dressed in a dapper evening suit; surrounded by the beautiful, the rich, the famous and the fraudulent; indulging in every available and unavailable vice alike. That is the expectation.'

'When one is in hiding, living up to people's expectations is really the last thing one should be doing. Besides,' he said, 'heights tend to make me gloomy.'

'Ha!' she laughed shortly and then smiled, almost bitterly. 'Look at you—the great Lord . . .'

The man held up a silencing finger. 'Now now, it isn't polite to name names.'

They both smiled. Names had power. And using them freely could always have unintended consequences.

The kettle started whistling just as the visitor ducked under the tile roof, shedding both sandals and hat to pour herself a cup in a manner befitting an aristocrat of forgotten years, when a good cuppa was saddled with its own baggage of ritual and getting it right was thirsty work. As the rain dripped in the garden, she inhaled the steam and took a careful sip. Jasmine . . . brewed to perfection.

She sighed, and sat across from the man, cradling the cup in one hand. 'Good tea,' she remarked. 'There's nothing like grabbing a quiet cup before things get really hectic. Of course, in cities these days . . .' She shook her head. 'The modern world is all well and good, but somewhere along the way, they forgot how to make tea properly.'

'Mortal memories,' said the man with a shrug. 'They forget, we remember. At least, this way, someone does.'

She took another long sip. 'If I didn't know better, I would think that being in hiding has made you sentimental.'

'But you *do* know better.'

'But I know better.' She set the tea aside. 'I was quite surprised to hear from you. Not worried I might tell someone where you were?'

'If you had, I would have been disappointed, and *you* would have been . . .'

She arched an amused eyebrow. 'Yes, I imagine the word begins with "d" as well.'

He nodded. 'Besides, you owe me a favour.'

She lowered her eyes to the shogi board, deftly filching a game tile and spinning it between her fingers. 'I suppose that's the nice thing about being you,' she said. 'You can vanish for fifty years, hiding away in a tiny house in the middle of nowhere, and still have an endless list of people who owe you.'

The man held out his hand for the tile. 'It does have its benefits. But tell me, I hear you took on a small inquiry for a certain Lord of Judgement.'

A flick of a painted nail sent the tile arcing across the table and into the man's hand. She shrugged. 'The rumours are everywhere. Everyone's whispering that we have a foothold back into this world. It's hardly surprising that someone wanted to check on one possible cause. And imagine my surprise when

I found that the Arcanus have been stolen from the Vaults of Elysium. That is rather dangerous knowledge to be out in the human world again.'

The man's expression gave away nothing. 'Knowledge,' he said calmly, 'is only as dangerous as its use.'

She narrowed her eyes. 'And then there are other whispers. The *wyr* are starting to flee the underworld in numbers that haven't been seen since the end of the Great War. Your dear friend Abby is reportedly dealing with humans on an unprecedented scale, and the disappearances around the Abyss are rising every day. You know, he'd stop if you just took the time to say hello. I think the poor boy's just feeling a bit neglected. He's really just an old softie under that bitter, murderous, black-hearted outer covering of his.'

'I'm sure he'd be delighted to hear that, but assumptions can be dangerous. Let's play this one traditionally. I tell you what I need you to do, and, for the sake of your obligation to me, you do it.'

She let her mouth twist into a grimace. 'Traditions can be so boring. Still, I guess there's no use in arguing.' She bowed her head mockingly and raised a hand to her breast. 'Your humble servant awaits her orders.'

'I want you to gather them,' said the man quietly.

She nodded slowly. 'I have to admit, I was almost hoping that it wouldn't be about this.'

'I would have thought you'd welcome the challenge. Besides, isn't this what your kind always look for? To get in on the bottom floor?'

She shrugged. 'Don't get me wrong. Opportunity is a fine thing. It's just . . .' She bit her lip before continuing. 'I've always been more of a local girl, you know. I mean, just look around you. This is my home. Sure, there are many of us who love this whole "world getting smaller" stuff—but me? I miss the old days.'

'Yes or no?' asked the man, patiently toying with another tile.

'Yes, of course,' she said. 'This is a once-in-a-lifetime moment, and if I can be rid of my obligation to you . . .' She grimaced. 'I've waited centuries for that. Where do you want me to start?'

'Things have been moving about, in this last decade of ours,' he said ruminatively. 'If I were to speak like a master manipulator scheming or plotting over some kind of strategy game . . .' They both looked pointedly at the shogi board. 'Then I would say that most of the players have been on the board for some time now, but some pieces . . .' He dropped the tile delicately on the board. 'Have yet to be placed.'

She gave him a curious look. 'You mean the Dreamer that everyone's been gossiping about?'

'Not everyone, I hope.'

'No. Not everyone. But Kali is rumoured to have taken an unhealthy interest in this one.'

'I'm aware—is that a problem?'

She considered the question, and then shook her head. 'No. Our "piece" hasn't awakened yet, and that means no one has an *exact* location. The rest is just a matter of being at the right place at the right time, which is something that I excel at.'

The man got to his feet. The rain outside was slowing down for an undoubtedly brief intermission. He walked over to the kettle, pouring out a steaming cupful of the fragrant tea.

'One thing puzzles me, though,' said the woman.

He turned to raise a quizzical eyebrow.

'I actually saw the Nepalese boy a while ago, when I was in Avici. Many would say it was a kindness saving him from the snow all those years ago, though I can't say I believe that. What he was learning . . . what he was *becoming* . . .' She looked at the man searchingly. 'The Dreamer, the Disciple, the Vessel, the Hybrid—they will not serve you.'

The man picked up his cup before replying. 'Do not forget that they are still children,' he said, 'and have much to learn about this world of ours. Personally, I couldn't care less if they never learnt of my existence, so long as they play their part in this cosmic game. Make no mistake, Trickster—one way or another, I will save *my* kingdom.'

The man took a sip and then smiled, his own inhuman eyes glittering with a darkness as ancient as human civilization itself. 'Besides . . . I've always had a soft spot for those who will not serve.'

Down the Rabbit Hole

Alice

Make all the looking-glass and white-rabbit jokes you want to. I've heard them all, and I'm 100 per cent immune to each and every one of them. And sarcasm. That doesn't bug me either.

Not that everyone makes *those* jokes. They generally just go on about the name. I mean, Alice? It isn't the worst name, but when you live in Hong Kong and look 100 per cent native (though genetically only 75 per cent), it becomes some kind of cultural flip-a-switch that divides everyone into these weird little uptight groups. Anything else would have been better—Fang, Lien, Jiao, Wei. Nice, normal, local names. Just like everyone else's.

But my parents just had to make me stand out—Sun Alice. Last name first, in keeping with their own cultural schizophrenia. So that's me, all awkwardly displayed, wishing to hell that the other girls in school (the ones with the normal names) would just shut the hell up. I mean, the other more 'global' kids at least have a local middle name to help them fit in (actually, I think it's a Christian thing, but bringing religion into it doesn't help).

And it really doesn't help that when people talk fast, I can't tell the difference between Cantonese, Suzhounese, Putonghua or even Japanese. That's really disgraceful, but my mind just switches off under the pressure of translation.

All because dear Dad decided to work in California just around the time I was learning to walk and talk, before uprooting the entire family back to Hong Kong. It's all the rents' fault, me feeling like an outsider. Which is still better than a freak.

Of course, I can keep avoiding the subject and keep going with parental blame, naming dysfunction and a whole lot of other stuff, but the truth is I'm just having a really hard time wrapping my head around being a freak.

And if you're wondering what being a freak looks like—it's being out of your mind with fear and panic, lost in a very isolated Hong Kong alleyway, trying to keep from shaking the world apart with every breath while staring into the bright green eyes of a fox stalking its way towards you.

But all that's later in the day.

You see, it started with a dream . . .

<hr>

'What was it about?' asks Dad absently, yawning as he tries to feed Gerry a spoonful of what I can only describe as 'gross yellow muck' (or baby food, if you want to be exact).

It's morning, and Mom's packing away paperwork, muttering to herself and keeping a strict eye on us all so that we finish breakfast on time. She's got two different types of cereal at either end of the table, and there's this complicated arrangement of toast, nuts, snacks and condiments, laid out like some kind of fort.

Mom loves forts (the old kind). Like, once we went on this trip to the back of nowhere and spent the entire time going through dusty ruins. Mom put on her oldest jeans every day and went rummaging through every nook and cranny the tour guide would let us into, coming out grinning even though she looked like she'd been buried back there. I think she was an archaeologist or something in a previous life. She'd make a great Indiana Jones if . . . well, if Indiana Jones were Chinese and a woman.

'I don't know,' I start out. 'It's like there were all these people, except they're not actual people. They're made of glass, moving silently and smiling and talking among themselves, and then I look around and everything's made of this same glass—except that I know it isn't glass.

'It's air. Just threads of air, and the people are made of it as well—but I'm not. I'm walking on the air. Not flying, just walking on solid platforms of air. And somehow or the other, they all look at me, and I keep getting more and more nervous as I keep walking. Strolling through a city made of glass, of air, of little dust particles trapped in between. And then there's this roaring sound, like thunder, except more . . . alive, and then . . .' I trail off. I can't quite describe what happened next.

'Don't worry your head about it,' he says, looking really satisfied that he managed to get Gerry to take a bite. 'Next time just close your window properly before going to sleep. It was probably a breeze or something. Or maybe a leftover science lesson.'

I mean, could there be a more classic dismissal of a mysterious, foreboding dream? I should have turned around, locked myself in my room and stayed there for the rest of my life . . . but since that would have been slightly crazy, I didn't.

People really shouldn't worry so much about *slightly* crazy. Not when the real thing's lurking just around the corner.

The day continues with packed lunches, goodbye pecks on the cheek from Mom and Dad dropping me off on his way to work. (He's a supervisor or something at some embassy or the other. I keep switching off when he talks about his job.)

Then begins act two. School life.

School life is not fun for me. Ninety per cent of the girls at school don't know who I am (which suits me fine); 9 per cent don't like me (I can live with that); and 0.9 per cent hate my guts and want me completely and totally dead. And I mean that literally and not in the girly, bitchy way that I could probably deal with. The remaining 0.1 per cent is divided into friends and whatnots.

Now this doesn't sound so bad if you're taking note of the fact that I only divided the percentages of *girls*. But wait . . . it gets better—it's an all-girls school.

I hate my life. Even without all the weirdness, I'd hate my life. My basic strategy at school is to avoid any and all eye contact until I meet up with Lin. For want of a slightly better word or phrase, she's my best friend and a 100 per cent, grade A wannabe. But not a freak.

So I end up telling Lin about my dream, and she gets all wide-eyed and amazed (I think she wants to be an astrologist or something) and says, 'It's probably about suffocating . . . Your life as it stands is slowly stifling you!'

My response: 'No, duh! What else you got?'

Lin has issues with sarcasm. She gets all annoyed, and the dream interpretation comes to an abrupt halt. Anyway, we already have enough to worry about, with our lives being in imminent mortal danger, courtesy of a small . . . um . . . disagreement with a very dangerous classmate of ours.

It goes back a couple of days, which was when the homicidal levels of hatred for me started building up and we completely moved past the usual bitchiness—and I'm saying 'we' because Lin is also neck-deep in this little problem. (I'd actually like to blame it all on her, but she is—was—my friend, and you don't go around blaming friends. Not when you don't have very many.)

It was just before lunch, and we were doing what we shouldn't: bunking class. Lin was talking about some movie that I've never watched. Some Italian thing. It's really weird how obsessive she is about foreign-language films. I guess it's like a wannabe subcategory or something like that.

'It had this whole surrealist undercurrent going on. It was just amazing! I'll burn you a copy.'

'Uh-huh,' I replied, thinking wistfully of the stacks of pirated foreign films that I'm never going to watch.

We were going by the standard class-skipping route. All neatly mapped out and handed down through generations, even if the school's only been around for maybe a decade. It ducks past the art room (no one's been there since imperial times) and then down two flights of stairs to the sub-basement, where all the really neat monsters go to hang out. And somewhere along that route, my hearing (which has always been great but gets me into lots of trouble) picked up the harsh, grating voice of Miss Cheng Daiyu.

Cheng Daiyu is one of the seniors and probably the most feared girl in the entire school, though you wouldn't know it to look at her. She's a slightly plain sort, and thin as a rail, but everyone knows that her dad's this enforcer-type chap for the Sun Yee On (that's the local triad gang) . . . and no one's going to mess with something like that.

So I pointed out the presence of Her Evilness to Lin, and—here's where it becomes her fault—she suggested we go and listen to what they're up to. As everyone knows, this is never a good idea.

'Bad idea,' I whispered to her, but it was only a half-hearted objection. This shows my remarkable presence of mind, but not so much strength of character, if we're going in for personality profiles.

She ignored it and had this evil little grin as she pulled me along the wall, and though I'm trying like anything not to hear anything, I just can't help it at this point. Yep—we eavesdropped.

No major info, no obscene boy–girl talk, no mob secrets from Cheng and barely anything of interest. They'd just got their hands on an exam that was going to be sprung on us all in a day's time, and they were happily discussing solutions in the most boring way. Can you see where this is heading?

No?

They got caught the next day. Actually, we got caught listening first, and after death threats, mocking jokes and taunts, we got sent on our way before Lin could even muster up a good witch's curse (she likes curses, even if they never work). And after that, Her Highness Daiyu and her sycophantic little posse got caught cheating.

Do they think it's because they all gave the same answers on the test? Answered in the same way and even got the exact same scores? No, of course not—because that would involve them using their own stupid brain cells! Instead they assumed that Lin and I had ratted them out.

Which leads me to lunchtime today and the impending mortal danger we're facing. In the school cafeteria, no less.

Have you watched *Prison Break*? I only watched, like, the first half of one season before the pirated DVD gave out and tried to do weird, illegal things to my computer. Anyway, from what I remember, the tensest moments were almost always the lunch scenes. All those macho men hanging around their cutlery and trays, their eyes darting all over the place. It's like they're all just waiting to stab something.

That's kind of what it's like in my school. This feeling of complete and total sorority, just blanketing everyone in a sense of loving harmony.

In case you missed it, I'm being *really* sarcastic.

The reason behind this cut-throat attitude is that there aren't any teachers around in the cafeteria, and we're generally left to the supervision of the lunch staff. And while they do make a mean teriyaki chicken, they're not very good at maintaining discipline. Actually, scratch that—they're really *bad* at maintaining discipline.

So lunchtime is always a step away from being a free-for-all, but since we all try to be polite little private school girls, it rarely leads to violence. Unless Daiyu gets her way, which was just about to happen.

Now, normally most grudges get settled with bad rumours, disgusting pranks and a promotion to the designation of local plague-carrier; but there are exceptions to every rule, and the reason we were so—shall we say, unnerved—was because Daiyu was known for being that exception.

Last year, Gabriela, a transfer student from Singapore, talked down to Miss Mafia Daughter, assuming that since she was the senior, this would fit right in with the older-versus-younger bullying order of almost every school.

There was a lunchroom 'incident' the day after that. Gabriela went home to Singapore missing her two front teeth, and, in a really suspicious turn of events, not a soul saw the actual fight happen. As one of those unseeing souls, I was really worried about my teeth. They're nice teeth—they don't stick out, and I never get cavities. I like my teeth.

At 1.17 p.m. we try and make a break for it. Lin gulps nervously and does her best to look absolutely casual, but I'm very ashamed to say that she only ends up looking like me— scared absolutely shitless. Seriously, mice probably have more quiet dignity when faced with an angry tiger than we did then— trays in hand, moving in a slow, zombielike lurch to the bin and tray-rack nearest to the door.

We're three metres from the bin when we run into Fang. Fang is—to put it politely—a big girl. Not so politely—she's an ogre who should be locked away from the rest of human society until the very end of time and only let out then because we're going to need savages like her to fight all the demons and ghosts that rise up on doomsday.

She's also Daiyu's second-best friend.

Daiyu's best friend, Heong, is right behind us—and here's a girl that makes that psycho Japanese chick from *Kill Bill* (what was her name? I can never remember her name) look like a geisha doll with tiny, inconsequential emotional issues.

Lin squeaks—I kid you not. A little gasp of air rushes out of her throat as she tries to stifle it and it comes out so unbelievably mouse-like that if I were scared of mice I'd be searching for a chair to stand on. I actually really like mice, but that isn't the point. It was a bona fide scared little squeak, and if I wasn't trying like mad not to whimper, I would have laughed out loud, resulting in the complete and total dissolution of my only lasting friendship in the fifteen years of my very confused life. So I guess it was a good thing that I was totally ready to jump out of my skin.

Faced with Fang, we did what any two not particularly big-built fifteen-year-olds would have done. We stepped back.

At which point Heong puts her hand on Lin's shoulder, causing her to jump, emit another, even more high-pitched, squeak and drop her lunch tray. It was then that, in the tradition of Bullies 'R' Us, Fang took two steps forward to our one step back and, with a hand that I'd just have to call very meaty-looking, pushed down on my innocent tray, sending it cascading to the floor along with a slight spill of over-salted mayo.

That's when the freak thing kicks in.

Whenever you recall a story, you always want to be able to say that time had suddenly crawled to a treacle-like standstill just so that now you can describe each and every little detail in enough depth to make your essay-writing teachers stand tall with pride and say, 'I taught her how to do that.'

I've never been great at essays.

Basically, I duck, and as Fang steps forward, all that fear and anxiety makes it hard to breathe and before I know it, there's this *rushing* sensation, followed by something like a thunderclap overhead.

What follows is complete pandemonium—or if you don't want to get into SAT words with all their baggage, complete chaos. And I know chaos. Chaos is Monday morning with Gerry crying, Dad searching for long-lost paperwork, Mom desperately trying to be in five places at once and me scribbling over spilled cereal just how much x is equal to and why, in the grand scheme of things, history is important. Now fast-forward that, multiply it by a random number and then compress it into half-a-minute's worth of existence.

That's chaos.

When I look up, both the ogre and the psycho chick are flat on their backs, Lin is pinned to the nearest wall with her eyes really wide and half the school is crouched in their seats, with anything smaller than a full lunch tray having been tossed to the winds. That includes food, so you can imagine the mess.

Oh . . . and Daiyu has apple pie pasted down the front of what was her clean white shirt.

Yep, I'm definitely a freak. A freak who can apparently create small, localized tornadoes in self-defence—but still a freak. On the plus side, it doesn't look like I'm going to live long enough to worry about it.

In the aftermath of the chaos, there's this little window of silent disbelief, and before the shock wears off, Lin grabs my hand, pulls me out of the cafeteria and into the nearest hallway and doesn't stop until we're all the way up on the school rooftop—a bright, open space that most people avoid like the plague since an unfortunate . . . um . . . *accident*.

If Lin was nervous or scared before, now she's gone all the way to total breakdown, and she's taking it all out on me and, though I'll admit part of this might have been my fault, she shows absolutely no consideration for the fact that I'm freaking out. Best friends are like that sometimes.

'What did you do?' she starts in this shrill tone that speaks volumes about the raw nerves underneath. It's not the best kind of sound.

'I didn't do anything!' I reply desperately. I've always thought I'll be great at debating as long as I don't have to actually justify anything I'm saying.

At this she points a finger at me, which is pretty much the highest physical insult short of a bitch-slap. Trust me, the finger is *quivering*. 'You did something! I was watching and when you ducked, you had these colours and stuff flowing down your arms, and next thing I know, the air feels thin and there's this bluish orb floating above you, like some weird anime energy sphere!'

'And then—BOOM!' she finishes sharply, confirming the worst of my fears.

'Boom?' is my timid reply.

She shakes her head and repeats, 'BOOM!'

I step back and try to keep my voice from shaking. 'I'm telling you, I don't know what happened!'

'What did you do??' she starts again, this time with one less question mark, so I'm guessing she's started to calm down.

'Lin, I honestly have no idea what happened in there,' I say.

'Are you possessed?' she asks.

I have no idea what kind of answer she expects, so you can't blame me for giving her a blank look. 'Yes, I am the host of the demon Xyzvyk—and I will now have to eat your brain.'

She actually backs away at this. Like I said, she doesn't get sarcasm.

'Joking,' I say by way of apology, though, to be fair, I'm not discounting the possibility of demonic possession.

She glares. 'Not funny.'

You'd think I'd get credit for wisecracking in the face of a very possible demonic possession, but no . . . people can be so touchy.

Sighing heavily, I go to the edge of the roof. They've installed this chain-link fence all around and, while it does ruin the view, there's nothing like a chain-link fence for fitting your fingers through and just hanging on.

'It's happening again . . .' says Lin worriedly, interrupting my metaphorical (and actual) hanging-on.

I turn around, ready to snap, with a frustrated 'What?' but reality decides to burst my frustrated diva bubble by allowing me to *feel* the full and total sensation of what's happening to me this time. You know how people talk about their skin crawling, or getting pins and needles and stuff like that? Well, it's kinda like my skin didn't realize those were metaphors and then decided to dunk itself in buckets of bright blue, yellow and green paint.

'This is what happened earlier?' I ask quite calmly, too freaked out to even freak out properly.

'Uh-huh,' she replies faintly, her voice being faint by virtue of her having retreated all the way to the roof door, ready to duck and run at a moment's notice. I could see why she would. Being a best friend is all well and good, but being confronted with weird forces twice in one lunch break is a bit much.

I'm convinced it's emotional stress that's causing this, which is really ironic because right now what's causing emotional stress is—this! But since I'm actually aware of what's happening this time around, I figure I should make the most of it and take it all

11

in before calmly and logically moving on to my next step. So I calmly, logically do one quick 360 degrees on the roof and then decide (also calmly and logically) to scream.

In hindsight, that was probably a huge mistake. It was a really good thing that I was facing away from Lin, because even though she was behind the door, I didn't peg her position as safe.

Yes, I know I'm drawing it out all suspenseful like, but a little latitude, please—this is all very emotionally scarring.

Sigh . . . There wasn't some bright little blue orb this time around. Instead it was like one of those moments on a still day in the middle of an open field and then, as you're happily gazing at the sky, you take one innocent step back just as a gale-force wind slams into you from the opposite direction.

It blew the chain-link fence off the roof. I don't think a combination of plastic explosives, shaped charges and scored wire links (special forces documentary—don't ask) could have done a cleaner or more explosive job. The unfortunate part of this was that Miss Zhuge, our PE teacher, was walking the grounds at that moment and, while she is a sturdily built woman, being the target of a falling chain-link fence is enough to put a dent in even the sturdiest of souls.

The *most* unfortunate part of this is me—still being calm and logical—looking over the side of the roof to find all this out, only to have everyone who isn't pinned down by a fallen fence whispering and pointing up at me. And trust me, what they were *not* saying was 'Oh, thank God that girl on the roof is all right.' So I did what any sensible, calm and logical girl would do in a situation like this.

Yep, I ran.

Some eight hours later, and I'm lost somewhere in the city, cold, hungry and really, really scared.

I'm 300 per cent certain that the rents are worried out of their minds, 100 per cent sure that Lin's wondering what happened to me and about 1 per cent sure that it's all going to work out fine. That's a whole lot of percentages for someone with a barely passing average in maths.

But even if it wasn't for the whole school drama and the inevitable Daiyu-endorsed triad hit, I still can't go home.

You see, the whole causing-explosions-in-mid-air thing? I really can't control it any more.

I feel like I've been running for days, all the while leaving behind a set of concussed casualties, including a set of dustbins, a very vicious stray cat—which, I'm not sorry to say, got blown into a tree—and a group of Japanese tourists, whose own blurry camerawork of being knocked over will undoubtedly be on YouTube any time now.

And somewhere along the way, I start noticing that there's a fox following me. Anyway, it was just there on that list of stressful things, but not really high-priority: causing massive air-current fluctuations, seeing foxes, being sure that something from lunch wasn't still stuck in my nice teeth . . . oh, and avoiding going home.

Reasons for not going home include the fact that I might just take out entire walls, not to mention family members; the possibility of the police looking for me; or having to tell my mom that 'Something weird is happening to me, and no—it's not *that*. We had that conversation two years ago, remember?'

Basically, when you realize that you're a ticking time bomb of an almost literal kind and you have a normal 'I don't want to be shot down by the police or get locked up for eternity' kind of perspective, you kind of try to avoid other people.

Which would be nice and easy if this wasn't Hong Kong. There are places that are more crowded, but I've never been to them; so for me, Hong Kong is the most crowded place on the entire planet. My plan (okay, my desperate idea) was to get out of the whole central area and head for the hills, where you have fewer people. Unfortunately, however, I had to go twist my ankle while scurrying down what I will now testify to be the loneliest alley in all of the city.

It's dark, damp, dingy and a whole bunch of other 'd's. It's the kind of alley where no self-respecting mugger would find himself, much less a panicked teenage girl; but when you're panicking, a sense of direction is suddenly not so much of a priority. Midway through, I realize exactly where I am, which triggers what I'm just gonna refer to as a 'panic attack' ('cause saying that you're going supernaturally critical just seems all kinds of tacky). The whole skin-turning-into-a-multitude-of-flowing-colours deal isn't really that prominent any more. Now it's more like, *Stop, breathe in, breathe out, watch the world rattle.*

I've always been objective about things. Which means I am totally qualified to watch my entire existence go to pieces and still be rational about it. So I can tell myself, very rationally, that when you've had a day when you're not exactly sure of what you are . . . it is very okay to curl up against a wall and try to make sense of things while crying. Quiet tears, of course. Sobbing is out of the question.

And there's a fox staring at me. Have I mentioned the fox?

How do I know it's a fox? Well, I'm thinking that the orange fur, white underbelly, pointed snout and ears, bushy tail and smaller-than-a-wolf size would be the telltale signs, but what do I know?

This is the point when I decide that the world really doesn't make *any* sense, that I've just been asleep since morning, or that someone's slipped me some weird halluci . . . hallocin . . . you know what I'm trying to say.

So I wipe my eyes, give the fox a terrified smile as it slinks its way down the alley and wave in what I hope is a 'I know this is all a dream, but please don't attack me' kind of manner.

And then it says, 'Don't scream.'

Yep. This is definitely, 100 per cent, genuinely all a dream.

So I scream. I scream loudly.

I don't wake up.

Blind Justice

The Snowman is coming!

The guest house shook in the blizzard, the night wind howling with vengeance and death, like the thin taste of tin, in the air. In the cold night, Chun fingered the old revolver. He'd taken it out of storage, making sure that it worked. He'd never missed with it. But would a gun be of any use?

The old house that had been their home, their fortress, was now their jail. Awaiting execution, one and all, the last remnants of the Paschid militants. They had never been many, little more than one of dozens of Kathmandu's gangs, vying for control of Nepal's underworld. Jhakri had brought them together, decades ago. And when he had left, they had gone their separate ways, left only with memories of the horrors they had inflicted on the world.

And today those horrors were coming back. In the last few months, many had already died. The survivors told fanciful stories. Of men being flung through the air like pebbles and ripped apart like paper. They spoke of a demon. They spoke of the Snowman. They spoke of the boy.

'We have to fight!' Inja had pleaded, fear dancing in his eyes. 'We have to take a stand, or he will kill us all.'

So they had decided to gather, and to fight. Lucky Zhao comforted his brothers-in-arms and told them not to worry. He had a plan.

Lucky Zhao was the first to die. The plan died with him. A broken stick, coming from nowhere, struck him through the heart. Blood poured out of the corners of his mouth, thin streams that dripped, drying slowly, until it looked like he'd died with a smile on his face.

It was a demon, they whispered among themselves, but Chun knew the truth. *They* were the demons. It was an angel coming for them, with death written on his hands, on his marked eyes.

The house shook. Boulders crashing against its walls, breaking through the thinner ones to pin the unprepared against the inner layers of concrete. Under the weight of stones that were no bigger than human heads, bones snapped and were mashed into pulp to the accompaniment of screams. The snow howled into those broken walls, relentless as it filled the house, draining the artificial heat and freezing hearts that beat entire marathons of the purest terror.

'The demon comes!' they screamed in their native tongues.

Chun wondered if Lucky Zhao even had a proper plan. The very foundation of the house quivered. Maybe his plan had been to die quickly. If so, he'd succeeded.

Chun locked the door of the inner room. The thin mattress scattered sideways against the wall, and Palam's collection of stolen *Playboys* scattered on the chest of drawers. He leaned back, his hands starting to tremble. *A man, a boy can be killed with a gun. That's how you deal with humans. With angels, fill them with bullets until they come crashing back to earth.*

He shivered as another scream echoed. An animal howled as his rage turned to fear, which turned to pain. And then silence. Death.

Two Ton rushed through the door, his swift bulk shaking in the dim light. 'The snow . . .' he said, horror in his voice. 'Look at it! Look at it, and tell me that he is no demon!'

With slow, dread-laden steps, Chun stepped out to the balcony, looking through the storm, at the white ground . . . no longer white.

'He makes the earth bleed,' Chun whispered and felt that single tear start to fall. He clenched his hand ever tighter around the gun. Still just a boy. A human being. He could be killed.

Two Ton, having followed him out, knelt tiredly on the wet balcony, his large, heavy knees sinking in the melting snow. 'He writes in the snow. He writes our death in the snow.'

The words. Anyone could see them as words, but Two Ton—illiterate as he was—wasn't able to read them. Chun could read them, though, stained in their crimson glory, burning ever brighter against the falling white snow. The message written in clear English was part of the symphony of fear.

'Justice is blind,' he whispered, despair making the world move just that bit slower. He watched each individual snowflake fall, shuddering in the wind, bouncing away and colliding with other flakes. He could no longer hear any screams, because there were none to be heard. There was only him and Two Ton.

The silence settled over them both, and Chun watched as Two Ton let out a long whimper, his ever-courageous heart failing in the face of a demon. He watched his companion turn and run into the house, only to stop just inside the doorway.

'Tun,' Chun called, his voice slow and echoing in his own mind, but his friend did not move. Gun raised, he started towards him, a single step, and time slowed even further. A moment of eternity, a foot outstretched, his gun ready, and Two Ton as still as water.

Chun watched helplessly as time moved forward a fragment at a time and heard the beginnings of Two Ton's helpless scream as invisible hands raised him in the air and, with power greater than Chun had ever seen, lifted him through the ceiling. The wood splintered and clay tiles shattered, and a crushing wet sound was all that Chun heard. Two Ton was dead, snatched through the ceiling by the demon.

He is a boy! Chun shouted at himself as he stumbled, dashing his knees through thick cloth against the stone of the balcony. *I have to remember that he is just a boy.*

And then, from the hole through which his poor dead friend had exited, *he* arrived.

Like an angel with arms outstretched, he fell. A graceful jump that was the landing of a predator, sleek of coat and sharp of tooth. No smile marking the lips that were set in a firm, unbroken line. Promising a death planned to perfection. A death as deserved as only blood vengeance could be. The boy. The demon.

He had grown tall. Not the height of a man, but tall for a boy. His hair dark, his frame skeletal and his eyes . . . marked. Marked with two bloody scars that marred the perfection of blank, unseeing eyes.

'Justice is blind,' whispered Chun once again. Without further thought, and the barest of movements, he looked down the barrel of the gun at the blinded youth.

And he fired.

Genesis

Eden was asleep.

The captain of the Black Rangers looked at the compound through his binoculars. In the darkness, the small oasis of buildings and gardens blended into the surrounding foothills. The Afghan night air embraced it all in a deep chill.

There were only a few sentries visible. Secrecy had kept Eden safe. So many false leads—abandoned villages and factories. Mountain warrens laid with countless traps. A thousand different local politicians paid to look the other way. And the masking technology—miles ahead of anything that should have been found in this corner of the world.

The captain had seen all the intelligence. His current employers had spent more than a decade trying to uncover this one elusive location. Ever since the Kharsans had defected from their ranks, stealing the technology that then transformed Eden into such a threat and hiding it away in this corner of a war-torn country.

He checked the time. Two minutes till the air strike. A helicopter would have been more useful, but the surrounding terrain had made that impractical. He looked around. Everyone was in position. The captain took a deep breath, hoping for no surprises. He hadn't told the Rangers everything. They wouldn't have believed him. They had sufficient clearance, but complete knowledge would have been distracting. There were too many unknowns and not enough evidence. Even he didn't know whether their target landed in the realm of the supernatural or science fiction.

Still, he trusted their skills. That would have to be enough.

He could hear the planes approaching. They'd take out the guard towers and then be on their way, leaving it to the Rangers to clean up what was left. He raised a fist and gave the signal to advance.

~

Adam awoke in what most people would call darkness. For him, though, there was more than enough light coming in from the crack under the door. So in the darkness that wasn't darkness, he awoke, but then again, it wasn't really waking either.

The door was locked as usual, but the rumbling sounds outside tugged at his curiosity. Curiosity was a failing, he'd been told, but he'd never understood why. Curiosity was how people learnt, even if it was frowned upon.

As far as the rules went, he should have just ignored the sounds and closed his eyes again for the length of the night. That was not what he did.

The metal of the lock felt cold under his small hand. He never told them that he'd stayed out of respect. They might have suspected it, but he never told them, and it wasn't their place to ask. He could simply shatter the lock; but there were more efficient ways.

He braced his bare feet on the ground and began to push, gently, against the metal square of the lock. Just as it started to bend outwards, he heard the lock click. He moved back as the door opened and found himself staring up at a face that he'd only seen twice before in his life.

The gangly boy stepped into the gloom, his pupils widening until he could see the small figure that hadn't bothered to lower his outstretched arm.

'*Come with me,*' the boy said in Farsi, his voice thick with tension as the explosions drew nearer.

'*Yes, big brother,*' said Adam calmly, and followed him out into the world.

~

The first part of the assault was executed with textbook efficiency. The watchtowers had been destroyed, and the squads had gone in from multiple angles, taking out all resistance. Eden's main defence had been their secrecy, and without that, they were little more than fools with obsolete guns, guarding stolen technology.

In less than ten minutes, the main building was silent and dark. They'd sabotaged the power generators. The captain led his squad in, staring out at the world through wide goggles that painted every edge in sharp monochrome. In that surreal night-vision world, the smoke from gas grenades and the spent shotgun shells rose up and twisted into disturbing shapes.

The captain suppressed a shiver. The gunfire outside had gone quiet, which meant the second division had finished their run. The brave, suicidal ones were all dead now, leaving only those, huddled in the dark, waiting for ambush or execution. He didn't like to think about that. Better to just focus on the objective.

Walking slowly, he made sure that he didn't relax or that any of his troops didn't let down their guard either. They proceeded in a scattered file, so as not to be wiped out by a single surprise attack, with one out of every three doing nothing but scanning for traps, tripwires and infrared signatures. Only once they'd given the all-clear did the Black Rangers move on to the next corridor. It took them a full half hour to scout the entire upper building, and only then did they turn their attention to the basement levels.

The door to the basement was open, leading down into an inky blankness that even the light amplification of his goggles was having a hard time penetrating. He signalled, ordering two guards to be left outside the door and two guards at the bottom of the stairs.

In the darkness, the sound of his own breath was deafening. Shadows threatened to shift as their footsteps slid silently forward. The unit scout, loaded as he was with every conceivable type of surveillance gear, was the first to notice something unusual. He raised his hand to stop them all and pointed at the T-shaped junction ahead of them. He stood still for a moment, looking at his instruments. Finally he shrugged and shook the portable scanner in the age-old gesture meaning 'Either this thing's busted, or there's something really unexpected waiting around the corner.' The captain was almost certain that it was the latter.

Breaking open a light stick, he tossed it around one end of the T, letting the scout use one of his many gadgets to peek around the corner. The display came up blank. Preparing to repeat the procedure around the other corner, the captain frowned as something moved just at the edge of his sight. He spun around, ready to call out a warning.

When the captain woke up, he was pleasantly surprised that it wasn't in hell. His mask and goggles had been knocked astray, so the darkness around was basically all he could see. What he could hear was a chorus of assorted grunts, which he put down to the waking pains of his fellow Rangers. A quick check revealed no broken bones or unusual bruises. The only thing out of place was a slight soreness at the base of his skull. A sensation that he'd only felt years ago while in training. A perfectly executed nerve strike. Their target?

It was the work of another dozen seconds to straighten his night-vision goggles. Looking around confirmed that it was his soldiers doing all the groaning and grunting as they fumbled back to awareness.

He broke the silence. 'Did anyone see what the hell happened?'

They hadn't. Only one Ranger at the top of the stairs had been conscious through the whole thing. He just sat there in the dark, leaning against the wall, the dismembered remains of his M4 resting in his lap.

'I don't understand it, Captain,' said the Ranger disconsolately. 'Trevain was out before I even knew something was going on, and then this . . . this kid appeared. He was moving like a snake or something, just flashing out of sight, and then before I know it, he's in front of me, and I'm pulling the trigger, thinking I'm going to regret it in the morning, but I figured I'd at least be alive in the morning . . . I mean, we all know these guys ain't above using kids in their bloody—'

'Sergeant, focus,' said the captain, trying to contain his own irritation.

'Sorry, sir. So I pull the trigger, but by then he's already taken apart the whole damn rifle! And even with night vision, I can see that this kid—couldn't have been more than eleven or twelve— he's smiling! Then I'm reaching for my secondary weapon, but he's got to that as well. I don't understand how anyone could move that fast, sir. It was just surreal.'

'What happened then?'

'He pushed me, sir.'

'He *what?*'

'Pushed me, sir,' replied the man with more than a hint of embarrassment. 'Stuck out his hand and knocked me down like a bowling pin. Felt like my ribs were going in or something. Thought he was going to kill me, but then the other one arrived.'

'The other one?'

'Yes, sir—didn't get a look at him, though. He just rushed past, grabbing the kid by the shoulder, and then poof—they were gone.'

'Just to clarify,' ventured the captain cautiously, 'by "poof, they were gone," do you mean they went around the corner and then probably snuck their way out from under all our noses, or do you mean a puff of smoke and instant teleportation?'

'Sir?'

'Just answer the question.'

'Uh . . . the former, sir.'

Well, there was at least that.

The compound was secure and the survivors had been secured for transport and interrogation. Given the secrecy of the mission, breaking radio silence was out of the question. He'd have to wait for the debriefing to inform his superiors that the raid on Eden had gone *almost* exactly according to plan. Unfortunately, that sneaky little 'almost' meant that it had failed in the part that mattered the most.

At times like this, he did not enjoy the honour of being captain of the Black Rangers.

Flight from Eden

Kharsan

My name, Khadim, means 'servant of God'. I've never liked it. Everyone actually calls me Kharsan, though. That's my last name, and I don't know what it means.

Very few people believe me when I tell them I was born in the hills of Afghanistan, which is just as well because I was actually born a stone's throw from Heathrow Airport. My *father* was born in the hills of Afghanistan, but that didn't stop him from emigrating to the West at a young age. My mother—as far as I know—was born in London, though her family was originally from the Philippines. If I were to dwell on memories, I would say that I remember her as a kind person with many sharp edges.

I don't know much about them, having pieced together what I do know from fragments of memory and stories that their friend E'Cha used to tell me. The story goes that they met at the University of Nottingham, both students of the mysterious science of genetics. And I was born some sixteen years ago. I don't remember much of my time in England. My parents' work as geneticists may have brought them together, but it also tore our lives apart. What I do remember is the secrecy; the whispered conversations. The mysterious calls. The strange equipment that they shipped out piece by piece.

The three of us left England for my father's home country when I was less than five years old, contacting old and very questionable acquaintances. No one would answer my whys, but I have long since grown used to that. There are questions that no one has answers to, and then there are questions that no one will answer. I generally made a habit of asking both.

Most of Afghanistan may be described straight out of any one of a dozen bad war documentaries, but that wasn't where we lived. We lived in Eden. A curious sort of paradise—part scientific outpost, part militant training camp, part residential nuthouse for religious fanatics. In Eden, my parents continued their work, trying to undo some mistake from the past. And about a year after that, my mother died giving birth to my . . . 'brother'. His name is Adam—it means 'Earth'.

The night the soldiers came, all I could think of was keeping a promise. Many make a promise like it at least once in their lives. I don't know how many people actually keep it, and if I'd made the oath to anyone other than my mother, and about any other topic, I would have broken the bloody promise without a second thought. But family is important.

That was probably the only thing that I and the rest of the people in Eden agreed upon, bunch of bloody zealots that they were. And with my mother gone, and my father having disappeared mysteriously in the intervening years, that left me in the unenviable position of actually having to keep my promise.

The night they came, I knew beyond a shadow of a doubt that they had come for him. E'Cha and the others, the scientists, the soldiers . . . they would have fought to their last breath to protect Adam, and I imagine that they did. They would never think of running. These were men who had spent most of their lives running, but here in Eden . . . I think they imagined that they'd never have to run again, even if they would have to fight. But me? I had a promise made to a dead mother—to protect him—and a dark warning delivered from an absent father—that there were many things that he would need protection from.

Sometimes parents are far more trouble than they are worth.

His alert eyes don't blink, and they don't dart from side to side as if looking for danger, but I know that he is a thousand times more aware of his surroundings than I am. A bit disturbing that, but then again, what part of him isn't? In honesty, I know almost nothing about Adam. We have only met twice, and both meetings have been brief. Most of what I know is what E'Cha shared with me. What he *is*, what he's capable of . . . and what he means to the people of Eden. He is human, I was told. Just *more* human than anyone else. That is all I know, and that's hardly enough to get a picture of what kind of person he is. But I do believe he knows every last detail about me.

He hasn't even asked where we're going. Just silently walking alongside, endlessly and tirelessly. I'd swear that the pack on his shoulders is twice as heavy as mine, but he doesn't show any sign of discomfort, even though we've been walking for five hours. I think I find that more disturbing than anything else. In appearance he is, after all, a normal eleven-year-old boy.

It isn't even a proper road. I'm pretty sure those damn soldiers are watching all the proper roads. This is more like a dirt track through a dust country, with a side order of funnily shaped boulders. We're definitely not in Eden any more. The path we're following is from the map that my father left behind. Everything marked out neatly—places to get water, supplies, how to ensure that we wouldn't be tracked by air. All itemized and neatly labelled.

Anyway, at our current pace it's a few days to the nearest town. From there I think we should manage to get something that moves faster than my feet. Though I imagine that if I just pointed Adam in the right direction, he'd probably run there faster than a cheetah that's swallowed a bottle of speed pills.

Even with supplies, the journey isn't an easy one. Though winter's at its peak, there is an unnatural warmth, and the cotton cloth bound around my head doesn't do much to ward off the drying heat. Adam wears a similar cloth, and it annoys the shit out of me, knowing that he doesn't need it. I don't know what his limitations are. I just know that he's more . . . more than me. More than human. But how much more is anyone's guess.

We stop for lunch. All right, I know that he doesn't need lunch, or to stop for that matter, but this is getting bloody ridiculous. We're in this together and, as everyone knows, a team is only as strong as its weakest link!

I'm trying not to have any qualms accepting that I'm the weak one, so if I stop for lunch, *we* stop for lunch.

It is a convenient spot. That's the good thing about this trail—there's no end of wind-worn alcoves in which to hide away from the sun. The entire godforsaken countryside is pockmarked with caves and hidey-holes. No wonder all these stupid foreigners have so much trouble tracking militants in these mountainous regions. It's like herding wild rabbits. Foreigners—ha! My old passport still says Khadim Al-Kharsan, citizen of the United Kingdom. What can I say about foreigners? Probably a lot, but anyway . . .

Adam still doesn't say a word. Politely takes a slip of dried meat from my hand, tears it in half and hands one half back, a small smile painted on his face . . . and he still doesn't say a word.

I offer him the flask, but he waves it away. Probably for the best, though. Even if the wells and springs are marked accurately, water is going to be our most valuable resource. Still, you'd think he'd have a camel's hump or something to show why he didn't need it. He looks so normal . . .

'Is something troubling you, brother?'

Yes, you perceptive little bugger, many things are troubling me. Men with guns and assault helicopters . . . and God knows how many satellite cameras are scouring the land for us while we're happily plodding along on foot into a viper's nest that almost no one comes out of. 'It's nothing,' I say instead. Since there's no one around to overhear us, it's easier to speak in English.

He opens his mouth—no doubt to tell me that he knows I'm lying—but a quick glare stops him. I might not be able to run like a cheetah for days without food and water, but, by Allah, I can glare. I chew slowly on a piece of hard biscuit. Iron rations, these are called. You need teeth of iron to chew them, a stomach of iron to digest them and intestines of iron to dispose of them. Having only flesh and blood, I'm not looking forward to the inevitable constipation.

Finally swallowing, I make up my mind that we might as well go over the rules once. Adam is sharp as the sharpest knife, but some things can't be counted on. By the time we get to civilization, I have to know that having Adam around other people won't go phenomenally wrong.

'Let's go over this one more time,' I say, looking him straight in the eye. 'What is rule number one?'

He smiles tightly. I guess this is just a game for him. But then, for him, what isn't?

'Don't kill anyone,' he says.

It's a very scary game.

'Rule number two?'

This is the one that he has trouble with and, sure enough, he hesitates before answering. 'Don't . . . don't ask them if they are infidels?'

'Yes,' I say. 'That isn't a polite question. If people are infidels, they're perfectly within their rights to be infidels. *You* do not need to know.'

Obviously, he disagrees. 'But, brother, I need to know. I have to know what people are.'

'No, you bloody well don't!' I can't help my voice dropping to a growl. 'It's nobody's business but their own. And if you ask that question at the wrong time, you're going to get *me* killed.' I know that nothing is going to happen to him, of course. But where we are heading, I can imagine all sorts of ugly things that can happen to me.

Sighing heavily, I let the growl fade. 'Look, it is probably better if you don't say a thing at all, but in case we get separated— you have to understand, you have to act . . .'

And that's where I run out of words. How do I tell him, 'You have to act *normal*'? What does he know about normal? For that matter, what do I know about normal? My normal is taken straight from books, rumours and the Internet. I might know a thousand different memes, umpteen pop-culture references and what every pornographic actress in the world looks like, but for something as basic as a conversation, I can only refer to what so-called normal people say in books.

'When we get to the town,' I say, 'watch everyone closely. Especially those around the same age as you. Try to act like them.'

He nods. 'Camouflage—we have to blend in.'

'Exactly.' I suppose I should be grateful that his extensive knowledge does include the foundations for subterfuge, but I do wish they'd taught him the more . . . *subtle* aspects of infiltrating a populated area. Then he could give *me* some pointers.

Still, the world is full of strange people, and these outlying parts of Afghanistan are reputed to be stranger than most places. I'm sure they'll forgive a couple more oddities. And if they don't . . . Well, I hope to all the demons in the world that I won't have to ask Adam to break rule number one.

'What's rule number three?'

'Don't talk to strangers, and only speak when spoken to.'

'Rule number four?'

'Pretend that I'm scared around people bigger than me, or if they have a weapon.'

That's going to be a laugh. Even if he's pretending, I can't imagine him scared of anything. Me, on the other hand—the escape from Eden nearly had me soiling my pants, and we didn't even see a single soldier after getting out of the building.

'Rule number five?'

'Don't take anything from anyone, and don't give them anything that they didn't ask for.'

'Rule number six?'

'Blink regularly.'

To underscore that, he blinks long and slow. On him, it's an unnatural movement. Those sharp eyes care not for the dust and grime that affects ordinary people. He sees everything. But he knows so little.

Only a few days to civilization. I hope it is enough.

And then, onward to the Valley of Shadow.

Sigh . . . this cannot end well.

Violets in Shadow

The Voca Arcanus, *the Book of Summons, was once the cornerstone of Santor.*

'Jack had a bone . . .'

'JUMP!'

'Which he kept at home . . .'

'JUMP!'

It was the only Arcanus left in the human world after the Withdrawal. Many an empire was built on its knowledge.

'And whose bone it was . . .'

'JUMP!'

'He'd never tell . . .'

'JUMP!'

When the survivors of Solomon's fall made their way across the ancient roads, all the way to this part of the world, they built the valley— Santor—to protect themselves, and to protect the book.

'Some said it was John's . . .'

'JUMP!'

'Some said it was Tom's . . .'

'JUMP!'

And then I came. I . . . tried to help. It still wasn't enough. It's been eleven years since they stole the book. I've tried to teach you about the consequ—Violetta, are you listening to me?

'And some said it belonged . . .'

'JUMP!'

'To his Uncle Mel.'

'JUMP! JUMP! JUMP! JUMP! JU . . .'

Sitting on the edge of the wall, Vi kicked her legs up and down, scowling at the ragged laces. She wasn't scowling at the raggedness or the shoes (which were equally ragged). Rather she was scowling at the world in general. In particular, she might have been scowling at the other children playing in the yard in front of her, but she'd never give them the satisfaction of admitting to it.

'I'm listening,' she said. 'The book that Father failed to protect. Go on.'

It . . . can wait. They'd let you join in, you know.

'It wouldn't be the same. They all talk and whisper. It becomes all . . . awkward.'

Because of me.

She shook her head decisively, messy hair falling over her eyes. 'No. I've told you, it's because of us.'

They're scared. They're only children.

'Yeah,' she said peevishly. 'And I'm all grown up.'

No, you're different. A different lesson, then. Pay attention. You can learn from this.

She nodded, letting the annoyance on her twelve-year-old face change to concentration. 'Here comes Cask,' she muttered, looking at the children playing. 'At least I'm not him.'

Don't watch the player. Watch the game.

Again, she nodded. She tried to take in every detail of the playing field—a large dusty circle with patches of brown-and-green grass as ragged as her shoes. The rusted see-saws to the side, lined up next to tire swings that swayed gently in the breeze. As a backdrop, the dark, dirty red of the school building loomed, the late afternoon sun reflected in its scratched and occasionally cracked windows.

And in the dying light of the day, the children hopped and skipped, playing their game. Three people at a time and one single rope; moving like a snake—over, around and then across. Jump and duck.

She kept her eyes on the two holding the rope as they started a new rhyme.

'There once was a codger . . .'

SNAP!

The rope flipped through the air, deliberately slashing Cask behind his knees and bringing him down hard. He yelled, but the sound was drowned by laughter that only grew louder as he started to cry.

'Don't be a baby!'

'Don't be a crybaby!'

'I'm next!'

'No, I'm next!'

'Me!'

Why did they do it?

'They always bully Cask,' she started, and then stopped. 'Except when he's not there, and then they pick someone else. They need . . . a target.'

Power only works when others know you have it. But who is the one wielding it?

She tried replaying the seconds in her mind. Then she unsteadily raised her hand and pointed towards a group of three children who stood a little away from the main gathering. Two girls older than Vi, one with auburn hair loose around her shoulders and the other with long plaits framing a dark face; and a boy around the same age, with a permanent half-grin painted on his face.

'Them. It's all or one of them.'

Look closer this time.

She looked closer as another player stepped into the whirling obstacle. She didn't know this one . . . she didn't know a lot of them. She didn't go to school with them. She didn't play with them. She barely talked to them. All she did was watch.

Because she was different.

The song went on, but this time she didn't listen to the words. The key was in the movement, and the rhythm kept boiling until one of the rope wielders glanced over at the watching three. And there . . . right there—the barest narrowing of the eyes.

The rope came around quicker than before, this time getting entangled in the heels of the jumper.

This time her hand wasn't unsteady.

'That one,' she said, pointing straight at the girl with the long plaits. 'I know her—Kava, that's her name.'

As if drawn by those distant words, the plaited girl looked over to where Vi sat, their eyes meeting for a second before Kava looked away, shivering.

She is the one who is most scared of you, Violetta. Do you understand why?

She nodded. 'Because over there, she's the one with power. She's the one with the most to lose.'

True. The power might be hers, but only because she knows the mind of the mob. She can channel that by giving them a focus. A beacon that they can flock towards. And she fears that you burn brighter than she ever will. Now, do you know why she doesn't stand alone?

Vi frowned, trying to work it out. If Shade said there was a reason, there was. It was just a matter of figuring it out. Like a puzzle, or a game . . . her own private game that none of the other kids could play.

'They're . . . protecting her, almost,' she said, rolling the thought around in her head. 'So that even if the others think that she's wrong, they can't think that all three of them are wrong.'

36

Exactly. Shade sounded pleased. *In the games of power, there is strength in numbers. It adds weight as well as deflects criticism. But, remember, there will always be a single light that guides the rest. The nature of the mob demands that—or else chaos will reign.*

Again, she nodded, trying to commit his words to memory. All of this was for a reason—that's what Shade said, and even Seidre, who hated Shade, agreed with him.

'I'm tired of watching,' she said suddenly. 'Let's go for a walk or something.'

All right, said Shade after a pause. *But there is still a lot to learn, and there isn't much time.*

'What do you mean?' she asked as she hopped off the wall, her feet kicking up dust all the way to her ankles.

The consequences of the theft of the Arcanus are now beginning to make themselves known.

Vi frowned, letting her curiosity and dread speak for themselves.

The child of Eden, said Shade finally, *he is coming here. This is where it starts. We will have to leave soon. The Arcanus must be recovered.*

She started walking away from the field slowly, ignoring the fading laughter and screams of the other children. Shade had long implied that she would be the first of the lineage to carry him . . . to carry the Shadow beyond the valley, but she'd always thought it would happen later. When she was older, like Seidre had been when she'd gone on her journey.

'I don't want to leave,' she said sullenly as they walked down the road. The sun sank in front of her and Shade trailed behind.

I know.

There was silence as she walked. In the town, only the children laughed and screamed. Everyone else had been through so much, Vi knew. Shade had told her much of what had happened. And there were the nightmares and the memories.

Now, as evening fell, people huddled deeper into their homes, lighting lamps, away from the darkness of the night. For centuries now, the town had reason to fear that dark.

Shade knew. He had been that reason.

They turned right at the end of the road. Shade was now beside her, drifting seamlessly over the broken cobbles and the overgrown flower beds of the villas.

'If we leave, who's going to take care of the town?' she asked, her voice sounding small in the depths of gloom.

The world changes, Violetta. Even if not for the book, if we don't go, the world will leave this place behind, until all here is as forgotten as the old world. No more than legends and myth—written in the dust.

'You don't tell me about your "old world",' she said, glancing sideways at his shifting shape.

I don't remember much, and you don't need to know, said Shade, his voice quiet but firm on the subject.

She stopped at the second-last house on the road, looking up at the broken windows and the creeping ivy. Mother lived there. Alone, since Vi had gone to live with Seidre. She wondered if she should go in. Just to say hello. Or goodbye.

'How long until we have to go?' she asked.

At least a week. Maybe a bit longer. The road to Santor is not as reliable as it once was.

Time enough, then. She could say her goodbyes later. With a sigh, she started to turn away, but then stopped, looking at Shade directly.

Her shadow was cast across the flower bed; but at the edges, Shade's presence made itself known, thin tendrils of darkness stretching out fluidly. The flowers seemed to shiver and the green weeds were the first to shrivel up. Drying to dead husks, they left only the ageing brown flowers, some small white lilies and three violets, blazing bright in contrast. Then, one by one, the flowers and their stems crumpled, until only a single violet remained.

'I thought I told you not to do that,' she said peevishly.

Sorry, said Shade.

Hellhounds and Vixens

Alice

In my defence, it wasn't a high-pitched, window-shattering kinda scream, and it wasn't hysterical. It was just long, loud and very panicked. It shows just how isolated this alley was that no Good Samaritan charged in to save me. I mean, really, what kind of world is it when it isn't even nine o'clock at night yet and a girl can scream her lungs out in an alley and not be rescued? That's just so very wrong. Okay, so maybe I'm straying from the point, but I *am* panicking. I'm totally allowed to stray!

In contrast to my non-hysterical screaming, the fox just sat down calmly on its butt and looked skyward in a way I'd never seen outside of a Pixar film. I can hear it sigh, for God's sake . . . Foxes aren't supposed to do that!

'Are you quite done?' asks the fox, and I'm kinda shocked to realize that I actually stopped screaming five seconds ago. Hmm, there's a lot to be said for straying, you know.

I can't but help point accusingly at the fox and say, 'You're talking!'

'So are you,' it says patiently. 'You don't see me yelling about it.'

My hallucination has a sense of humour. This is not good. I try arguing with it. 'But you're a fox . . .' Fine, so there's a reason I'm always picked last for the debate team.

'Vixen, actually.'

'What?' I can almost hear that tiny trace of desperate hysteria in my voice.

'As long as we're speaking English, it's good to be precise. You do learn things like gender in school, don't you?'

At first I'm wondering what the hell she's talking about, and then I just realize that I've thought of the fox as a 'she' and that the voice does have a . . . girl-like quality to it. Figuring I'll try out all the angles, I take a deep breath and start saying, 'This is only a dream,' but I only get to 'This is only . . .' before this talking *vixen* bounds closer and interrupts.

'Not to rush you or anything,' she begins, 'but do you believe in life after death?'

As might be obvious, I'm not sure what to make of that. Still, I manage a real eloquent 'Uh . . . wha . . .? I s'pose, um . . . yea . . . no?'

What was the debate team thinking, passing on a gem like me?

'In that case,' she says, and only now do I pick up on this total sense of urgency, 'you might want to follow me.'

And the vi . . . whatever—I'm just going to call her a fox— tilts her head towards the other end of the alley. Which is no longer deserted. While I was hoping for saviours to have heard me scream (while secretly expecting men in white coats holding up a straitjacket), the *things* that were now occupying the mouth of the alley were definitely part of the same reality as the talking fox.

Unless people regularly see black shadowy creatures the size of small bears with wolves' heads and what looks like very spiny armour plating across the back and tail. They also have burning red eyes and are drooling a lot through very wicked-looking teeth, but I figure that part goes without saying, really. And behind them, as if it's a weird trick of the light, I can barely see someone else—all shady and ominous, dressed in black robes.

While my brain does a backflip, my legs have thankfully fully analysed the situation, and realized that even if this is all a really freaky hallucination, getting ripped to shreds in it is not going to do anyone any good.

The . . . I'm thinking 'hellhounds' is appropriate . . .? So the hellhounds lurch forward a couple of steps, and I can definitely smell fire and that rotten-egg smell, but by this time my legs have started propelling me desperately towards the other end of the alley. I'm actually shocked to find that I'm not screaming, but I figure this is just because I forgot how to. The fox leads the way around the corner, my legs follow and the hellhound stampede follows.

Sigh . . . I'd give anything for a nice, normal, tardy white rabbit right about now.

I broke my right arm when I was ten, while trying to climb a tree. I have a small patch of permanently dark skin on the back of my left hand that is the remainder of a hot-tea incident that resulted in a three-year delay in my ability to make my own tea. And I'm almost positive that I've already had my share of sprains, bruises and scrapes that comes with being an active sort of kid.

But I can honestly say that I never knew pain until one of those really freaky hellhound things bit down on my ankle. Burning, piercing, stinging, crushing . . . whatever type of pain you can mention, I can bet that for those five seconds you could have found it at the end of my left leg.

Thankfully, while I'm analysing all this and screaming bloody murder at the same time (which is really kinda great for stress relief, or would have been if not for the excruciating pain), my other leg has the presence of mind to kick out and catch that snappy creature straight between the eyes, resulting in a momentary respite for me, and, since I'm currently trying to clamber up a fire escape, a brief lesson on gravity for the hellhound.

Blasted toothy, snappy, spiny hellhound! I hope it ends up in . . . well . . . hell.

Still, beyond the excruciating pain, there is this teeny ray of hope. And that is that other people (who can see the particular fire escape I'm clambering up) are now screaming. When it comes to being chased through the back alleys of Hong Kong by vicious (possibly mythical) creatures, it's always nice to know that someone else is also in mortal terror, or is at least as completely and totally freaked out.

So, gasping for breath while still in serious pain and feeling just the tiniest bit relieved that I might not be insane after all, I turn to the fox and ask her, 'Can those things climb walls?'

'No,' she says as I wonder if she's actually saying it (because I'm still pretty sure real foxes don't have the vocal range) or if the words are just arriving in my head. 'Also, they're a bit on the shy side, so with the crowd around, we won't have to worry about them.'

And sure enough, when I peep down the iron frame, the monster-ish creatures are totally backing into the shadows and vanishing as the few brave people who aren't terrified are rushing forward to see what the whole commotion is about. For the second time today, people are suddenly pointing up at me and talking. Let me tell you, even when it's out of concern, it's not a nice feeling.

'Calm down,' the fox says. And for a second, I'm choosing between shouting about the reasons why I really shouldn't be calm and wondering why she's making a point of it, but then I look down and, once again, there's this whole rainbow just rippling around my right arm.

Most people try deep breathing, meditation and other stuff like that, but given the extreme nature of my current circumstances, I think I can totally be forgiven for choosing to relax by shooting one hand forward and grabbing the fox by the scruff of her neck.

'What *are* you?' I ask the scruff-held fox. 'And what the heck is happening?!'

Instead of answering, she kind of twists in my hand, whacking me across the face with her tail, and then darts up the fire escape to the roof of the building.

So with one leg still on fire from a hellhound bite, I just stand there thinking about how people are definitely gonna lock me up and throw away the key for all sorts of stuff, including injuring a teacher with a wire fence, unleashing hellhounds on Hong Kong and, of course, spraying food on a gangster's daughter (I don't think they can arrest me for that one, but they can probably kill me, which is, well . . . worse).

Then I have this moment of complete limbo, like I can climb down and forget all this ever happened (until I'm killed by the triad, of course) or I can drag myself up to the roof before people come and take a closer look.

Stupid me, I drag.

Three long, painful minutes later, I'm on the roof. And instead of the fox, there's someone just standing there patiently. She looks human, Japanese, tall (enough to give me an inferiority complex), beautiful (only reinforcing that) and is dressed in really tacky clothes (which kinda makes up for it).

For a second, I'm just staring and trying to figure out where the fox went, when I hear its voice coming out of the woman's mouth! So I listen.

She says, 'You're definitely an unlikely one, I'll give you that. No, it's all right—you don't have to get all worked up about being confused. I get that you don't have a clue as to what's going on; but the thing is, I don't have a lot of options and, honestly, I don't care if you think this is all some hallucination. You hear me out, and then we'll see how this thing goes, 'kay?'

I nod.

She continues, 'By the way, you can call me Kit.'

The Fox's Tale

'Everyone tells stories. Some are true. Some are not. Sometimes a story is just a way of trying to make sense of a world that seems to be completely mad.

'If you want to make sense of all this, just whisper to yourself quietly, "People have believed in nonsense and fairy tales for centuries beyond count, but just because a lot of it is nonsense and fairy tales doesn't mean that it can't also be true." Or I could just say, "Keep an open mind," but everyone says that these days.

'Let's start with one such story. It's not one that immediately concerns us, or you, or the present or anything really. It's just a story about a long time ago and stuff that happened that isn't really important any more, but once you get a grip on that story, this one becomes a little easier.

'You see, a long time ago, there was a war between men and gods. When I say men, I basically mean humans, and not just of the masculine gender. Same goes for the gods, though maybe they weren't really gods in the way you'd look at it, but, say, rather that they were called such and they had that kind of power. Anyway . . . so, there was a war between men and gods. And the gods lost . . .

'Before I go on, I might as well say this: don't bother your head about theology. We're not talking about some ineffable, all-powerful mystic being that created the universe. I've seen pretenders to that particular throne, and not one of them was or is worth a single prayer. We could call it mythology instead, but that's not the right word either. A different sort of history, maybe.

'In this history, the universe always had a mind of its own. Maybe not the way we have minds or thoughts or desires, but it was part of all that cosmic energy that people go on about. It was whiling away the aeons, waiting for something to talk to.

'And that's where you lot came in. Somewhere between the cave paintings and the pyramids, when a species was learning to talk, to build, to tell stories and to *imagine*—the universe decided to talk back. And in that space, where imagination met reality, you had "magic".

'People conversed with these primal forces. They've been called many things—the Primordials, the First Ones, the Titans . . . The names and numbers change from legend to legend and story to story, but they were supposedly personifications of the building blocks of the universe—Earth and Time, Creation and Destruction—walking among men, granting favours and taking delight in the curiosity and wonder of a fledgling species. Gaia and Kronos—Titans from the Greek sphere of influence. Izanagi and Izanami—whose legends formed the heart of my homeland. And so many others . . .

'Humans learnt from them, and their own imagination and study took them further, until some were no longer human. They built kingdoms to protect their own people, and they began to gather more and more power.

'These humans were the first "gods". Each building their own Pantheon and area of influence over different parts of the world and moving civilizations forward. And maybe their intentions were good to start with, but they didn't stay that way for long. Where once they protected, now they ruled; and when that rule became tyranny, the war began.

'In that time, before and during the war, these gods built countless heavens and hells from nothingness, just barely connected to the bedrock of reality. Realms of dream and illusion, weaving together shadow and sleep and raw imagination.

'This earth of yours—we helped shape it and it shaped us. We played and danced to the scripts of mortal minds; we created stories and were created by them. And then the war happened and things changed. It got . . . complicated.

'I don't know all the details. Some stories have been lost or twisted to untruths—and I have to say that the creative liberties and whitewashing undertaken by some of your poets and major religions are honestly breathtaking. Like, you would not believe the shenanigans that happened around the original Tower of Babel. The first-hand stories I heard were positively scandalous.

'No, I wasn't there. I'm definitely not *that* old.

'What am I? Broadest category: spirit. Something wild that became attached to a story, and then made that story her own. We'll leave it at that for now. If this were Japan, you'd be pointing your finger at me and excitedly shouting my name.

'But let's set aside the history lesson. Focusing on the here and now, I'd say the urgent stuff on your mind is: "What the hell is happening to me, and what the hell were those creatures just now?"

'For the first, think of it like waking up. As if there's a part of you that's been asleep all this while and has suddenly opened its eyes. In ancient times, there were those that fought for humans against the Pantheons. Think about it—a war between mortal and immortal kind, back in those days when a small pointy piece of metal was considered a decent weapon by mortals? How do you think your kind won? Trust me, it wasn't all garlic and holy water. No. The gods weren't vampires. I was just trying to make a metaphor. Forget it.

'Once, there were others like you. Now . . . this is also complicated. When the war ended, the rule of "magic" ended with it. Civilizations built on fantasy crumbled into ruin, and my kind retreated to their own pocket realms, to the edges, to the wilds, to the in-between places.

'You're feeling lost, aren't you? Good. Hold on to that feeling. Because there's no other way that you'll ever believe your own eyes, your own senses, your own brain. But if you just drift for a bit, you'll realize that the connections are all there. The threads of why you dream and imagine and indulge in little hallucinations and fantasies, without it being completely insane. Just wait, and listen. It won't all make sense, but there isn't much that does.

'Keeping it simple—in the last fifty-odd years, things have started to change again. I don't know why, though I've got a few theories. Things are starting to become a lot more like the old days, which means that suddenly a story isn't just a story any more, and while magic can be a lie, it can also be the truth. And somewhere along the way, the wrong kind of people started picking up on it.

'There's a lot of the wrong kind of people, if you really want the specifics. Greedy, power-hungry megalomaniacs, or weird nihilistic fanatics, or just very righteous and unselfish people who think that they know better than everyone else. It's a long list; though on priority, I'd say there's a demon or two causing some real trouble, a few of the remaining gods looking for a fresh toehold in the world and one global human paramilitary group that has so many intertwining operations, plots and schemes in motion that I wouldn't even know where to begin.

'But, summarizing, what you are is a consequence. Something to help balance the equation. Don't worry. Don't freak out. No one's asking you to save the world. This is not about you being "the chosen one". You're basically "the unlucky one". Sorry.

'As to what the hell those creatures were . . . If you have to know, they were creatures from hell.

'I don't need to tell you that your life's just got very interesting. Judging by that shocked expression on your face, and your earlier hysteria, you seem aware of it.

'By the way, the whole by-the-scruff-of-the-neck thing does hurt. Try it again, and I will bite you. Also, you might want to get that leg treated. Some hellhounds can be venomous. If you're feeling a bit dazed, it's probably not just the whole situation. You might actually be dying.

'Still, you managed to crawl all the way up here with that leg, and you're still conscious and hopefully making a little sense of the weird world around you—so that's a good thing.

'As to where I fit into this whole mess . . . I'm not going to lie—though, trust me, if I were, you'd never know it—I need your help. You're not alone. There are others like . . . well, not quite like you, but still close. Like I said, no saving the world. I just need your help to find them and also to track down a very dangerous book that's fallen into the hands of . . . um . . . the wrong kind of people.

'You do have a choice, though. You can say no, try and ignore whatever's happening to you, head back home and see if you can salvage a normal life after today's chaos; but the thing is—you're not going to succeed. If you stay, those creatures are going to be back. And if you don't learn to control what you've started doing, you might just die before that happens. And I know I'm being cruel when I say this, but you will hurt those around you.

'So . . . with all that laid out before you, this is the part where you make that very simple yet very hard choice.'

Blood Judgement

The bullet stopped in front of the boy's outstretched hand. It hung in mid-air, the air around it shimmering for a brief second as the sheer kinetic force of the projectile bled into it. And then it was still—frozen in time as the boy's hand came around, just under the floating metal slug. It dropped gently into his hand.

'Did you really think that would work?' he asked softly, in clear, unaccented English.

The revolver in Chun's hand shook as he stared up at the boy's face. Too old for a child, yet far too young for a man. Bland, unassuming features shaped around narrow lips and framed by ears that stuck out slightly. But it was the eyes that marked his true nature. Red half-healed scars cut down diagonally from the brows, lining both lid and eyeball, as they stared, sightless and unmoving, at the world around. The eyes of the dead. The eyes of the demon.

Chun swallowed and dropped the gun. 'No,' he said. 'But I had to try. You are him . . . You are . . .'

'Take not the name of the dead,' came the reply. The boy turned away casually, pacing the length of the corridor before stopping and turning back. 'For now I am simply the judge and executioner. Your name would be Chun, yes?'

Frowning, Chun nodded.

The blind youth nodded back. 'I spent a lot of time learning about the Paschid,' he said as he walked. 'Learning the names, how they walk, move . . . live. Your own people helped me, of course. The ones left alive at each gathering. Getting the exact descriptions was not an easy process.' The lips lifted for a second in a mirthless smile. 'Not for them anyway. From their information, I figured either the one called Zhao or you would have the sense to hold back, and they did say that you kept a revolver handy. Which one was Zhao, anyway?'

'The first one you killed,' said Chun.

'Hmm . . . I suppose he was obligated to try something.'

The revolver rose from the floor, as if bound to the boy's will. He stepped closer, tilting his head to one side with an expression of faint, almost forced, amusement. 'As, apparently,' he said, 'were you.' The gun shattered in a fraction of a second, the scrap tumbling carelessly to the ground.

'Would you care to guess why you are still alive, Chun?'

'Because I am useful,' Chun said and then slowly sat against the wall, a smile of mocking despair painted on his lips.

'Correct.' The pacing finally stopped at the opposite wall, and the boy slid down, folding his arms over his legs with an air of practised weariness. He seemed frail in that moment, but Chun knew too well that it was only an illusion.

'Zhao, the figurehead, and Chun, the thinker—the last pillars of the Paschid. Beyond that, there is only one name, and you know what that name is?'

'Jhakri,' said Chun without hesitation. 'He is no longer here. Torturing me won't help you find him.'

'Jhakri,' repeated the boy slowly. 'Yes . . . that is the name you know him by.'

Silence reigned for a minute. Outside, the wind howled as streams of white snow spun in the blizzard. More than a few flakes found their way in through the hole in the roof, and a pile of frost was collecting in the corridor.

'How old were you?' the boy finally asked.

As the question was asked, every doubt that Chun had evaporated into the icy wind. He was going to die.

'I was seventeen,' he said. 'I stood watch at the door.'

'Why?'

And that one question almost brought a laugh to Chun's lips. *Why?* He settled for another headshake and slowly got to his feet. 'Come, demon,' he said. 'If the kitchen is still intact, I'll make tea. I'll tell you everything, and then you can kill me.'

The boy nodded after a moment's thought and then blew hard into his palms, almost blue from the biting cold. 'As you wish,' he said.

The kitchen was still intact and, more remarkably, so was the stove.

Crushed leaves, water and milk—all dunked into a single saucepan and brought to a boil. Even if there had been poison in the kitchen, Chun knew better than to try adding it to the mix. The blind eyes saw everything. That much, at least, was clear. Two candles were lit, one placed on the counter next to the stove and another on a high shelf, filled from end to end with dusty spice jars.

'Would you like ginger? Or mint?' asked Chun, unable to stop exploring the sheer absurdity of the scene.

Again, the boy's head tilted in what Chun could only translate as a moment of curiosity. As if the mind behind the scarred eyes was trying to explore every possible response to such a question. Finally, he simply said, 'No.'

The tea boiled quick enough, helped along by the altitude. With a sigh, Chun lowered the heat and covered the saucepan with a steel plate. Best to let it brew a while. It brought out the flavour. He decided to fix his gaze on the candle before speaking.

'Jhakri was kind enough to lift me from being a *sukumbasi ka baccha*—an orphan on the streets of Kathmandu. That's where a lot of the Paschid were recruited from. Whatever life, education, *existence* . . . I had, it was because of the Paschid.' He shook his head. 'Call us what you will—militants, terrorists, gang, mob, a cult even—we were all those and more.' Chun hesitated as he tried to find a way to address his would-be executioner. 'Surely there must be another name by which to call you?'

'You may call me Tao,' the boy said quietly.

At that, Chun couldn't help but laugh. 'That which is beyond all words and definitions—nameless. Yes, I suppose I can call you that.'

Tao nodded, the small, mirthless smile passing across his face again. Idly he turned to the candle next to the stove and waved a hand over it. Orange flame and grey smoke melded for a single second into the immortal symbol: a disc of dark and light, divided by a sinuous line. 'The tea is done,' he said as the candle flickered back to normal.

And, indeed, the tea was done. For a moment, as he poured the mixture into two metal glasses, Chun considered throwing the hot liquid in the boy's face and trying to make a run for it. Strangely, even as he predicted the bloody end to that scenario, he only smiled. It was as if the halted bullet had exhausted all the fear and desperation of the last few days, and now all that remained was a tranquil certainty.

Chun held his glass with a ragged cleaning cloth, insulating his hand from the heat. Not surprisingly, the boy didn't even seem to notice the heat as he clutched the metal in his thin hand. There was no sugar, so Chun didn't bother offering him some. The boy didn't seem to mind.

'We were loyal,' continued Chun. 'Slaves freed from the chains of poverty and bound again with those of violence. But poverty brings despair and violence, hatred. Hatred will keep a man alive long after all else fails.'

55

Silently Tao inclined his head in a shallow nod.

'We thought we had a higher purpose. That one day we would rise up and destroy the unfair world that had wronged us all. We would cheer around the tables as our pipes smoked and we fired bullets into the air, drunk on adrenaline and swill that would have blinded . . .' He couldn't help glancing over at Tao's scarred eyes. 'Well, you get the idea. We served Jhakri, and we did whatever was needed to be done. We bullied and threatened, stole and shattered, killed and tortured . . .' Chun smiled bitterly. 'And we told ourselves that there were good reasons behind our actions.'

He sipped the tea. 'Of course, I was a bright lad, and we all know what happens to bright lads in such company.'

'Why don't you tell me?' said Tao, his voice maintaining that calm softness that seemed far more threatening than the hoarse growl of demons.

'Well, either we drink and drug ourselves until we don't have brain cells left, or we get killed or kill ourselves, or—finally—we watch.' Chun allowed himself a reflective shake of the head. 'And we wait, and eventually we aspire to be like Jhakri.' He raised his eyes to stare at Tao defiantly. 'I followed the thread of my life and, though I regret much, I will not say that I would take it all back.'

Tao drained the glass easily, a thin stream escaping from one corner of his mouth to drip down his chin. 'That is how it should be,' he said quietly. 'We cannot change what was, and though repentance may be genuine, it, too, is powerless to change the past.' He set the glass down gently on the floor. 'So what happened after that night, Chun? After the Paschid came for my family?'

Chun swallowed. 'That night was the last official act of the Paschid. Jhakri left, never to be heard from again. After that we were just a gang, a mob forgotten in a country that had too many other problems to worry about. We made our living by hiring out to bigger organizations. We managed to scrape by, dreaming that we were just sleeping until the call came to awaken.'

He put aside the glass. It was still half-full, but the taste had turned to ash in his mouth as he'd brought back the past. 'So we waited, and waited . . . and then you came,' he finished.

Tao nodded once and then, with a wave of his hand, extinguished the light of both candles. In the almost impenetrable gloom, he walked over to the kitchen window and stared out at the frozen landscape, moonlight reflecting off the white snow and the words that were written in the blood of the slain.

'Did you know what was going to happen that night?'

'Yes . . .' answered Chun slowly. 'Both Zhao and I knew what was going to happen . . . and Jhakri also told us what would happen after that. We didn't believe him at first. We thought he had gone insane with his talk of "sacrifice" and "gods". And yet he seemed so certain.'

'I dare say he was . . .' Tao's voice trailed off, as if escaping to the winter world outside. 'It was a winter's day just like this, wasn't it?'

'Just like this,' said Chun.

'Then I promise you this, Chun: it will be a winter's day just like this when I kill you. Even if you should leave this place and flee to the sunniest beach in the world, know that when the storm winds blow in December and the snow is thick on these mountain slopes, I will come and I will end your life. But for now,' said Tao, 'you are more useful alive. There is yet a road that leads to Jhakri. Someone will come soon. I want you to deliver a message.'

'What . . .?' asked Chun hesitantly. 'What message?'

Tao's eyes were far away, as if looking at the possibilities of the future unfolding. 'Tell them that I wait in the forest in which the Snowman dwells.'

Chun nodded and then shut his eyes tight as the boy raised his hand. There was a deafening sound as wood and stone broke and the howling blizzard rushed into the kitchen.

When Chun opened his eyes, the snow had already started to powder the floorboards, entering from a hole in the wall around where the window had been.

Of the boy-demon there was no sign.

Debriefing at Deacon's Hill

The crooks and crannies of the vast mountain ranges of the Hindu Kush, dividing the countries of Afghanistan and Pakistan, have been host to many a mystery through the millennia. From forgotten legends and temples and buried treasures, to mountaineers vanished, to terrorists hidden away in caves.

And one modern mystery was the presence of a well-camouflaged military installation built into the side of a mountain that, on the surface, looked like any one of a thousand other mountains. The installation was called Deacon's Hill, after one Roger Levinson Deacon. Not too many people knew the name, and even fewer understood its significance. Understandable that; for most, good ol' RLD was just a name buried in old intelligence archives. A single-page employment record that indicated a two-year work period with three days off for illness and then subsequent termination.

What the record does not show is a detailed listing of Deacon's work, preferring to hide it under the label of 'strategic consultant'. And what the record does not show is that Roger Levinson Deacon was *not* fired at the end of those two years, and that he kept working for various intelligence agencies until he died, some twenty years later, in an accident that involved an electric fence, a strong breeze and an umbrella.

This was only to be expected, as Deacon was the personification of the unassuming character that is 'the man with a plan'. And like all purists of the genre, he was lamentably destined to meet his end anonymously and senselessly, leaving nothing behind but his ideas.

With one prominent idea being that there had always been places in the world where reality was thin enough to connect to *other* places. And while many civilizations had decided on temples, or pyramids, or burial grounds for such locations, in times of war, what was really needed was a guardhouse.

As far as commanders of top-secret paramilitary bases went, Roth fit the physical characteristics reasonably well. He had the greying, short-cropped hair, the biting temper and the world-weary aura of someone who had tried to save the world so many times that he was half inclined to destroy it himself for the sheer convenience of it all.

And days like this didn't help.

The captain of the Black Rangers continued his report.

'We followed the orders to a T—our attack time was under ten minutes, we had guards posted at thirty-metre intervals and we had all sections secured before we went down there. And then the subject breezed through without a care in the world.' The captain shook his head. 'We could have had the time to put snipers on every rooftop, and I'll still wager it wouldn't have made a difference. We tried tracking the subject's movements, and all we found was the remains of a camouflaged escape tunnel. The damn thing must have been lined with explosives or something, because it was completely collapsed by the time we got to it.'

'All right,' said Roth, raising his hands in surrender. 'We'll agree that there's nothing you could have done. At least we have a backup plan.'

The captain hesitated. 'Do you really think they'd head to Santor? Wouldn't Kabul or a city make more sense if they want to get lost in the crowd? They must know that we will be watching.'

'By your own report, Captain, "they" is the subject and a teenager. While I would not underestimate them, I do expect that they're trying to follow a previously laid-out plan. And what with the intelligence recovered, Santor—that damned valley—seems a likely destination. Speaking of,' said Roth, 'I trust that your troops have their orders? Under no circumstances are they to attempt to enter the valley. I won't have any more lives thrown away, Captain.'

'We have that in common, sir.' He nodded. 'My men don't understand it, but they'll follow orders.'

'Well,' interrupted the other recipient of the briefing—a woman of chiselled features and indeterminate age, who seemed to exude an aura of gentle, almost comforting authority, 'if you want to explain to them that we can only attack the valley at specific cosmological intervals, the last of which was eleven years ago, please do tell me how they react to it.'

Roth glanced at her. Madeline White was still quite an enigma to him. She'd been assigned by the Central Command to liaise with Deacon's Hill but seemed perfectly content to let most things run their course with minimal interference. It made him uneasy.

The captain shot her a glare. 'They'll think I'm crazy, ma'am,' he said stiffly. 'And then they'll do as I command. *That* is what matters.'

'Of course,' she conceded graciously. 'But, Roth, what makes you think that intercepting them en route to Santor will work any better? I'm sure the captain would agree that the subject has proven himself to be quite adept. And the road to Santor isn't even the contained sort of environment that Eden was.'

'That's why we have a backup plan for that as well.' Seeing her arch an eyebrow, Roth raised his hands to forestall further inquiries. 'We'll get to that later. For now, I believe you,' he pointed towards the captain, 'have good news, and you,' he pointed towards Madeline, 'have horrible news. You first, Captain.'

With a grunt of effort, the captain swung his bag off the floor and on to the desk. 'The spoils of war, sir. The two prisoners who didn't manage to kill themselves will be in with the rest of the troops, but I thought you'd want this immediately.'

Roth's movements were slow and deliberate as he undid the straps of the bag, but it was that very caution that belied the trembling excitement hidden just beneath the surface. Within a minute, the canvas bag lay discarded on the floor and, with care, Roth ran his long fingers across the jacket of the book taken from Eden. 'The *Anima Arcanus*—the so-called Book of Souls,' he said with equal parts reverence and scepticism. 'Eleven long years, Captain. Eleven years spent trying to recover this second piece of the puzzle.' Roth shrugged. 'It does seem very anticlimactic, but I guess the drama is all out in the field.'

'I suppose you could call it that,' said the captain carefully. 'What I don't understand,' he went on, 'is why we found that tome in a bloody storeroom, locked away under enough dust to kill a man. They've had contact with places like Santor. They obviously know that this shit is real, but instead they're mucking around with things like that boy. It doesn't make sense.'

'It makes perfect sense, *mon capitaine*,' said Madeline with a smile. 'You have to understand that the current proprietors of Eden do see themselves as "men of God", as it were . . .'

62

She waved a hand towards the book. 'And this volume here is undoubtedly . . .'

'The work of the devil,' finished Roth. 'I guess we should be grateful that Eden didn't dabble in these black arts. That would have been a headache even the Rangers would have had a hard time dealing with. Still, we have the book now and, combined with the information gleaned from the *Voca Arcanus*, we can put it to *constructive* use.' He turned to Madeline. 'All right, now that we're all cheerful and optimistic, I think it's time for the cold water.'

'We have confirmation,' she said simply.

There was silence as the words sank in slowly. Roth sighed heavily while the captain just waited for further explanation.

'Our Nepal team has managed to check at least three different sites and, judging by what they've seen and what they've heard, the Paschid can now be considered to be wholly extinct.'

'Fourteen years ago, I would have been overjoyed to hear that,' said Roth. 'But not today. So Jhakri succeeded there. Do we have any indication as to what we're dealing with?'

'Something or someone who is destructive, messy and extremely unconventional. The former militants seemed to have put up a token resistance, but it didn't do any good. Bullets halted before impact, grenades crushed or rebounded back into the safe houses. At the very least, a high-level telekinetic.'

The captain raised his hand. 'Excuse me, what are we talking about here?'

'It appears, Captain,' said Roth, 'that our troubles are no longer confined to Santor and Eden. And this time our "enemy" does indeed appear to be a product of the dark arts.'

'And there's one more thing,' said Madeline calmly. 'As you know, we've been trying to track the uptick in supernatural activity—strange animals in the wilds, more missing persons in older cities, visitations and contact with the so-called

Edge realms. So far the increase has been worrying, but still under control.'

'Why do I get the feeling that you're about to tell me that's no longer the case?' asked Roth.

'Today, something new awoke. We don't know what it is. Or why. Or anything, really, except that it's powerful.'

'Where?'

'As far as we can tell, somewhere in the vicinity of Hong Kong.'

Something new . . . New variables always complicated things. 'Make sure that Central is in the loop, you can put Marcus and Beryl on ESP-scanning to see if they can find something more specific, but for now, our priority is still the boy. We have to find him before he gets to Santor.'

Wanted

Kharsan

The path from Eden to Santor is a lonely one. From the old maps left with my father's directions, it borders the wilds of Afghanistan where the Hindu Kush begin their rise. Santor—or the Valley of Shadow, as Seidre once called it—is protected in ways that Eden could not manage. I never quite understood how, but the valley was supposedly impossible to discover through satellite imagery, airplane mapping or any modern technology.

There are a few small settlements on the way, though. Little shelters that know about and are known to the world, but cheerfully ignore each other, resting assured that a meeting will only result in mutual headaches all around. These little oases aren't so much isolated, or traditional, as they are just . . . old. People just live there the best they can.

Eventually they will die out, because they have nothing beyond their existences. They have no larger world. They are good people. But they will not survive. If the ravages of nature do not destroy them, civilization surely will.

On arriving at one such place, and after making sure that Adam wasn't going to cause some bloody catastrophic scene, I struck up a conversation with a boy a bit older than me. He speaks more Urdu than Farsi but somehow we manage to converse.

'No. Not many people come by. Lot of people are leaving because of the drought. My brother, he is in Kabul. We do not get letters, but next year I plan to go join him. They say the fighting is less now. Have you been there?'

Kabul—that was a long time ago.

'No, never been,' I reply cagily. 'From east. Relatives in north that we are visiting.' My Urdu is bloody awful.

'Really? North road is good. Stay away from the west, though.'

Santor lies directly due west of here.

'Why? Fighting?'

He shrugs carelessly. 'Don't know. But west is a bad place. And there are lots of warbirds that have gone there recently. They never bring good with them.'

'Warbirds?'

'You know . . .' He makes a whirling motion with one hand.

Helicopters. 'Do they stop?'

He looks at me quizzically, so I make this ridiculous show of pointing towards the ground to ask if the helicopters had ever landed here.

'No. We do not have anything that they want.'

At that, I can't help but glance to the side and look at where Adam is . . . that is, where that bloody idiot should have been.

I turn back quickly. 'My brother,' I ask, deliberately keeping the urgency out of my voice, 'did you see?'

He looks around quizzically for a second, which just lets me know I'm about to be led on a wild goose chase all across this stupid village, and even if it's not that big, neither is Adam.

'I think he went that way . . .' says the boy with absolutely no confidence.

Sigh . . . I hope he at least remembers rule one.

I start with worst-case scenarios. Crowds of people screaming, perhaps; though in this village there aren't really enough people for a crowd, even if you include the livestock.

Maybe he's facing off cheerfully against some water buffalo and beating it into the ground with a single movement. Actually, it's more likely he's made friends with it. He's rather good with animals, going by that cobra he managed to save me from the other day. Quite terrifying. Also embarrassing, given that I was trying to take a piss at the time, but mostly terrifying.

What else? No tall buildings for him to climb. No bar or gathering spot to cause a commotion. There's a small building in one corner of the village, where the children go to learn; but it's late afternoon, so there's no one there.

The children . . . I won't be surprised if he went searching for someone his own age. Where would they play? The area is still dangerous. Especially the caves and dried riverbeds just south of the village, filled with all sorts of creepy-crawlies, dangerous falls and moments of mortal peril. If that isn't a perfect playground . . .

Sighing heavily, I turn south.

Just once, I'd like to be wrong. I'm usually not. I have a very realistic, pragmatic view of the universe that prepares me for almost anything. It also makes me feel a lot older than my sixteen years, but I suppose, on a journey like this, it's probably better to be older and wiser. Or at least older and grouchier.

I have to admit, the warren of caves makes for quite the impressive arena. Pillars of rock carved by howling winds and long-lost waters; hollows where the softer sand and stone have been torn away, leaving nothing but the bare bones of the earth. A naked skeleton for children to play in.

I have a somewhat morbid personality. I blame Eden for it.

They're playing something that looks like cricket, in that there's a plank that might be a bat, a rock that might be a wicket, a stretch of slightly less rocky surface that might be a pitch and a ball that might be . . . uh . . . That *is* a ball.

My momentary relief that Adam is neither at bat nor in possession of the ball is gone the moment I notice where he is. Towards the back of this makeshift 'cricket stadium', there is a single spire of rock jutting upward into a very pointed tip. I should be thankful that the attention of the rest of the children is focused on the game, and not on the grinning idiot balanced barefoot on the very pointed rock.

'Adam!' My shout doesn't disturb a fragment of that inhuman balance, and he just spins and flips forward and down before looking up cheerfully.

'Yes, brother?' he calls.

While I have to yell to be heard across the distance, his voice just seems . . . louder. No. Wrong word. Tighter. More focused. I look up at the sky. When we arrived, the noon sun was burning all shadows away, and only an hour later, matters haven't improved much.

If helicopters do come by this area, it would be better to move during the evenings, but we can't stay. The longer we stay, the greater the chance that Adam will be noticed. I'm almost certain that our pursuers already know about Santor, but this particular path is unlikely to be known to them. Still, there is no sense in taking chances.

'We leave in ten minutes,' I shout back. One of the other boys then looks up and shouts something that my limited knowledge can only identify as not being something obscene. Then he tosses the ball at me, and a sick realization dawns. Bloody hell! They want me to join in.

I fumble the catch badly and, with a resigned sigh, walk over to where the ball has rolled and toss it back. I can walk with the best of them, and back in Eden, boredom, more than anything else, forced me to keep fit. But for some reason, even the simple hand-eye coordination in a game of catch escapes me. I'd like to say it's some illness or the other, but I fear it might just be because I'm clumsy. So I calmly hold out my hands in the universal symbol of 'Much obliged, but no thanks' and take a seat on an uncomfortable shelf of rock.

Resumed shouts and the sound of the ball bouncing signal the game's continuation. I lean back with a sigh, just dreading every moment of the future. But this is better than it sounds. I'm very comfortable when I dread. I have this delusion that expecting the worst prepares me for it somehow.

Tilting my head up, I take in the very surreal blueness, unbroken except for a single, solitary white cloud. A thin cloud on the verge of being burnt away by that merciless yellow eye. I close my eyes for a second.

~

'Wake up, brother.'

No sleep has ever faded that fast. My eyes open wide, the pupils narrowing before the pain of light can force their contraction. Nothing . . . no sense of fatigue, no muzziness. Nothing. Bloody hell!

Sitting up, I look at Adam, crouched there beside me. The only thing I want to ask this wretched child is 'What did you do to me?' but the intensity of his gaze somehow forces the words to change. 'What's wrong?'

'It is time to leave,' he says and stands up to look at the horizon, prompting my very reluctant self to get off the hot stone and do the same.

By the look of the sky and the sun, I must have been asleep for at least an hour. Strange, I hadn't been tired at all till I sat down on that rock-shelf. Goes to show how fatigue can catch up.

'What can you see?' I ask, because as far as I can bloody well make out, there's a whole lot of nothing in the sky.

He shakes his head and taps his left ear once. 'They are too low to see. Three helicopters—coming from there. One will stop at the village. Two will pass half a kilometre south of here.'

I sigh. My internal sense of dread snickers a told-you-so in the back of my head. 'Do you think it's the same soldiers?'

'Yes,' he says quietly. 'It is them.'

A part of me wants to ask how he knows it's them. Maybe it's the way they're flying. Maybe he can just sense them. But now is not the time. The two that will pass south, they're probably heading towards Santor or the other settlements en route. But the words of the village boy come back to me. *We do not have anything that they want.*

Now they do.

'All right,' I say. 'We'll take the riverbed route. With the rough terrain, the helicopters won't be able to land near there. Let's go.'

We move slowly. Running is a last, very noticeable, resort. Still, I thank Allah that I had the foresight to keep our supplies near the dried-up riverbed. Or maybe I just thank my natural sense of dread and paranoia. Whatever it is, it's time to be moving again. Time to be gone.

Souls and Visions

At Deacon's Hill, there were buildings within buildings and rooms within rooms, and the sort of floor design that would have left both Theseus and Minotaur completely at sea, even with a guiding ball of string. There were meetings, committees and various levels of subterfuge strung in disparate knots along the chain of command, with it not being so much a case of the left hand not knowing what the right hand was doing, but rather that of the head not being aware of what the neck was doing—and, dear god, what was that elbow planning?

It was the perfect place for keeping secrets—and since everyone knew that, it could be said that the only secret it couldn't keep was the fact that there were secrets. Roth knew this well, and encouraged the convoluted non-secrecy about secrets. He ensured that fresh gossip was supplied to the rumour mills on a weekly basis, and took an hour off every Sunday just to read about and chuckle over the new theories that had popped up.

At one point, back in the days when the organization had been more or less legal, they had toyed with the idea of just telling everyone who joined the blatant, unvarnished and completely unbelievable truth. The number of psychiatric breakdowns had quadrupled for that year alone.

So it had been decided that all secrets were best kept secret. Especially secrets like these. The book recovered from Eden, the *Anima Arcanus*, lay open in front of Roth. Interpretation had been relatively easy. For decades, his predecessors had worked on deciphering similar texts. Even now, different fragments of knowledge were being tested around the world.

But as far as he knew, this ritual was unique. Location was of importance. Inside Deacon's Hill, this room had been built around the specific point where reality thinned. Here, the runes he had carved into the stone had meaning. Each emblem giving shape to an idea. A bargain to be constructed piece by piece. It was not a gentle process.

The shivers had finally stopped. Tiny spasms that ran up and down muscles he never even knew he had. The blood from a bitten lip had crusted over, and his heart had finally stilled from its marathon pace.

'That,' he hissed softly, 'was decidedly unpleasant.'

'There is a price for everything,' said the other occupant of the room—a person who might be called a 'man' for lack of a better description. He was dressed in combat fatigues and seated on a box in the corner, smoke escaping lazily from between his lips. A visual highlighted by the disturbing lack of a cigarette, cigar or pipe. There was a beret perched on the man's head, tilted forward until it half hid the light-sucking voids that were his eyes.

As for the room—it was a relatively small chamber, lit by two standing lanterns next to opposite walls, a bright gas flame burning in each. In the centre was a raised stone platform that a Gothic-minded fellow might call an altar, and the rough stone floor was now littered with the runes that had been carved.

'Still,' said Roth reproachfully as he straightened, 'you'd think there'd be a more civilized way to do this. This is the information age, after all. I don't suppose you lot take bitcoin?'

'The suggestion has been made,' said the man non-committally. 'But for now, mortals have their expectations. We have ours.'

Roth shrugged, moving over to a side table where a shallow bowl filled with water and a clean towel awaited him. 'Fine. Fine. I have no intention of bad-mouthing tradition, but the binding is done and the bargain made. Shall we move to a different venue?'

The man inclined his head in acquiescence.

In the outer chambers of the test area, Madeline was waiting.

Her calculating gaze took them both in without the faintest of reactions. 'It's a pleasure to meet you . . .' She let the sentence trail off. A courtesy for their visitor, allowing him to choose both rank and alias.

The man inclined his head again. 'You may call me Sheol.'

Roth nodded towards the inner door. 'In there is the end result of ten years' work. During which we've had teams of scientists beating their heads against the wall of . . . well . . . black magic, if you will. The Arcanus recovered from Eden was invaluable and, when combined with the volume we recovered in Santor a decade ago, we finally had the theory necessary for this experiment.

'It was probably a good thing it took us this long to get it. We needed most of the last decade to update Loew's research. Like it or not, clay is hardly a durable material in this information age of ours.'

'Others have used iron, stone, bronze,' said Sheol reflectively. 'Why, even gold has been used, and, on one rather disastrous occasion, glass.'

'You'd know better than me. Madeline, are we ready?'

She nodded curtly. 'We've cleared out all non-essential personnel. The "shells" are securely locked down in case of any mishaps, and we've blanketed the staging area in an insulation field. Nothing is going to get in or out.'

'How comforting,' commented Roth dryly. He looked over at the "shells", or sentries, as they had been nicknamed. Though they differed wildly in size, depending on their purpose, they were all humanoid in shape, their burnished metal-plated faces blank and unseeing.

He turned to their visitor. 'Now, Sheol, shall we discuss the price of a soul?'

~

The forest of the Snowman had slept through the ages. On the surface, evergreens and snow covered the expanse, the monotony tempered by a rustling wind. 'Gentle' was a word easily applied to these woods. As if the forest slept peacefully in its niche, uncaring of and unchanged by the rigours of eternity.

Appearances could be deceptive, though.

In the forest of the Snowman, dark things had dwelt forever, and they didn't take kindly to strangers. Still, Tao was no stranger here, and 'dark things' evoked little fear in his heart.

He sat in a small clearing, where an aged tree had toppled under its own weight to form a natural bench. In front of him, a circle of stones enclosed burning kindling, the flames dancing in the wind, while the trees around the clearing swayed, enjoying the warmth without fear. Both the forest and the Snowman had survived since the Great War, when he had been created by the Elementals to be an enemy of the Pantheons. And like the Exile of the Nephilim and others, his kind had paid the price for defying divinity.

Now the Pantheons were long gone. The gods dead or shadows of their former selves. And yet the forest endured.

In Tao's sightless gaze, the heat of the flames was alive. It roared across the clearing in waves. And all around, the contrasting world was as cold as death itself. Both frost and fire brought old memories to the surface, which he suppressed. Yama's teachings had been clear. Memory was a gateway to emotion. And that was one thing a disciple of Yama could not afford.

A crack sounded in the woods, louder and heavier than any normal animal. Without moving, Tao let his awareness of his surroundings grow. Within an instant, he had found the culprit, and relaxed, focusing once more on the flame ahead. Tao had never quite found the right words for his abilities. Bit by bit, it had just become a natural part of who he was. In his own mind, the world was an extension of that bare void in which Yama had summoned him, the emptiness now filled by a never-ending vortex of chaos. Matter and energy whirling in a cosmic dance for as far as he could reach.

And what he'd learnt from Yama was to find the currents within that flow of matter and energy and redirect them accordingly. That the natural state of the universe was chaos, contained by bonds of natural law, waiting to be bent or broken.

The flame leapt under his mind's touch. Contained in its circle, it was forged by him into the likeness of a thousand flaming men, and each one then slowly extinguished until only two remained.

The Snowman entered the clearing, the heavy footsteps thudding to a halt on the other side of the fire.

'The Paschid are dead?' the Snowman asked, its dull, flat voice soft in the gentle wind.

Tao nodded. 'All save one. And Jhakri, of course, but he was never truly one of them.' The two flaming figures merged into one; bright orange and red, laced through with dark threads of burnt carbon. *But then, whose was he?* The thought stirred his long-subdued curiosity. *I was offered to Yama. But who did the offering?*

A grunt echoed around the clearing as the Snowman eased its large bulk to the forest floor. 'And now?'

'There are other matters to consider. The Lord of the Abyss walks with humans. With each bargain, more seeds of chaos are sown and the world is drawn that much closer to the brink of war. And then there are other variables . . .'

The flame flickered again, now a delicate form shaped by Tao's will. Two dark tilted voids marked serpent-like eyes, horns grew from a ridged forehead and the long, tapered snout was filled with dagger-like teeth. The dragon raised its head and stared down at the Snowman.

'So for now,' said Tao gently, 'I wait.'

The Snowman stared up at the figure that Tao had shaped from the flame and shook his head in quiet admonishment. 'Be careful, young disciple. The dreams of the Elementals are not to be intruded upon lightly.'

It was hours later, and the ashen complexion of Roth's face had only grown worse. Sheol was gone, but now he could almost feel *them* . . . the energy flowing from the other side as part of the bargain.

He slumped back in his chair, squeezing his eyes shut against the hard glare of his office lights. 'This cannot end well,' he said finally.

'Yes,' said Madeline. 'But the directives are clear. The bargain had to be made. You didn't have to volunteer, though. There were other, more expendable candidates.'

Roth shook his head. 'It's better this way. I have enough on my conscience. What did we find out about our visitor?'

Leaning forward, Madeline tapped a neat black folder on the desk. 'Nothing good,' she said. 'We had every kind of sensor imaginable pointed straight at him, and we got nothing.

Even after decades of research, I think we need to accept that we have no idea what these creatures are, or what they are capable of.'

Roth ground his teeth together for a moment. 'So instead we rely on folklore, fairy tales and frayed old texts. Do you believe in demons, Madeline?'

She arched a curious eyebrow. 'You mean . . . after having met one?'

'Yes.'

She shrugged. 'Certainly not in a theological sense, but I believe that they exist, and that humans do not understand them. But I wouldn't believe that they cannot be understood.'

'Then I guess we'll just have to keep trying.' Roth pulled the folder towards himself and opened it at random. 'What about the *espers*?'

'Beryl managed to get a glimpse, and that's left her semi-conscious in the medical wing. From what she said, the whole thing—opening the portal and using your life force to keep it wedged open, as well as the flow of energy through the shells . . . The structure of the ritual may have helped, but as far as the power required goes, Sheol was the one doing the heavy lifting.'

Roth frowned. 'Beryl? She's our second-best esper. What happened to Marcus?'

'We'll get to him in a moment. First, you realize the implications of Beryl's reading.' It wasn't a question.

'Sheol has all the real power in this equation.'

'And that means we're playing his game.' Madeline twisted her mouth sourly. 'He's using us, Roth. And we don't know what for.'

'The bargain . . .'

'I believe in demons,' she interrupted. 'But I don't believe a word they say. We have to find out what he . . . what *they* are really up to.'

'And so we treat our fairy tale friends as cautiously as we would alien invaders . . .'

'Which they might well be.'

'Which they might well be,' agreed Roth. 'And in the meantime, we use them to our ends just as they use us. Deacon's doctrine: all resources exist to be exploited. And this is a resource we can't afford to ignore.'

'I suppose so. But, as you said, this cannot end well.'

Roth nodded firmly. 'Always good to keep in mind. Now, what's the situation with Marcus?'

Madeline tapped a second folder on the desk. 'You've been busy with this ritual, so I haven't had the chance to update you. Given the magnitude of the Hong Kong incident, we thought it would be a good idea to take a closer look. So we hooked Marcus up to the dream-reader machine—you know, to just amplify the ambient psychic readings and maybe isolate the person or persons involved.'

'And?' Roth opened the second folder and froze, the blood draining from his face.

'There was a bit of a psychic backlash. Either he wasn't prepared, or whatever he sensed sort of sensed him back. We're still cleaning his brains off the wall.'

Forcing himself to look, Roth scrutinized one particular photograph. 'You're kidding? The wall was actually stained in that . . . in that pattern?'

'Yes,' confirmed Madeline. 'You can guess what it's meant to be.'

'If I didn't know better,' said Roth with an uncertainty that indicated that he actually *didn't* know better, 'I'd say that was a bloody dragon.'

What Is Left Behind

Alice

It stretched across the sky, black as midnight, vast as the horizon. Its claws were lightning. Its eyes were hurricanes. The beating of its wings was the breaking of a world, and its breath . . .

Wake up screaming: check.

Yep. That's definitely how I'd planned to start today. And it's not one of those times when I've been screaming in my dream and then I'm shaken awake by concerned parents all ready to comfort me about it and say stuff like, 'It's only a dream'. This was way more sudden. Sleep to waking, silence (I don't snore) to screaming in five seconds. And then cold sweat, shivers, breathlessness and the very real possibility of heavily dilated pupils, all while listening to footsteps, bumping and cursing (in that order) as said concerned parents try to make it in time for the second act.

Okay, on the positive side, this is home, this is my bed and those are my concerned parents trying to fumble their way around in the dark. On the negative side, the pain in my leg tells me that yesterday did happen, and I just woke up screaming.

What the heck was that thing? It looked . . .

The door opens and concerned parents come in (without knocking, I might add). Dad takes up the watcher's position at the door, leaving mom to close in and ask, 'Are you all right?'

'Yeah . . . it's just a bad dream,' I respond in a very shaky voice.

A glance is exchanged between the two adults, which doesn't tell me anything other than the fact that vast amounts of data are being transferred in an instant. Mom turns back with a comforting smile.

'Come on, I'll warm up some milk. It'll help you sleep.'

Oh, great . . . my parents are plotting to send me *back* to that nightmarish vision. Though I guess they do mean well. I suppress a sigh and nod. 'Sure. That sounds great.'

And as I follow mom out of the room, I almost manage to completely ignore the pair of eyes gleaming in the far corner of the room. *Don't worry*, I tell myself. *It's just the fox.*

I pause at the door after thinking that, with what I know has to be an exhausted expression on my face. Yep. This is what it's like to want to bang your head against a wall. Last night didn't go as bad as it could have, which isn't really saying much because my 'bad as it could have' was a scenario of me being sold out by my parents (who were actually aliens in disguise in this scenario) to the Chinese government and then locked up and dissected within hours because it had turned out I was also an alien. I'm still not sure about the alien thing, but I am thankful that the rest was just my overactive imagination.

After the whole rooftop storytelling session, Kit kind of escorted me back home and played the concerned stranger who found little old wayward me after I'd been shell-shocked (her words, not mine) by weird events at school and was suffering from a concussion . . . and had also been attacked by some animal.

Still, the real shocker of the evening was Kit. She was totally right about the fact that if she were lying, I'd never be able to tell.

After Dad got me back from the doctor, she was just sitting there, sipping tea and laughing lightly. 'Yes,' she was saying with a bright smile, 'I never thought my first visit to Hong Kong would be like this. The city is *such* a change from the countryside in Hokkaido, and I think I just got lost. And then I bumped into your daughter. It was an astonishing thing, really.'

You can imagine the depth of her acting skills when she pretended to leave and Mom turns to Dad and says, 'What a nice lady! We should invite her to dinner while she's still in the city,' completely ignoring the fact that Kit didn't give them her name (*any* name), address, phone number or anything.

I'd like to think it was magic, but then Kit's warning about not to use that word as a sort of all-round 'fix it' incantation comes to mind . . . No, I think the magic was just all in their heads, and in the way she just darted past every question without leaving any room to even remember those questions. I mean, if I were a morally dubious kinda person (which I'm totally not, honestly), that would have been something like a lesson from a master. As it is, I just sat there trying to get over the inoculations and the stinging in my stitched-up leg, with my mouth slightly open, as I thought, *Wow, my life would be so much easier if I could lie like that.*

I think it was the poison from those hellhounds, but I couldn't get to sleep for ages. Basically from eleven o'clock onwards, I was just tossing and turning and trying my best not to think about tomorrow.

So much for that.

The clock on the kitchen wall reads 4.25 in the morning, and I just know I'm not getting back to sleep. Dad's retreated, muttering apologetically about work early tomorrow, but Mom's keeping me cheerful company. It's sometimes scary how she can completely switch off all sleepiness when she wants to.

'I used to have awful nightmares when I was a girl,' she says in that forced casual kinda way. 'I blame my grandmother.

She used to read me stories from *Journey to the West*. Before I was twelve, I was seeing demons in every corner.'

Demon . . . I wonder if that's what Kit really is.

'Warm milk never helped after a really bad nightmare,' she says. 'So I always ended up reading under a small lamp in the living room, right until dawn, and then everyone would ask me why I was so sleepy through the rest of the day.'

I nod, not really listening.

Kit said that it wasn't going to stop. Not what was happening to me. Not those . . . *things* that came after us in the alley. Maybe they were after her? Okay, that doesn't solve it. I'm still potentially causing minor hurricanes with every major sneeze.

'Mom,' I start, not really knowing why.

'Yes?' she says, surprised at being cut off in the middle of what I'm guessing was supposed to be something really interesting.

'Is there . . .' I take a deep breath. 'Is there anything that you haven't told me?'

She looks at me with her head tilted to the side, a bit confused. Then she smiles. 'Dear, there's lots of things that I haven't told you.' She winks and puts a finger to her lips. 'Even a mother has to have her secrets after all. But I promise, I'd never keep anything important from you unless it was absolutely for your own good, and even then—I'd tell you straight away that there was something I *couldn't* tell you.'

Now I furrow my brow in confusion. I've totally got a hang of this furrowing business, by the way. 'So . . . you'd tell me that there was a secret, but not what the secret was?'

She looks at me kindly. 'Don't put it like that, dear. You make me sound sadistic.'

My mom's a lot of things, but yeah, I'll totally admit you'd never find anyone less sadistic than her.

'Okay. So . . .' I look up at her. 'Is there any secret?'

Now she just looks surprised. 'No,' she says.

I don't know what I was expecting, or what I was hoping for. Maybe some story that she and dad were actually wizards or something, or that I was actually adopted under some weird, mysterious circumstances . . . or, you know . . . *something*. Anything that's replayed in some weird story somewhere and could just explain all this stuff too.

Because I do believe it now. I do believe that this isn't a dream or a hallucination, or whatever . . . It's real. It's happening. And it's totally terrifying. And if Mom doesn't have the answers, that means that I can only rely on Kit, and that . . .

'Alice,' Mom continues. 'What exactly happened yesterday?'

I reply without a moment's hesitation and with complete honesty, 'I really have no idea.'

She just looks at me for another long moment, and she's doing that thing where she's deliberately painting emotions on her face so I can see that she's worried and wants me to know that she's there for me but is going to wait until I'm ready to talk or whatever. Then she nods.

'Would you like something to eat? There are some cookies in the larder, or I can make breakfast if you want. You're not going to school today—so maybe we could start the day early, and if you get tired later on, you can take a nap.'

'Nah, it's all right.' I make a show of downing the warm milk. 'I think I'll try and get some sleep.'

And there's that look again. Yep, if my supernatural weirdness is genetic, it's totally from my mom's side. There's something so freakily psychic about the way she can just know when I'm lying.

Of course, she doesn't *say* anything, because that would totally undervalue the whole psychic aura thing, and instead just smiles comfortingly again. 'That's probably a good idea,' she says.

'Still, if you need anything, I'm going to sit up for a while in Gerry's room.'

Maybe it's just that I don't have that whole maternal instinct thing yet, but I really don't understand it when Mom says she finds it 'soothing' to watch him sleep. I mean, all I get is the urge to draw funny faces on him with a permanent marker.

A couple of 'goodnight's later, I've marched back to my room and, with the door shut firmly behind me, I don't bother looking around. I just go right to my bed, turn off the bedside lamp and sit, staring straight ahead with what I'm hoping is a fierce expression. (According to Lin—whom I've tried it on before—it generally just comes out sulky.)

Kit is standing in front of the window, and is totally ignoring my fierceness.

'Okay,' I start, 'let's say that I do believe you. Why now? And don't tell me it's just a natural teenage thing. I know how these things are supposed to work, and there should have been warnings, indicators—*something!*' I can hear every bit of doubt and desperation in my own voice.

Without looking at me, she smirks. 'Have any strange dreams lately?'

'Everyone has strange dreams,' I reply, stubbornly refusing to accept that a couple of out-of-the-ordinary subconscious hallucinations could result in all this.

She still doesn't look away from the window. 'One would be enough. An odd dream that happens for no reason, that has a meaning that you can't quite understand, that seems alien compared to the rest of your dreams, but somehow . . . it's also really familiar. Stop me if I'm wrong.'

She's not wrong.

'Sometimes a dream can be a beacon, or a warning. There are whole worlds out there that almost no living human knows anything about, and that one special dream can be a lot louder and brighter than you could imagine. I think it's because of what you are.'

'Um . . .' Trust me, this is a real 'um' moment. 'So . . . what do you think I am?'

'I'm not sure.'

Since I know by now that she's an amazing liar, I also know that now she's not really bothering to conceal the fact that she's lying. Still, I'm really in no mood to just let it go.

'You're lying.'

And then she does look at me, and I realize that she isn't.

'I'm not . . . sure,' she repeats, this time emphasizing the last word. 'And what I suspect isn't going to help you. I found you because of your dream, and I'm definitely not the only one who could do that. The hellhounds confirm that much at least. And tonight you had another dream, didn't you?'

'Well, yeah . . . I mean, no. It wasn't really a dream. It was more like . . .' I trail off, not really knowing how to put it.

'Like the end of a dream,' she whispers. 'Like the story and the images have all been and gone, and there's nothing left but something as hard and certain as the waking world . . .'

'Uh . . . I suppose you could call it something like that.' All right—*exactly* like that. Plus a lot more terrifying, with whatever that . . . that thing was.

She nods. 'The metaphorical door is now open, Alice. Whether it's through a dream or people hearing about hellhounds and unexplained explosions in mid-air, there are other people who can find you.'

'That's nice' I find myself snarling. 'I hope they're better at explaining all of this stuff than you.'

Her face just freezes over. And I mean cold, expressionless and very scary. 'Alice,' she says, using the name almost like a question.

'Yeah?' I ask, all cautious like.

'Don't be an idiot.' She turns away from the window and sits down at the foot of my bed. 'There are some things you should know. And you need to start packing.'

Not liking where this is going, I don't move an inch. Kit just shrugs and starts rummaging through my stuff without any care for privacy or anything and keeps talking in this kind of whisper that's both casual and also really ominous.

'The thing about fairy tales, about stories . . . is that they only have happy endings when they're read out of books in a comforting tone of voice. I've been around for a decent amount of time, and fairy tales generally don't end well. In fact, nine times out of ten they end with blood and limbs everywhere, and they sometimes start with blood and limbs as well.'

'What are you trying to say?' I try asking, not sure if she's trying to threaten me, or scare me . . . or what?

'I'm saying that in stories there exists an archetype called "the reluctant hero". It's someone who just wants to live a normal life, but all sorts of weird things just start happening around them and then they have no choice but to plunge headlong into murky waters, all the while grouching and griping and staring wistfully into nothingness as they try and remember a time when things were simple and non-perilous. It's a huge metaphor for growing up, if you ask me.'

I guess she sees my eyes begin to glaze over because then she says, 'To get to the point—it's already too late. There is no going back. Those hellhounds were just the tip of a very dark, very disturbed iceberg, and unless you take up the mantle of the story, it will be forced upon you, drenched in the blood of your friends, your family and very likely your sanity as well.'

(Well, no great loss on that last one.)

She looks at me, as if expecting some kind of answer or response, but I don't know what to think. I mean, this makes my head hurt in ways that I know it just wasn't meant to hurt.

'Get out!'

I didn't even plan to say that, and the weird hiss-like tone was so far from the horizon that . . . And my hands, my arms . . . The colours are back with a vengeance, and I just know I'm a hair's breadth from just blowing her out of my room along with the wall behind her.

And Gerry's nursery is right behind her.

She hasn't moved an inch, but somehow the shadows around her seem to be so much darker, and those eyes are just staring right through me. The minutes crawl past, and my breathing sounds ragged in my ears. I know that she's waiting for me to calm down, and, honestly, I'm also waiting for me to calm down, but I can't stop wishing that she'd just get the hell out of my room. I'm still wishing that I could just go to sleep and wake up and find out this was all a dream.

Reluctant hero? Try reluctant, scared and possibly schizophrenic half-freak, half-teenage-wannabe! (Okay, so I have a few self-esteem issues, but can you blame me?)

The ripples fade away, leaving me just completely . . . drained.

She pulls out a large old camping backpack from under the bed. 'You have until daybreak,' she says gently. 'I'd suggest a note.'

❧

It's later. My eyes are red, my nose is frozen and I'm shivering in the cloudy 7 a.m. light. I'm holding the backpack with all that I could carry in it, and wishing upon anything and everything that I could just be back home, cuddled up in bed.

KUBER KAUSHIK

But I'm standing next to Kit in the middle of Victoria Harbour, and my own tear-stained words keep haunting me.

Dear Mom, Dad . . . I'm sorry. I can't explain, but by the time you read this . . .

I look up at a rust-covered cargo ship that's docked just left of us. Kit's scrutinizing it all too carefully, but I can't seem to really care. I'm just trying to keep from bursting into sobs again. It's all a lie. Every story I've ever read. Every happy ending I've ever believed in. There is no Hogwarts. There is no Neverland. There is no guiding star. There are no kindly old wizards or fairy godmothers. These things don't actually happen to ordinary kids. Or at least, when they do, their lives don't turn into some weird and wonderful adventure.

Instead, everything changes.

88

The Most Horrible Boat

Alice

I want it on record that I hate boats.

My mom always says that 'hate' is a strong word and really shouldn't be used except when you really, really can't think of a nicer way of putting it. And I've thought long and hard, and I've come to the undeniable conclusion that I totally *hate* boats!

Especially large, decrepit freighter type boats that sway around on the waves and just go from side to side in an endless repeat motion of rising and crashing, with the horizon bobbing up every minute and . . . Oh my God—I need to throw up again.

I'm given to understand that the disgusting, undignified— and socially acceptable—thing to do on a boat is to simply throw up over the side. Doing so when the boat is rocking like crazy is a technique that takes a lot of practice to master, but I'm repressing certain memories there—so let's just say I've got quite good at it.

The *Zui Jidan* is the most horrible boat that has ever existed in the history of horrible boats. There have been more cramped, more unhygienic and definitely more evil boats. But the *Zui Jidan* is definitely the most horrible. Throwing up over the side for three days now might have prejudiced me slightly, but I'd like to think I can still be objective while my internal organs have been twisted into a giant knotty mess.

To describe it, the boat is a 4000-ton cargo freighter painted a dull, matt grey and striped with bright crimson, built from the salvage of thousands of wrecked vessels and held together entirely by rust. If anyone poured oil over the tanker, I'm sure it would just fall apart. But the majority of the crew is not what anyone would call a shady lot. If you removed the piercings, tattoos and the attitude, I wouldn't be surprised if they came across as younger and less cynical than me.

And the captain . . . Well, on the surface of it, he seems to think he's a Disney pirate or something (the non-drunken ones), all charm and looks and all that, but it's hard to tell anything more because he spends half his time chasing after Kit and the other half vanishing after she lets herself be caught. I'm not going into more detail. See, I'm trying to be very non-judgmental about the whole thing.

There are other passengers. Wide-eyed, broke tourists turned crew-members, trying to get a taste of real sea-life. A small group of potentially illegal immigrants who get off at every port of call to feel the place out before scurrying back. And there's a smelly old dog named Iawandanaheh, which took me all of these three days to learn how to spell. In any case, barring a sympathetic young boat janitor by the name of Benjie, I don't really get along with most of the rest of the boat. Which leaves me plenty of time to try to control my weird air-control powers between bouts of nausea while trying not to be obvious about it, in case people freak out and want me thrown overboard.

Kit promises that's not going to happen, but still . . .

We're headed to a place I've never even heard of.

All right, I've seen it on a map and all, and I vaguely remember the name (Kolkata), and it's in India (which I have heard of)—but other than that, I've never heard of it. I don't know exactly why we're going there, but whenever I've tried to bring it up, Kit's generally just muttered something about 'finding someone' and I've been too sick to pursue the topic any further. On the plus side, I'm sure all this throwing up is a great way to lose weight.

'You just need to get your sea legs,' says a concerned voice from behind me.

I bite back the reply that it's my stomach and not my legs that's the problem. Instead I just try out a wan sort of smile and turn to face Benjie.

'Any idea how long that usually takes?' I ask with a note of despair.

'It takes a while,' he answers rather less confidently than he did when I first asked the question and got a solid 'It only takes a day or so' for an answer. 'Me—my father says I was sick for five days on my first boat trip. And I was only two years old at the time!' He says it with such a lot of pride that I really don't know how to respond.

'Um . . . okay?'

'But after that, not a single twinge of nausea! Not even when we all went to that offshore seafood restaurant with the green squid and the rest of the crew was sick for three whole—'

He stops, interrupted by my sudden, violent lunge to the side of the deck and the retching sounds that followed. I think it's a rule of the universe that there is always someone who will talk about disgusting food around a nauseous person.

'I want to die,' I say in a very soft, very matter-of-fact tone of voice.

'That is no way to talk!' says Benjie cheerfully. 'Just give it time, and then there'll be nothing but the refreshing smell of salt water and this wonderful weather to enjoy!'

Cheerful people normally make me depressed, but, I swear, it's like he's infectious or something. 'The weather is nice,' I agree with a half-mutter. 'Now if only the horizon would just stay still for a minute or two, I'd be happy as a peach.'

'That's the spirit! Optimism is the flavour of life!'

I don't want to know where Benjie learnt to speak English, but I keep imagining a blotched, torn book titled *Popular Idioms and How to Mangle Them*.

'Oh,' he says suddenly, 'I almost forget to tell you—that Japanese lady is looking for you.'

I nod weakly. I suppose I should be chasing her for answers and stuff, but all I've got is this deep reserve of dread. That and seasickness. Not a great start to an adventure.

❦

I find her in our 'room'.

The cramped space with a single thin mat is about as far from any boat cabin I've ever imagined (though, to be fair, I've never really devoted all that much time to imagining boat cabins). I thought there'd at least be a bunk or something. There is one of those round window-like hatches, though I really don't want to look at it because I now have traumatic seasickness memories.

'You look like you just swallowed a sea urchin,' says Kit observationally.

My stomach lurches at that. 'You,' I say, glaring at her, 'are a very evil spirit.'

'So I've heard,' she says with a small smile. 'Anyway, I've got something in mind that should help distract you for a bit.'

'Really?' I ask sceptically. 'Morphine?'

She opens her mouth as if to answer, which means it's a total surprise when her arm flicks around and there's suddenly a small but very heavy-looking piece of scrap metal flying at my head.

There's a thick sound, like someone struck a gong and took all the loudness away so that all that's left is that teeth-shaking vibration. Sheer power surges inside me, and using it is suddenly as easy as breathing, except breathing isn't easy any more. It's like this massive movement . . . It's me trying to figure out what all this means, and *knowing* what it means but not understanding. For a second, I'm just frozen there, the air around me as solid as a wall and the piece of metal quivering in front of me.

In the next moment, it flies off, deflected by an almost perfect ninety degrees, and buries itself in the bulkhead. The blue-green's already fading from my arms, and for a moment I'm just too shocked to be anything but shocked.

Okay. Moment's over. I think I'm perfectly justified in being absolutely *furious* now!

'So the reflexes have settled in, then,' she says, completely ignoring my first splutters of outrage. 'I thought it would have taken longer.'

'You just . . . You could have killed me!' Fine. So maybe the metal thing wasn't really that big or sharp or thrown *that* fast. But it would have definitely hurt!

'I was aiming over your left shoulder,' she says with a hurt expression.

'I'm sure there are easier ways to—'

'No,' she interrupts. 'There aren't. This isn't something you get better at by sitting in a corner and meditating. This is *power*. Something melded into blood, bone and brain, and we don't have time for easier methods. Maybe I could find you some great sage teacher and you could take decades to gain full control, but I'm not going to, and you won't be able to find another teacher. Now sit down.'

I allow myself a full five seconds for glaring before complying. 'You could try being nicer, you know.'

She nods thoughtfully. 'I could, but then you wouldn't be seething with rage right now. Anger can be a powerful motivating factor.'

Sigh . . . Welcome to the dark side of the force. All I want to do is stay alive, and she's going on about power and whatnot, and . . .

It's weird how awful this whole thing feels. This isn't normal. Maybe I should be all 'I've got superpowers—cool!' but this doesn't feel like a superpower moment. It's more like a 'I haven't studied for the test—crap!' moment.

'So now you're going to teach me about all my powers and stuff?' I ask.

She shrugs. 'Not really. I can't teach you anything you probably won't learn better on your own. But we have time, and there are a few pointers that might make things easier.'

'Like?'

As if doing a magic trick, she flicks her fingers and a sharp iron nail appears in her hand, which does make me lean back a bit. She grins, and starts scratching lines into the floor.

Leaning in closer, I can see, in very rough lines, the sketch of something that looks like a fox. I try not to make sarcastic art-critic comments.

'Now,' she says finally, when a tree and a globe have joined the fox, 'I'm not going to teach you anything about magic and power and all that, but I can teach you about something that I know very well, and it's something that can help you.'

Suddenly the nail's no longer in her hand and the scratches on the metal floor are curving and shifting all on their own. The fox is suddenly everything that I ever imagined a fox to be—with sharp eyes, quick feet, a toothy grin and, for some reason, two tails. The tree rustles in a breeze that I swear I can feel blowing on the surface of the deck, and the globe . . . *is* the world.

She says, 'I'm going to teach you about stories.'

The Truth about Stories

'I've told you a little about our history. This seems like a good time to elaborate,' Kit said, trying to keep from smiling at Alice's green-tinged face. Hopefully seasickness would mean fewer interruptions.

'So imagine that you were there a long time ago. When the world was more alive than ever before. The ability to communicate with the elements and bend and break the laws of the universe—to bargain with reality—was becoming commonplace. And your leaders—the most skilled in 'magic'— were becoming more powerful. At that time, the first covenants were sworn, and these leaders tapped not only into the power of the world around them but of the beliefs of their people. The bargain was simple: the people were protected, and their rulers became even more powerful.

'But then they were no longer content with simply bargaining with the elements. They wanted more. Immortality. The power to bend reality and time to their will.

'Alliances were formed across the world between these rulers, and they made a pact. They would abandon their humanity, overthrow the Primordials and create a new reality, crafted by their desires alone. To do so, they waged war on the forces of nature itself, on the very things that made existence possible. And they almost succeeded.

'The surviving stories say that the Primordials were not like humans. They didn't fully understand conflict and the perils of human ambition and avarice. They didn't know how to fight or how to stop these people that they had once been fascinated by. So instead, before they came under direct attack, they retreated beyond the reach of their tormentors, giving up their human forms and returning to be part of the silent cosmos again.

'It was too late for this world, though. Where once were kings and queens ruling justly over their people, now there were gods and goddesses. And though their power was not absolute, it was enough. They divided the world between themselves, each Pantheon ruling over a region.

'Thus we enter an age of legends.

'Palaces, prisons and playgrounds—these gods began to spin entire worlds out of nothingness. Countless heavens and hells connected to the bones of reality by the thinnest of threads. Entire realms created and destroyed in the span of a season.'

She said the last thing almost sadly, but smiled before diving in again. 'It was a time that would make any poet jump for joy. There were stories beyond imagination, lost now to myth and legend. Around every corner, in any part of the world, you could take a quick glance and find wonders that would make you gasp and horrors that would leave you weeping.

'It was also a time when your life could so easily slip out of control. When you could be reduced, in the blink of an eye, to nothing more than a toy for powers beyond your understanding. Hades, Diyu, Avici, Naraka, Xibalba, Gehenna . . . We may speak of paradises beyond living sight, of the green fields of Elysium, the white pillars of Olympus and the Jade Palace, but it is the hells of this world that carry the truth of the battle. Our beliefs, our existences were smelted in that fire, shaped by an ageless struggle and quenched in the blood of all who came before—'

'I don't get it,' interrupted Alice suddenly, her face screwed up in confusion. 'Are we talking about the afterlife here? I mean, it's fine if you want to go on about different religions and beliefs and things. That's . . . well, weird, but not really . . . unless you're telling me that it's suddenly Armageddon and the dead are rising, and then that's . . .' She frowned, lowering her eyes, before muttering in a small voice, 'Stupid.'

'Alice,' said Kit quietly, 'look at me.'

When the girl didn't react, Kit reached forward and gently took hold of her chin, raising it to fix her with a piercing stare. 'I am as alive as you are, but different. And all those worlds are also part of reality, just in a different way than you're used to.'

She released the girl's chin. 'What I do know is that god or demon, spirit or human—all things die. And then they are no longer part of this story. Death is still the last unknown and, for all their longevity, the gods of that time were not immortal. That was the last secret that the Primordials managed to protect. And it was in search of that secret that the gods began to tear this world apart.

'Entire civilizations enslaved as workforces to create and imagine ways to prolong their rule and to conquer death forever. Life in a thousand different forms, shaped to their whims, to do nothing more than serve. The monsters and heroes of legend, born out of living . . . well, I suppose you could say living souls.

'I do not know where this road would have ended. Perhaps an eternal paradise, created here in place of a universe subject to the laws of time and space. Perhaps the creation of a separate world, given entirely to magic and all its forms. Perhaps an endless age of tyranny, where the powerful fed forever on the weak. Perhaps the end of all things. But they never got the chance.'

'Is this "perhaps" where that war of yours fits in?' asked Alice not quite sulkily.

97

'We call it the Great War,' she said. 'Remembered and misremembered a thousand times in a thousand different tales. Fragments remain. Different battles. Different heroes. The epics of old—Gilgamesh and Beowulf, the Mahabharata and the Iliad—parts and pieces of the same struggle. Even among those like me, there are so few who know the whole tale. Among all the secrets of the underworld, there are only two facts that seem to remain constant.

'The first is that of all those who stood against the gods of that time—those who defied the Pantheons—first and foremost was a group of four, who made pacts with the Primordials before they'd fled, who sacrificed their humanity to become Elementals—vessels for the elements themselves.

'The second is the name given to those four. A name forgotten in this realm, and only whispered in others.

'They were called the Children of Destruction.'

Into Limbo
Alice

Okay . . . consider my blood chilled.

There are so many questions I want to ask, and I don't even know where to begin. First off, how do I prove that I haven't had a complete mental breakdown and am not currently locked up in a padded cell somewhere? I think I need to see a psychiatrist, and instead I'm . . . Okay, I'm over the shape-shifting-cum-talking fox thing. Totally.

But there's more. What exactly were these Elementals? By gods, are we talking about all the millions of Greek, Norse and Hindu varieties? And she doesn't know what comes after death? Really?

But I'm not asking any of these aloud, and I've got this sneaky suspicion it's because she is actually a good storyteller. It's more than the words. It's the tone, the body language . . . It's this feeling of staring at something that's completely grand and, you know, awe-inspiring . . . And you just want to know what happens next.

'So they fought, and when the Great War ended, the age of the Pantheons was over and what some call the Withdrawal began. Magic began to fade from this world and all humans were left with were stories. The heavens and hells went on with their own lives, all the people in those worlds just fighting to survive as best as they could. And now the connections to those worlds are growing stronger again, and it's not a good thing.'

'Are you sure?' I manage to force out a question. 'If everyone could use magic, then maybe that would be a good thing.'

Kit looks troubled. 'Before all this, there were a lot of rumours about the other realms dying. Some had already been lost to chaos and war, and it was only getting worse. And then this renewed connection to the physical realm—the human world—happened. As things get worse in the other realms, a lot of nasties are going to find that easy access to this realm is a great way to escape the destruction of their homes. Having fled, befuddled and downright hoodwinked many of those nasties, I assure you—you don't want them anywhere near your world. Though I'm hopeful that, with your help, we can maybe put a stop to some of this.'

My eyes are wide with alarm and the other questions are ready to spill out, except Kit puts up a hand, as if listening to something. Then the whole stupid ship decides to turn ninety degrees on its side and back, tossing me around that small cabin with many a bump that even my air-thickening powers can't seem to cushion.

'What was that?' I yell at her, but she's already on her feet and heading to the door.

'Stay here!' she shouts at me as the ship continues to sway and roll. She clambers out, running towards the stairs.

Unfortunately, the sensible part of me must have been knocked senseless by that little tumble, because instead of staying there safely, shivering in uncertainty and trying not to throw up, I end up thinking that if I'm really going to have to swim for my life because we've hit an iceberg (or reef or whatever), it's probably better to be up on deck. So I follow her, the terror and adrenaline overriding the seasickness.

Other crew-members are bolting out of their cabins, abandoning below-deck duties and heading in the same direction as me. A few take the time to shout things at me that I'm sure are on the same lines as Kit's command. Thankfully, with all the chaos and confusion, I can safely ignore them while trying to make sure I don't get thrown off the deck ladder. Scampering in the opposite direction is Iawandanaheh, threatening to trip everyone up as he charges down, moving faster than I've ever seen that dog move.

Bursting out into the daylight, my first sight is that of a huge wave slopping over the side, white and grey foam everywhere. I make my graceful appearance by slipping and sliding right out of the hatch and into a nailed-down deckchair. The boat rocks again, and I'm just aware of Benjie rushing forward and bending down next to me.

'Are you all right?' he asks, shouting to be heard above the crash of the waves.

'Just fine,' I reply, spitting my own hair out of my mouth. 'What's happening?'

'Don't know. It was not the weather. We might have hit something.' He looks up uneasily, eyes darting all around.

Scrambling to my feet, I pick up on an immediate focus. Kit's near the deck railing, her hands gripping it tight enough to turn her knuckles totally white as she stares over the side into the churning sea.

Careful not to be washed overboard, I manage to lurch forward half a dozen steps to get closer, before shouting, 'What is it?' at her.

She shoots me an immediate glare, almost as if she really expected me to follow her 'Stay where you are' orders. 'Whales!' she shouts as a fresh spray of white swamps everything.

'What?' I shout back, not really sure that I heard her right.

In irritation, she stabs a finger down at the water. 'Whales! A pack of baleen whales! They're all around us!'

'What?!' I shout again, this time in total disbelief. Whales! *Really?* Is this some kind of environmental revenge?

Kit rushes to my side between tilts, gliding across with an enviable grace. 'It's not natural,' she says when she's close enough. 'They wouldn't gather or attack a ship like this, or even be able to. Something's behind it, and I would bet you the truth about my story that it's because you're here.'

'Is this like those hellhound things?' I ask, the panic in my voice nearing delightfully shrill levels.

She opens her mouth, as if to explain something long and complicated, and then stops. 'Yes,' she says confidently instead. 'Let's go with that.'

This time, the boat dips at a perfect forty-five-degree angle; and, for a second, looking to my left, it's almost like the surface of the ocean is this huge, endless wall, all blue and frothy white. Just a second, though, but still long enough to have me hanging on like mad to the side rail. I wasn't really aware that I was screaming until the boat straightened and decided to go the other way. Oh, it's so good that I'm scared. Otherwise just imagine how seasick I'd be.

'What do we do?' I shout at Kit, noting with irritation that she's somehow managing to keep her balance very well.

For a moment, she looks frustrated, as if being attacked by brainwashed whales was not something she planned for, and then she grins. That should have made me shiver and go run under the deck and just wait to drown, because it would have been quicker and less painful. But, being just the teeniest bit distracted, the implication of that grin doesn't fully register.

So when she jerks one arm up and points over my shoulder and says, 'Look over there,' I actually turn around.

The only thing I remember is a sharp pain at the base of my neck.

And then I'm here. Wherever here is. It's as if the world is made of shadows and smoke. Or glass and mirrors. Or blue-white fire. Or . . . Looking down, it's all I can do not to gasp. Though, it's more like I can't gasp. It's like those times with the colours running across my skin, except now someone's done a magic act so there's no skin, no body, just . . . colours. Is it weird that I feel totally naked?

Realization and the memory of pain kick in. She *did* something to me! That complete . . . *Urgh.*

So I'm here. It's still the boat, except the deck is all ghostlike, the ocean is still in a creepy way and seems to have traded its stormy grey-blue water for endless acres of cloudy ice. Oddly, I still seem to feel wind on my face. It's like someone took away the movement and left the *sensation* of movement, if that makes any sense (which it probably doesn't, since none of this does).

Of course, none of this prevents me from looking around desperately and then looking down, which is when things get scary.

Below the ghostlike deck, and the equally insubstantial sea, there's something . . . there. I can't see it at first, but there's this deep, gnawing . . . *wrongness*. And the more it freaks me out, the worse the wrongness gets, and then it starts to take shape . . . Or maybe it's my mind telling my eyes to give it shape, I don't know . . .

It's like one of those cool graphics of a nervous system—all lines and sparkles, but shaded in this ugly, angry red, with each nerve ending a gruesome black spike existing only to cause pain. This is the benchmark for horror film directors everywhere.

If I could feel my stomach, I'd throw up.

'Disgusting, isn't it?' The voice is a cold, slow drawl from somewhere behind me, and where I'd normally whirl around and stumble or something, I don't. I guess being slightly insubstantial has weird effects, because as soon as my ears tell my brain to turn around, I'm already turned around, trying to shake the feeling that I just twisted the two halves of my body in two totally different directions.

I don't know what surprises me more. That there's someone else here, or that it isn't Kit. He's standing about twenty feet away, right where the control deck is. Unlike everything else around here, though, he seems to have . . . substance. Going by the face, I'd say he's maybe a year or two younger than me, but taller, and bony to the point where you could reconstruct a sketch using only straight lines. He's dressed in a shabby black cloak, all trailing threads and patchy repairs. But it's the eyes that really grab the interest.

There are red lines, like cuts, above and below each eye, as if someone just slashed across both . . . but the eyes themselves seem untouched. Pure black pools, without even a hint of white. He's also smiling, but it's not a normal kinda smile. I want to say it's a cruel smile, but I've seen cruel smiles and what makes them cruel is the touch of sick humour around the corners of the lips and eyes. This is worse.

The smile is an expression of judgement, weighing every last part of my existence and declaring without any real malice that the sum total isn't worth the effort of a frown.

'Yes, I imagine you have a lot of questions, but we do not have a lot of time,' he says. 'Who am I? You'll figure that out soon, and, if you behave, one of these centuries I'll show you what I *really* look like.'

He definitely doesn't *sound* like a kid younger than me. Actually, the voice reminds me of an old teacher of mine, so

I'm guessing this is just a perception thing. Or else the entire conspiracy dedicated to making my life weird actually started in kindergarten, which is a way creepier thought than I want to think about.

'Huh?' I could have sworn I had a better question than that lined up.

'We are going to have to learn to work together after all. It's been ages since I've been up and about, and lurking around in the back of your head for the last decade has not been a fun awakening.'

'*What?*' I'm torn between panic and outrage.

'Oh, yes, you don't remember. It's fine. Near-death experiences can have that effect. But on to more immediate matters. It's good that you're getting more comfortable with our abilities, but there's still so much you don't know.' He lifts up three fingers. 'Power over matter. Power over mind—or energy if you prefer. Power over magic—or rather, the intersection between the previous two. These are the basics.'

'Excuse me,' I say slowly, 'I think you're skipping some important stuff . . .?'

'Like I said, we don't have time. Now, come on—look down, if you please.'

Now, this is a teacher's voice, and one that promises a combination of detention, homework and brutal evisceration for any type of disobedience. Having watched one horror film too many, I can honestly say that I'm not too keen on being brutally eviscerated. I look down at that spiky underwater dream forest.

'In this . . . *realm*,' he gestures all around us, 'a mirror of reality can be seen, bereft of most life. It's easier to pick out magical constructs or other things that are affecting *your* world.'

He points at the tangled spikes. 'What we have down there is a "spell", as you might call it. A classic example of a mind-warp.

The psychic construct is designed to entangle itself into the minds of the whales, and inflict pain enough to give rise to violent impulses. And those impulses can then be targeted at someone or something else. Do you follow me so far?'

'Uh . . . n-not really.' I stammer, trying to decide on a question that doesn't make me sound stupid.

'It's a nasty way to enslave poor creatures who cannot fight back.' For a moment, the boy (or whatever he is) sounds reflective. 'It's a fine piece of work. Haven't seen the like in aeons. In any case, now that we understand what the object in question is, the next problem is how to remove it.'

'Uh . . .' A part of me totally wants to shout, 'No, I really don't understand at all, you freaking weirdo!' but I suppose I can get on board with this . . . Here we have a problem, and now we move on to the solution. It seems all reasonable and orderly. Like algebra. Although, it's not a good time to be thinking about how much I suck at algebra.

Focusing on the warp thingy feels really weird. With each second, it's like it's more alive, and aware, and bigger, and . . . closer.

Oh.

Looking around, it seems I've somehow managed to sink right past the insubstantial ship and am now in the insubstantial ocean, heading fast towards that really substantial and evil-looking warp thingy. This might be a very good time to panic.

'So how do we remove it?' I yell, doing my best not to think about talking underwater and frantically trying to see where my 'teacher' has got to.

'We?' says a voice both uncomfortably close to my ear as well as kind of far off. 'This, dear child, is *your* problem.'

A Dance in the Thorns

The girl's shrill scream as the first spike pierced her arm was likely more out of surprise than actual pain. Pain was possible here, though. Deep psychic pain far more damaging than any mere physical wound, but the girl seemed strong enough. Indeed, after that single sound, she yanked her hand away with admirable deftness, her posture instinctively shifting within the web. The thorns shifted around her, sensing the intrusion, but when the next one struck, she had already moved.

It was an awkward movement. She stumbled backwards as if she'd forgotten how to walk, but it was still enough to dodge the barb.

The watcher reflected on this. In time, the girl would have found her own path here—into the void that bound reality with imagination—but to think they would force her here before she was ready . . . It could smell the fox's imprint on her mind, but that wasn't it. Tricksters like that were not ambitious enough to take independent action with such powerful pieces. The watcher had slumbered for so long, without the thoughts or purpose that came with a human vessel. How much had the world changed since the war? What had happened to its brethren? Why was the interaction between the realms so fragile in this time? And, perhaps most importantly, what was the emptiness it felt on the horizon? Something that was so eerily alien, and yet somehow . . . familiar.

The girl moved again, falling away from yet another stab. On some level, the instincts were there, lurking underneath the surface, but there was so much miscellaneous clutter that they had to work through. If she had been ready, this little web would have been nothing. She could have danced between the cracks, moving as a phantom of the mind, and shattered it all with a single touch. Instead she was flailing around wildly, a clumsy child trying to balance the feeling of this world with what she knew as reality. It was enough to elicit a sense of impatience in the watcher, which was in itself an unusual feeling. After all, it had been patient for so long.

The girl moved again, her head whipping back and forth as she tried to look in every direction at once. *Foolish.* The idea of vision was obsolete in this place. If she were to let her eyes guide her, then this would be a remarkably short journey. The web was starting to twist around her in ways that no physical vision would be able to follow. Even if it was a passive web—bereft of its maker's will—it was alive enough to sense the threat of the girl.

Her stumbling movements were taking her deeper in, towards where the fragile strands lay—the vulnerable parts of an external web, linking it to the physical realm. The best way to break the web was to break the link, and it seemed as if instinctive memory was guiding her there.

The watcher frowned as she stumbled again, this time her arms flailing about as if looking for a handhold, of all things. Another thorn sliced past, grazing her right near the neck. She yelped and jumped back, unaware of a spike that shifted into a potentially lethal position.

The watcher sighed heavily. It focused, and the spike burst into ashes behind her. She didn't even notice, which was just as well.

'You might want to finish this quickly,' it said, the voice projecting to her mind with the barest effort.

'If you could tell me how,' she snarled back through gritted teeth, 'that would really, *really* help!'

'I'm sure it would,' it said with enough patience to make it clear that it wasn't going to. It could tell she was getting angry. That would help; strong emotions would bypass the cluttered memories, tapping into instinct. In the long run it would kill her, but that was for a later day.

As the next spike struck, she dodged awkwardly again, but this time reached back. For a brief moment, there was the illusion that her arm had grown longer and she grabbed the threads of the weave. They shattered under her touch, throwing her away from the now disconnected thorn.

In her surprise, the watcher could also see a spark of elation. Touching magic, touching power itself could be intoxicating. Now, if only she could channel that feeling into determination.

She didn't, and it was only a dozen awkward dodges, near misses and surface wounds later that she was able to repeat the breaking. The entire mind-warp trembled visibly this time. She was close enough to the centre that every movement upset the stability of the link.

She noticed the change, her movements becoming more controlled and her eyes focusing inward. She had at least learnt how to gather and release power prior to being thrown in here.

The spikes approached her and, though she made no move to avoid them, this time the watcher let matters take their course. They moved towards her with lethal precision, but before they struck, she raised both arms in opposite directions, palms facing outward with the fingers spread wide. If sound had truly existed in this realm, this move would have resonated as the deep toll of a bell.

It was a weak reflection of her power in the physical realm, but, this close to the centre of the warp, it was enough. The monstrosity shattered around her, the breaking of the thinner threads severing the thicker ones until the fabric of the web came undone and it collapsed around her.

She was trembling uncontrollably with her arms still outstretched when the watcher approached her. 'This way, please,' it said, putting a hand on her shoulder and shifting them back to the reflection of the deck.

Still shaking, Alice lowered her arms. Looking around, she wondered how they'd got back here. It hadn't felt as if they'd moved, but then she hadn't noticed the descent into the mind-warp before it was too late either. She examined herself, as if expecting to see blood dripping from her not-quite-corporeal body. But there wasn't anything that dramatic, though angry splotches of red marred the flowing colours from before. They were fading slowly, but while they were there, she could feel the pain of each wound.

It wasn't like when the hellhound had bitten her. These didn't hurt nearly as much, but somehow they felt deeper. Each one felt like a week's worth of forced nightmares. Fear, anxiety and an aching dullness. She felt more tired than she could ever remember being.

'Oh,' she said in surprise, 'I did it.'

'Yes, yes, well done,' said the boy sarcastically. 'You fumbled through that most admirably.'

'If you'd just . . . given me a few pointers, I'm sure I could have done . . . better,' she said, trying her best to sound angry, though the tone didn't manage to break through that wall of sheer weariness. 'So, does this mean . . .'

She felt herself collapsing. It was like falling forward endlessly, with all her senses blurring together. She wanted to fall. It would have been a relief. But something was holding her back.

'Can I go home now?' she mumbled, not really sure where she was. Maybe this was all a dream, and she'd finally wake up in time for school. Maybe . . .

She turned her head to look hazily at a boy a little younger than she was, with scars across his eyes. 'Who're you?' she tried, though it seemed like she wasn't making any sound.

'A face that you will see soon enough,' he seemed to say. 'Listen carefully, girl. I do not know what has brought you here so soon, nor do I know what lies ahead, but you must remember.'

'Wha . . .' She could feel her eyes closing. As the world grew dark, she wondered vaguely why she'd thought he looked like a boy. It didn't even look human. Its eyes . . . like thunderclouds . . .

'Remember, Alice,' the words followed her into nothingness, echoing deeply, 'this is the world that you chose.'

Home

By the time Violetta reached home, the sun was already hidden behind the mountains. All around her, doors were locked, windows barred and shuttered, and the only sound was of the wind rushing through the trees, rising from a sinister rustle to a piercing howl. She walked down the street, looking at the dry gardens filled with brown grass. Shade walked with her.

She passed by one house, and tried hard not to notice a set of eyes glaring at her through the bars. Eyes filled with an emotion that she could almost smell around her.

I'm sorry, Shade whispered.

Vi shook her head firmly. 'It's not your fault.' She meant it, but the words did little to rid the air of that sickly scent. Fear. This was the Valley of Shadow.

Once, they had flourished in their isolation. An oasis of wonder, separated from a world living through a dark age. But then Shade had come. It wasn't his fault. He had only tried to survive, tried to help . . . and in the beginning, he had helped. Now generations had passed. From blood to blood, the Shadow had passed. And when the soldiers had come eleven years ago, when they had killed her father and stolen the Arcanus, peace had followed.

But the people did not forget their fear.

She turned down the narrow lane that led home. Almost eclipsed by ageing trees, the faded brown paintwork created the impression that the house had somehow grown out of the woods.

In one window, a single candle flickered fitfully.

Raising her small hand, Vi knocked firmly on the old wooden door. It opened a minute later, first by a crack and then swinging back to reveal Seidre. She stood with her lips pursed and arms folded, and looked Vi up and down with careful concern. Then she nodded and drew Vi into a quick hug.

'You're late, little sister,' Seidre said.

After dinner, Vi talked about Kava and the other children as she helped with the dishes. As always, they stood near the sink with an oil lamp placed to Seidre's right, so that Vi could stand in between her and Shade.

'It felt wrong. They shouldn't have to behave like—' Vi was saying.

'Why didn't you stop them?' interrupted Seidre.

'What?' The question surprised the young girl. *Stop them?* The thought had never occurred to her. *Why . . .* Her eyes darted towards Shade.

Seidre dried her hands quickly before gently grasping her sister's head in both hands and turning her gaze away from the other being. 'Violetta,' she said quietly, 'I want to know what you were thinking.'

'I . . .' she tried. *Shade?* A part of her was still searching for an answer from him.

It's all right, said Shade. *Answer your sister however you can.*

Why hadn't she stopped them? She wouldn't have had to do *anything*, really. Just walk forward and meet Kava's gaze in front of everyone else. Teach her the right rules . . . *No!*

113

The thought was violent, welling up from the dreams, from the memories, with the impact of a hurricane. *I am not like them!*

She gritted her teeth. 'It wasn't my place to step in.'

'Why not?'

'Because it wouldn't have made things right. If they don't want to be bullied, they should stand up for themselves. Otherwise they'll always expect me to . . .'

'That's not it, Violetta.' Looking down at the kitchen floor, her sister sighed. 'I will not say whether you are right or wrong in this, but you must be able to say it out loud. You must be honest with yourself.'

Vi's frown deepened. 'It wouldn't have been right. Even if you and Shade and Aurin . . . even if you say that I'm normal, I'm not. The reason that they even feel the need for a . . . a *leader* . . . is because of me. If I went over there, it wouldn't have mattered how nice and how kind I was. They'd all still be scared, and that would just make them hide under Kava's skirts more.'

Seidre nodded, finally letting go of Vi's head and sitting down on a tall wooden stool that looked like it had seen better days. 'And?' she asked leadingly.

Don't sulk, interjected Shade as Vi's face threatened to turn itself into a stubborn pout.

Suppressing a few choice thoughts that would have shocked both her kitchen companions, Vi nodded glumly. 'And because I was afraid. Not of being different,' she said hastily. 'But because . . . I didn't want to use . . . I didn't want to be like . . . like Kava.'

They understood, and so did she. It wasn't Kava she was scared of being compared to. Those who had borne the Shadow before her had done so much worse.

Seidre patted Vi's hand gently. 'It's probably a safer idea to think like that, but just as you can't be ashamed of who you are, you also have to stop being *afraid* of who you are. Maybe it's not going to be those children over there, but you have your life ahead of you and a whole world waiting outside this valley. And there are millions of people in it who let themselves be bullied around by people like Kava, even if it isn't as obvious. And sometimes, all those people need is someone to show them what it's like to be strong.'

The lamp flickered as Vi sat thoughtfully and drank her hot chocolate. The sweet, spicy taste seemed to flow around her tongue and directly into her limbs, setting her fingers and toes tingling. Try as she might, only one part of what Seidre said really stuck in her head. *A whole world waiting . . .*

You need to tell her, prompted Shade.

You're in a bossy mood today, she thought back irritably. When in company, she did her best not to speak aloud to Shade. Especially not in front of Seidre.

Time is short.

Something must have shown on her face because a moment later, Seidre frowned and asked, 'What is it?'

'It's . . .' Vi sighed inwardly. 'It's almost time.'

Seidre's dark eyes widened, and her fingers had tightened around her cup. 'Already?' she whispered. 'Are you sure?'

'Yes,' replied Vi nervously. 'Shade says he can sense something coming. About a week away.'

'No . . .' said Seidre, biting her lip in thought. 'It's not something. It's someone, isn't it?'

She turned away before Vi could nod, and seemed to mutter to herself, 'Eden has fallen . . . That must be why. We said we'd help, but . . . Not this soon. Not now.'

Vi waited quietly. Two years ago, Seidre had visited this Eden and stayed there for almost six months, travelling with some of the elders from the valley. She had been the only one to come back, and just after that had been the first and only time she'd spoken directly to Shade.

Finally, after what seemed like an eternity, Seidre turned back. Her face was pale and worried, making her look a lot older than her nineteen years.

'You . . .' she started, and then just let the words fade away.

You can't be leaving.

You aren't ready.

You don't have to go.

Every unspoken sentence seemed to fill the gap between the two sisters, and even as she brushed them away, Vi couldn't help but be glad for them.

'You'll have to say goodbye to Mother,' said Seidre after a long moment.

'I know.'

'I'll come with you, of course. And . . . and maybe after that, I could come with you as well. I—'

But Vi smiled and shook her head. 'I'll be fine,' she said. 'I'm not alone.'

Across Hill and Dale

Kharsan

Leaving ahead of our pursuers was the easy part. Keeping ahead—well, let's just say the stitch in my side wasn't helping. It's all very well to walk miles and miles every day with all sorts of supplies slung over my back, but a single hundred-metre dash and . . .

Fine—so I could have just handed my pack over to Adam, who just happens to be slowing himself down to keep me company, but as far as normal human pride goes, there has to be a line that I won't cross, and handing over the pack is that line. It might just be the line that's going to get me killed, but I'm trying not to think of that.

The terrain isn't making things any easier. We're not really in desert country, but what with the year's drought, it might as well be. A sandy, dry riverbed snakes through the landscape, marking our trail, but I have a suspicion that following it might just make it easier for them to track us.

'How far behind are they?'

'Not far enough. But they are moving slowly. They will have other groups headed to the valley entrance as reinforcements.'

'Shouldn't—' I try not to gasp as a particularly steep stretch demands the use of muscles I was sure had atrophied from disuse. 'Shouldn't they be trying to surround us?'

Adam shakes his head, patiently waiting for me to catch up. 'There is no reason for us to go either north or south, even if there were trails to use. Santor lies to the west, and they know the connection between Eden and the Valley of Shadow. They will wait there.'

'And we, bloody idiots that we are,' I mutter, 'are headed straight for them.'

Adam throws me a small smile. 'Do not worry,' he says, but he doesn't bother with telling me why I shouldn't worry, which only means that I now have my original worries along with the worry of what he might be planning lumped on top of them. That's a lot of worry to sort through while scrabbling over a rough, rocky trail.

I keep glancing up nervously, expecting to see more of their bloody reinforcements screaming across the sky. Such a bright blue that it's damnably annoying, and not a single cloud from horizon to horizon. It does little to raise my scorched spirits. If the maps that my father left me are accurate, we should be approaching Santor early tomorrow. Or if we just keep walking, we could probably be there in the middle of the night, and I have a suspicion that this is the reason for our undue haste. No. This time around they will be ready, and the cover of darkness will not be to our advantage.

My father had said Seidre and the others in Santor could help hide Adam. But I worry about taking him there. Despite his upbringing, I believe he is more than a weapon, but that doesn't mean he isn't dangerous.

Glancing in his direction, I realize that he's stopped.

'Don't tell me,' I say, already resigned to the worst, 'they're right behind us.'

He shakes his head again, and I take note of his hand on the rock. Unless I've missed my guess, that touch on the rock reveals much, the vibrations of distant movements having been distilled into a kind of vision by his uncanny mind.

'No,' he says, and my worry levels immediately amplify, because I hear something in his voice that I've never heard before.

Doubt.

'What is it?' I try looking around but, with my meagre human senses, all I can make out is sun, dirt and rock. Not the most informative of viewpoints. He lowers his hand and then looks straight ahead.

'I think,' he says slowly, 'that we need to hurry.'

There needs to be a law against saying ominous things like that.

A few hours later, the sun is just beginning its dip behind the low mountains that surround us. And with the light starting to fade, the universe—the ironic bastard that it is—decides to end our lovely dried-riverbed trek and present us with a dried waterfall, which looks a lot like a towering 200-foot climb with a high possibility of falling, followed by an even higher possibility of death.

I hate the universe.

'We're going to have to climb this bloody thing, aren't we?' I ask.

Adam grins slightly. 'Yes, brother. Unless you've learnt to fly.'

A few days out of Eden, and he's found a sense of humour. Bloody brilliant. 'I don't suppose you can carry me?' I mutter, now quite willing to shelve my pride in the face of mortal peril.

He seems to give serious thought to this. 'I do not believe so,' he says. 'But it is a good idea to use rope.'

After we're tied together (which would have taken less time if I hadn't tried to help), he starts up the rock face with spider-like nimbleness. As soon as he's about ten metres up, I begin my own, far less graceful ascent.

The first five metres aren't that bad, and I make the mistake of thinking, 'Oh, we should be done before the sun fades away entirely.' The next fifteen metres repay my optimism with a jagged cut on my palm, a bump on the side of my head and a wrenched shoulder from avoiding a spiny-tailed lizard.

A while later, with twilight now all around us, I take a short rest, only to realize that I've almost caught up with Adam, because he's not moving. Before I can call out to him, he whispers, 'Be still, brother,' and I find myself frozen to the rock face.

Below us, there is a curious mechanical noise. Like hydraulics or a well-oiled tractor. I try looking down, only to instantly regret it. There is something down there, patrolling the riverbed. I can only make out a large figure. All angles and with a matt black finish. A machine of some kind? Beams of light stretch out across the riverbed below.

I try not to breathe. Though perhaps I should have been trying not to slip. Because at that precise moment, my foot slides off my precarious foothold, leaving me hanging by the fingertips for a second . . . before falling.

The rope goes taut in an instant, Adam's expertly tied knots digging deep into my flesh. Gasping, I scramble back on to the cliff face, unfortunately dislodging a shower of pebbles.

Adam is next to me in a flash. He pushes me forward, and we both flatten ourselves against the rock as the light from the 'machine' stabs upwards. Adam's hand reaches the back of my neck, and a sharp and sudden chill runs through me as my body heat dissipates into the cold evening. I should be shivering. But, instead, I'm just frozen in that instant, struggling to breathe, to stay alive.

More than Adam's superhuman agility and strength, this is what terrifies me. It is one thing to be able to train your own body to lower its temperature to undetectable levels, but no human should be able to do this to another.

The lights scan over us slowly. Back and forth. Thankfully, we are not alone. A nearby juniper tree, growing out of the cliff, shivers when the light passes over, and a small family of marmots poke their chubby faces out from a hole behind it, dislodging more pebbles, chattering angrily and then hiding.

The light lingers over them for a few more seconds, and then snaps back to the valley floor. Adam releases me a second later, and I feel the warmth flood back in.

I try to keep from shaking as mobility returns. We wait in silence for a few more minutes, and then, with considerably more caution, we keep climbing.

Near the top, we find a small mountain cave, just big enough to squeeze into.

The sky is the gentle purple of late evening, with a few pinpricks of light starting to sketch the constellations. The distant mountains have already faded, and the rock itself is alive at this time, each grade of shale and granite a different stripe of colour, and when the wind blows, the surface ripples as dust shifts, just barely visible.

Only once my breath has returned to a mere painful wheeze do I look over at Adam. He squats crouched at the cave entrance, scanning the area with an eagle-like gaze.

Does he see the same world as I do? Are the colours the same brilliant shades? Or does he look into the very heart of this universe, staring straight at a sight awesome enough to blind mortal eyes? *What do you see, my brother?* These are the questions I cannot bring myself to ask him.

But outside, I can still hear the muted sounds of the same mechanical movement echoing in the hills. 'Is it still nearby?' I ask.

He lifts an arm and points in the distance. 'Over there, on top of that rise,' he says. 'Lower your head, so that you can see it framed against the horizon.'

I do as he says, lowering myself so that my head is almost flat on the ledge surface, and squint suspiciously in the direction of his pointing finger.

Against the sky, something about twice the height and three times the width of a man clambers clumsily to the top. And then the moonlight hits, a silver sheen peeking out from a curtain of wisp-like clouds. The angles shine with a dull finish, and the shape is turned from an overlarge, angular human to a nightmarish image.

'What is that?' I hiss.

Adam closes his eyes. 'It is an abomination,' he says simply. 'We should rest, brother. Tomorrow will have its own challenges.'

❧

In the morning, there are no signs of those . . . things.

An 'abomination', he called it. Adam does not grant labels easily. Though given the fanatical nonsense they tried to teach him at Eden, I should be glad of it. Personally, when we first set out, I was fully expecting him to be a rabid psychotic hiding behind the innocence of a child, but now I see that he has an uncomplicated view of things that somehow has a way of sidestepping all the BS.

Still, as relieved as I am that monstrous mechanical abominations aren't about to tear us apart, I have an equal certainty that they are waiting downhill from here, where the entrance to Santor awaits us.

We take our time. According to my father's notes, Santor can only be reached at noon.

There's an odd belief that going downhill on mountain paths is easier. On a perfectly constructed path, with stairs, safety rails and anything else built for the sake of tourists with expensive digital cameras, this might be true. On a path that was rejected outright by mountain goats, going downhill is even easier. It's stopping yourself from going downhill that's really hard. And it's bloody murder on the knees.

Still, we manage to make it to a more plateau-like area without accident. We hadn't really climbed that high; it's just the terrain here that makes it feel like no matter where you stand, it's either mountain or desert. Hiding behind some rocks, we take note of the scene ahead.

Just where the foothills level off completely, there's a small expanse of absolute nothingness decorated by a few large rock formations, and beyond that is a sheer cliff wall rising up a good couple of hundred metres from the ground. I squint, trying to spot where the valley might be, but the folds and cracks of the cliff are shrouded in a thousand shadows.

'Can you spot the entrance?' I ask him.

He shakes his head. 'It won't be there till noon.'

'I was afraid you were going to say that,' I mutter back. 'What about our friends? Can you spot them?'

'Yes. There are five camouflaged outposts within a kilometre's radius of the outpost. Additionally, there seem to be three other vehicular units hidden near the foothills.'

'How can you tell?'

He taps his left ear. 'They are not as silent as they believe.'

I sigh. Even one man with a gun is more than what I would have liked, but if they've got an entire bloody platoon down there, not to mention . . . 'What about those . . . things . . . from earlier?'

A flicker of disquiet passes over his face. 'One waits ahead. Two are following, staying near high ground. They know roughly where we are, but they are keeping their distance.'

Probably to avoid spooking us. A bit late, if you ask me, but then no one seems to be asking me anything about any of this. 'Let me guess—you can hear them as well?'

He half nods, but then stops. 'It is . . . odd, brother,' he says. 'I can feel them.'

'I . . . see,' I say with a blissful lack of any form of seeing, understanding or basic comprehension. I can't help but let out another very weary sigh. 'What are they?'

'They are . . .' His hands move in front of him, as if he's trying an idea that he doesn't have words for. 'Like dolls,' he finishes, but from the expression on his face, he seems unhappy with the description.

I open my mouth for a follow-up question but shut it just as quickly. There are more pressing issues than the exact nature of the threats around us, such as how to slip past them.

'Do you have a plan?' I ask with knotted apprehension.

The thoughtful expression on his face does give me a moment's hope of a rational, foolproof plan, equipped with an equally foolproof plan B, which is further supported by plan C, which is not foolproof but is still very safe. Then he grins. Perhaps it's just me, but when people grin, it's generally followed by bad things happening. Usually to someone else.

'Tell me, brother, can you drive?'

❦

I hate being right.

Within the hour, I've discovered just how unsurprising it is to have the tires shot up, the vehicle swerve wildly, and topple and tumble three times before crashing against a rock with me still inside. On the surface, I am obviously screaming bloody murder because that is fully expected, but I assure you, inwardly I am calmly reflecting on how this is exactly as disastrous as I imagined it to possibly be.

Now, going back a good ten minutes before being placed in immediate mortal danger, there was me, desperately trying to keep up with Adam's nimble steps as he rushes *towards* one of the hidden units. (The logic of this action is very debatable, but there is a time for debates—and I really, *really* wish this was it.)

I'm fifty metres behind when I hear the first shouts, and the disturbing way in which they are cut off halfway through. I do hope he isn't killing them but, in this mess, I would probably be able to stomach an 'us or them' sort of mentality.

It's still a relief to round the last set of rocks to see the last soldier slump, unconscious, to the ground from a carefully placed nerve strike. The others all seem to be breathing as well. Just five soldiers and two vehicles parked in the shadow of a rock formation that reminds me of an Easter Island head. He moves quickly to the nearest vehicle—an armoured Hummer-like monstrosity—and begins rummaging in the back. I concentrate on stopping the wheezing, since it appears that despite a hardy trek across miles and miles of rocky wasteland, I am still, compared to Adam anyway, as athletic as an asthmatic koala bear.

'Do they . . . know . . . that we're here?' I finally gasp out.

He doesn't answer, hauling out a flare gun. Before I can object to what is no doubt a part of his brilliant strategy, he fires a flare into the noon sky, which explodes in a very visible red burst. 'They do now,' he says, gesturing towards the driver's seat. 'Hurry, brother, there isn't much time.'

I do as he asks, stoically ignoring the voice in my head that says driving a small supply wagon around Eden's main compound is not a qualification for gruelling off-road motorized pursuit. Still, it is a sop to my growing inferiority complex that this, at least, is something that Adam cannot do. Even if it is just because he can't reach the pedals.

It takes a few tries to get the vehicle started. But once it's going, it handles remarkably well on the rough terrain, a fact that is somewhat less comforting when I spot the columns of dust that are undoubtedly the other vehicles, which are also handling remarkably well as they begin to catch up.

Adam rides on the roof, the flare gun swapped for a very lethal-looking assault rifle. As the bursts of gunfire start to sound, I try to focus on driving directly towards a specific spot on the cliff wall ahead.

It's not easy, mind you; and, in my defence, it was a perfectly natural reaction to look backwards as one of the pursuing vehicles spun away, its tires shredded by Adam's meticulous aim. And it wasn't really my fault that there just happened to be a large rock just *there*, causing the entire vehicle to jump into the air, forcing Adam to discard his little toy and cling to the roof. Which, in turn, allowed the second vehicle to close in and start firing at *our* tires, resulting in our unsurprising crash.

What *is* surprising is being alive after the crash. Really amazing safety features. After extricating myself from the wreckage, I see Adam some distance behind. I'm guessing he jumped off just before I lost control. The crash has kicked up enough dirt to hide an army, so I can't really make out where our pursuers are, but I imagine it's not far.

Adam looks towards me; and, even from this distance, I can spot a disturbing degree of confidence in his smile as he turns away and rushes into the dust clouds. Thirty seconds later, the second pursuing vehicle breaks free of the dust, carried by its own momentum, with its bullet-ridden engine smoking gently.

It comes to a slow halt, without any sign of its occupants. Adam follows behind, as if he's posing for a bloody photo op. I swear that boy has an over-heightened sense of the dramatic.

There's about two minutes left before noon. Enough time for one last desperate dash towards the cliffs, and the waiting valley.

Then the dust clears, and the abominations arrive.

The Implacable Soldier

The last five sentries were lined up against the far wall of the engineering bay, staring straight ahead through blank optical lenses. These more human-sized versions were intended for the fortification of the interior of a facility. Oddly, their smaller size made Roth far more uneasy than he'd been when overseeing the field tests of their giant brethren. Perhaps the near-human size made them more . . . real. He turned towards the chief technician, Edward Merkaut, an owlish-looking man who seemed to exude a sense of permanently affronted dignity.

Merkaut shook his head, a dour expression on his face. 'We can't do it. We have taken apart one of the activated models and tried replacing each part piece by piece, but it makes no difference. The . . . um . . . energy flow is non-transferable. As per the original activation, we have five scout-class sentries, three assault-class and seventeen security-class—no more, no less.'

'All right.' Roth sighed inwardly. The entire robotic sentry program had been gathering dust for years now as people stumbled towards the breakthroughs that might have made it practical, but even the most optimistic scientist would have placed field-testing as far down the road as fifty years. With 'Sheol's' help, he had managed to do it in ten.

'How are the tests on the energy matrix proceeding?' he asked. That was the key. If the energy could be replicated, along with the method of 'linking', then there was no need for Sheol.

'Not well. The living energy is flowing into these shells from the other end of the link with almost perfect efficiency and zero loss or lag during transference. Now, if we had access to the *source* of the energy . . .'

'I doubt we'll be able to manage that. For now, keep doing what you can,' said Roth. This was still a promising start. With the *Anima Arcanus* in hand, they could really make a difference here. And not just against supernatural threats. With this kind of power, they could change the world.

His earpiece chimed. 'Yes?'

'Madeline here. We just got a coded message. The Black Rangers and their sentries have made contact with the subject.'

In hindsight, the captain of the Black Rangers considered that sending out the other vehicles to check on the emergency flare had probably not been the best of ideas.

It had taken less than five minutes for the boy to take out all three motorized response teams and place himself within range of the cliff wall. But the plan was set. Everyone had been given their orders pre-deployment, and now it was just a matter of seeing them executed. Teams two and four were already closing in quickly, and three and five had set up enclosure positions in case of a breakout attempt.

His team was already in place. The pursuit had given away the end point, and they'd set up a sniping position. He'd originally recommended gas and other wide-area countermeasures, but those had been vetoed on the basis that there was no way to know if they'd have any effect. A bullet through the leg, on the other hand, should be suitably difficult to ignore. The rifles had been modified heavily for small-calibre, high-velocity rounds, designed to cripple rather than kill.

'On my command,' he said harshly to the cover team, equipped with long-range assault rifles. 'Now!'

The bursts of bullet fire were not aimed at the centre of the rapidly fading dust clouds, but towards the cliff wall, the hollow-point bullets shattering as they hit and ricocheted off the rock face with the purpose of keeping the targets from approaching the cliff.

Over the consistent chatter, the captain signed for the snipers to take aim. They already had their orders—limbs were the primary targets, otherwise the lower body. The main problem was the vast quantities of dust eclipsing the wreckage of the hijacked vehicle, which made precision or even general targeting something of an impossibility.

A few seconds later, it seemed as if his hopes had been answered. A strong wind whistled through the space between the foothills and the cliff, funnelling the dust out with unnatural speed, revealing the tiny figures that were the targets, and around them . . .

The guns of his squad went silent. 'Keep firing!' he shouted. 'They're on our side!'

One of the snipers looked at him, her mouth half open, as if to say that the allegiance of those things was not the foremost question on their minds; but the captain fixed her with a glare promising a vengeful court martial until she turned back to her scope.

He bit his lip as he turned his attention back to the field. Roth had brought him in days earlier to watch the initial tests, those monstrous sentries towering over him like in a scene out of *Invasion of the Killer Robots*. And the way they moved . . .

Not like machines. Despite the outsize nature of the scout-class sentries, they'd seemed so disturbingly human. He should have been glad that they were on his side. Instead he had just felt nauseous.

Golem

Kharsan

My father kept a book of legends, filled with tales of gods, of monsters in the shape of men, of miracles and wonders, and of dark things that haunted the night.

The third story was of a Jewish rabbi named Loew. To protect his people, he shaped the figure of a man out of clay and brought it to life by writing the word *emet*, 'truth', on its forehead. Thus was born the golem.

These are creatures of steel and silicon rather than clay and there is no word etched on their foreheads; but looking at them, I know that this is what they are. Adam called them 'dolls'. And for all the world, they look like extras from a Transformers film. But from this close, there's something so tragically alive about them. The posture, the deep menace behind those gleaming lens-like eyes. It's almost as if I can hear them screaming soundlessly in pain and rage. I now know why he called them abominations.

Of course, this is hardly the time to be analysing their philosophical existence, what with the near-constant hail of bullets and the fact that these . . . golem creatures seem remarkably agile for their size, and are closing in fast. And Adam is just standing there, trembling. Not with fear.

Anger.

'Adam!' I shout. 'We have to go. Now!'

The first creature closes before he turns. Even from here, I can see its arm extend, the fitted joints and burnished metal interspersed with fixtures for a thousand different types of military hardware. A thin line shoots towards Adam with all the hallmarks of a taser gun.

He catches it with one hand and, despite the distance and gunfire echoing all around, I can hear the buzz of the current. Logic should dictate that he fall unconscious, but logic has never met Adam. Sparks erupt around the machine's arm instead, and Adam moves forward like a viper, the taser cable held tight in his hands as he slips through the metal giant's legs and around.

As it falls, he's already moving back towards me. For once, there's not a trace of ease on that face, grim determination having taken over completely. The second creature is already starting to close, which makes me think that running for the cliffs frantically might actually have some merit.

Adam catches up before I'm a quarter way there but paces himself to keep from overtaking. I get this cold knot in the pit of my stomach when I realize that he's staying just behind me and to the left—the same direction as the bullets are coming from. While I'm reasonably confident that he could survive being shot at point-blank range without serious injury, it is still very unnerving to have one's little brother act as a human shield.

Particularly when he stumbles after apparently being shot in the leg. He makes no sound. There is no blood. He just stumbles for a moment, and then keeps going. I imagine it's something about the adrenaline and heightened reflexes and all those bloody things that actually allows me to keep track of these details and still run. It's really very fascinating, in a completely morbid sort of way.

'There!' Adam shouts, pointing towards a shadow on the cliff face. In the noonlight, every irregularity casts its own shade

133

of grey, but this particular shadow is deeper, splitting the cliff in an irregular vertical line.

Santor.

Unfortunately, they seem to be consistently firing a line of bullets between us and the valley entrance. Seeing as there isn't much choice except to keep going, I decide to fall back on praying, which has never appealed to me as a reliable solution.

'Slide, now!' Adam's command bypasses my mind completely; and the next thing I know, I've already leaned back, my legs scraping a path as momentum carries me forward through an eerily timed gap in the consistent field of fire. Before I can come to a complete halt, I'm already scrambling to my feet, trying to ignore the bloody scrapes on my palms and elbows. I do hope they have tetanus shots in Santor.

Almost to the valley. The adrenaline rush seems to have burned out, and it feels as if my lungs are a hair's breadth away from imploding. Everything narrows now, a field of vision focused completely forward. It's only just before we hit the valley that I slow down, uncertain of whether or not Adam is still with me.

I start to turn when I hear his voice close to my ear. 'Keep going.'

I tell myself that it had that same core of command to it. That I had no choice other than to stumble forward into the shadow, before turning to see Adam struggling with one of the remaining metal creatures. He's trying to keep its outsize hand from closing around him, but even his strength seems insufficient against the sheer power and will of whatever is driving that thing. I start forward, without any clear intention other than to get to his side and try and help.

I tell myself that it was too late. The shadow was already closing all around, and the path out was closing with it. Before I took even two steps, everything had turned to darkness, leaving only the last image of Adam turning towards me with a resolute smile.

I have to tell myself these things. And I have to believe them. The alternative is that I just left my little brother behind. And that is not something I believe I can live with.

Call of the Dark

The house with the broken windows seemed to hold darkness all around it. Seidre knocked twice on the door. Then, without waiting for a response, she pushed it open, gesturing for Vi to enter first.

There was little light inside, the deep gloom broken only by a few gleams that managed to penetrate the thick curtains. The large living area was bare, causing each step to echo against the wooden floorboards.

Keep close, she warned Shade.

He knew better than to venture far in this house, but it was still a relief to feel his presence concentrate around her feet. There were too many . . . fragments . . . scattered here. It was a place where memories of terror were etched deep into the walls; and Shade's presence could trigger them all too easily. After all, he had helped create them.

'Mother?' called Seidre as she shut the door behind them.

There wasn't any reply, but the sound of soft scuffling came from upstairs. Vi let Seidre take the lead. It was better that way. They found her in the second bedroom upstairs, with the cat scratching against the door. It gave them a level green-eyed stare, as was its habit, before stalking off. The woman inside was seated at a small round table, animatedly gesturing and giving all the signs of being engaged in silent conversation with someone who wasn't there.

Seidre pulled up a stool and gingerly sat down next to her. Vi stayed near the door. It took a minute for their mother to notice their presence. She stopped her ghostly conversation abruptly and turned to face Seidre with a wan smile. 'Hello, dear,' she said. 'I didn't see you there.'

As she turned, Vi took a long look at her face. Even though she knew that her mother wasn't any more than forty years old, she looked so much older. Her hair had turned a silver colour that was neither truly white nor grey, and the wrinkles around her eyes and mouth were few in number but set deeply enough that, in the dim light, they might have been mistaken for scars. The beauty was still there—cracked, perhaps, but preserved nonetheless—somewhere around the high cheekbones and large eyes.

'We just got here, Mother,' said Seidre, bowing her head slightly. 'How have you been?'

There was a considering pause. 'I am quite well,' came the reply in a matter-of-fact tone. 'My companions are not so fortunate, I fear. There is something in the air that has them rushing about like headless chickens.'

Vi had once asked Shade if the phantoms were real or not, but she had got an answer that was both yes and no. *They are not real in that they exist only for her, but they are real because they were also created only for her.*

'I'm sure it will pass,' said Seidre soothingly. 'Mrs Azare says you've been eating less lately.'

'Are you certain?' She shook her head once, before continuing briskly. 'Well, you know best, I'm sure. I'll try and do better.' A shadow of a frown appeared. 'You look a little different, Seidre—how old are you now?'

'Nineteen, Mother.'

'Really? How odd . . . I was almost sure it was some other number. But something else is different. What is it?'

'I . . .' Seidre swallowed. 'Violetta is also here to see you.'

Vi made no move to step forward. If anything, she had to fight the urge to step back and fade into the shadows.

'Oh, I see . . .' She seemed to shrink into herself for a second, before sitting forward, a mixture of eagerness and fear on her face. 'Is that you, Vi? Come in, please. Don't skulk around the door.'

'Mama,' said Vi in greeting as she obliged, standing next to her sister.

Her mother's gaze was fixed on her face, but she could see the eyes fighting to keep from looking down.

'Look at you, Vi—you've grown so little, and you're still so thin . . .' Rather than expressing concern, she could almost have been wondering aloud. '*He* was also very thin . . .' Again, her eyes seemed to strain with effort. 'It's unusual to see you both. Is there an occasion? You'll have to forgive me if it's a birthday.' There was that weak smile. 'I'm afraid I've forgotten my own.'

Seidre tugged on Vi's hand, urging her to speak. She took a deep breath. 'Mama—I . . . I will be leaving the valley for a while.'

This time, her mother's gaze locked on the floor as fear took up residence. 'You can't!' She shook her head vehemently. 'That's why, isn't it? That's why they're restless. They know!'

'Mother . . .' started Seidre.

'This is your fault, isn't it?' She turned on Seidre. 'You left. You left the valley, and you didn't think there would be consequences!'

With an inward sigh, Vi rounded the small table to stand next to her mother. 'I have to leave,' she said, hating the silence that came after.

After a minute, her mother looked up at her face. 'Death waits outside,' she said in a small voice. 'That's what he said. This is the Valley of Shadow, and if the Shadow leaves . . .'

138

'I will be fine,' said Vi with as much confidence as she could muster. 'And the valley will also be fine.' She paused for a second. 'It'll be different. But that's better than nothing changing.'

Shade was silent. He always kept that way around their mother. He had been part of her life for so long, before Vi, before Seidre.

'Are you . . . sure?'

Vi was opening her mouth to respond when the feeling hit. It felt as if the world had grown immeasurably larger for a single second and she had been watching it happen from a great distance.

'What happened?' asked Seidre, seeing her reaction.

'They're close.'

'When?'

'Soon.' She jerked around. 'They're at the boundary. I have to go. If I'm not there, they could die.'

The boundary was where the dead waited. All those that the Shadow had killed over the centuries were bound there.

'Violetta . . .' said her mother, the fear still strong.

Vi swallowed carefully. 'Everything will be fine,' she said firmly and then started out.

Shade followed in silence.

Into Shadow

Kharsan

In every direction there are only shadows.

That is not to say that it is dark, but rather that the world itself seems carved from darkness. The craggy outlines of the seemingly endless valley are all too well-defined, but it is coated with a shifting cloak of black and grey, lending the entire landscape a most . . . *alive* texture. And one that has all the telltale characteristics of a hungry predator. As for other details, it appears that the sky no longer exists. Perhaps it might be better to say that I cannot see the sky, but I cannot shake the feeling, when I look up, that the sky has simply vanished—as if it had always been some great big blue hallucination shared by all of humanity.

Going back is definitely out of the question. Every time I tried, the shadows swarmed even thicker around the exit, threatening to suck the very life from my bones. I suddenly wish that I had read a lot less horror fiction. It would have made my imagination so much more manageable.

Time is another thing that I start to lose track of. For all I know, it might just be an hour since Adam and I raced towards the valley entrance. Or maybe it was a year ago.

As might be gathered, I am quite possibly on the verge of losing what is left of my sanity. It's only understandable, I suppose, after having spent my childhood years in what can only now be described as a cross between a scientific laboratory, a military academy and a religious school (quite a dangerous mixture, if I stop to think about it), being invaded by some random commandos, being chased across miles of barren countryside, being attacked again (this time by metal golem monsters), having watched my brother be kidnapped by the same metal golem monsters and finally being trapped in the creepy valley of interminable shadow . . . This has not been a good month.

I try thinking about Seidre, about more pleasant times. She could be here, in Santor.

Their odd delegation had come to Eden two years ago, right before Father had left. I'd never really met anyone even close to my age, though she was still older. Meeting her had been like feeling the first breath of spring after a long, hard winter. I remember being friends . . . being more . . .

The shadows seem to be much closer. They're starting to pool at my feet, with thin tendrils stretching up around my ankles, dragging them to the ground with each heavy step. Hunger, thirst and weariness may be gone, but the tight knot in my throat is a clear reminder that fear is all too present. And that all the positive thoughts in the world aren't enough to keep it at bay.

The walls of the valley are closing in now, sheer pillars of darkness on either side, and I can almost hear them move. I can almost hear them speak. It's getting harder to walk, or to think . . .

Hello, what are you doing here all alone?

And I think I just thought something that I didn't actually think.

Leave him alone. Ha ha ha. The Shadow will take him soon enough. Then we'll have all the time in the world.

Excuse me? Are you new? Are you alive?

Are you scared?

No. I'm not scared. I'm bloody well terrified. What are you? What are you doing in my head?

We're not in your head. We're over your head. We're under your feet. We're all around you. Can't you see us? Can't you feel us? Can't you . . .

Stop it! Don't scare him away.

Away? Ha! Where is he going to go? Where is he going to run? There is no escape.

Let's take a look. A peek.

He's trying to fight it. How hilarious. Don't fight it. Trust me, these are your own thoughts speaking.

Don't believe it. Don't believe anything.

Look what I've found. Look what we have.

What is it? What is it?

So solemn. So dramatic. It's a deathbed scene. Come on—everyone, take a look!

Everything seems painted in shades of white. The sheets, the walls, the sterile tiles lining the floor; even her dark face seems so pale. There's a hum in the air, emanating from the nearby bank of isobaric chambers, where the child sleeps silently.

His mother's gaze flickers and wavers towards the chambers and then returns. There's an emptiness around the edges of the scene that's eating its way inward with each passing moment.

Why, she looks absolutely horrible.

It's a deathbed. She's dying. It's expected.

He never expected this. They'd always said that everything would be fine. That it was safe. That this was a wondrous thing—a miracle beyond that of life itself.

They had lied. She had lied.

'I'm sorry,' she says. Her arm is raised, as if to make a comforting gesture, but then it falls, arrested by its own weakness.

Apologizing and dying at the same time? Is that allowed?

Of course not, but people who are dying tend to ignore such commonplace rules. It's really very uncivilized of them.

Shush. You're making him angry.

142

He knows he shouldn't be angry, but he can't stop it. He's almost trembling from the rage of unanswered questions. Of why this had to happen, why they're here in the first place . . . All the unreasonable whys in the world seem to be bubbling in his mind. Not the whats, though. He knows what's happening. And he knows what's going to happen next.

That's why he can't let the anger show.

He doesn't say anything, but he does meet her eyes.

'I know,' she says. 'I wish there was more time. There is always much left unsaid.'

'It's okay,' he says. It comes out as a sullen mutter, but it's the most he can manage.

There's a slight smile on her face. She knows. She knows everything about him. 'You must listen to me, Khadim,' she says. 'You are the eldest. Even if blood does not bind you, I ask this . . .'

In his mind, he wills her not to ask. He hasn't even seen the child yet, but a part of him wants nothing to do with him.

'You must protect them.'

Stay away from my memories!

Now, now—there's no use getting agitated. We only want to get to know you.

Stay out of my mind!

Do you think it really works that way? You came here. You're the intruder! Walking over our graves and scuffing your shoes on our bones! Do you know where you are?

Calm down. He doesn't know. How would he?

Share and share alike. Let's give him a tour.

No!

Too late.

There are no clouds in the sky, but the sky itself seems to have turned an overcast grey. The people have gathered, forming a half-circle in front of the manor. They maintain their silence, their faces carefully kept blank of either anticipation or horror. They have been summoned to witness. No more. No less.

He is forced to a kneeling position in front of them. There are no restraints. There are no guards. There is just the Shadow. And the man behind the Shadow.

The man paces in front of the crowd, his hands clasped behind him and his head bowed as if in reflection. He keeps at it for minutes, never once showing any awareness of the people around him or the kneeling man. They don't show any signs of impatience, naturally.

Finally, the pacing stops and the man comes to a halt in front of him. 'Look me in the eyes!'

The thought drives deep, jerking his head up to look into that face.

Such a thin face . . . sunken eye sockets, hollow cheeks framed by lank black hair. The cheekbones and high temple stand out, forming the framework of what might have once been a handsome face. But now there are only jagged angles, casting deep downward shadows in streaks. And the eyes burn with the purest form of wrath that he has ever seen.

'Do you have anything to say? You have my permission. Speak your defiance, if you will.'

'I have no words that are fit for those present,' he says. They won't listen. There is too much fear in them to listen.

That's when it hits him. Now, at the very end, he is no longer afraid.

The rage in the man's eyes dims for a moment as a cruel smile flickers on his face. 'Good. Accept in death what you could not in life. From my rule there is no escape.'

Then the Shadow closes.

Stop it! Stop this! Leave me alone!

Calm down. It's all right—they're gone now.

Sight is the first faculty to emerge from that chaos. Everything seems dim and unclear, as if I am entering a dark room after having walked in daylight. But as I breathe in, the sensations are reversed. The air is sharp, cold and clear, filling my lungs and clearing my mind.

There's stone, dust and dry grass beneath my hands, and the remnants of tears are on my face. It takes me a moment to realize that I'm no longer surrounded by claustrophobic walls and endless shadows. It takes a further moment to realize that I'm kneeling on the ground, and am completely incapable of moving.

It will take a moment to readjust. Do not be alarmed.

And here I thought I'd left all the voices behind. Maybe I've just gone crazy.

'He's just trying to help.'

I try looking up and, while my head doesn't seem to want to comply, at least my eyeballs manage a partial rotation. There's a young girl standing there. There's something very disturbingly familiar about her, but in my current state of mind, I can't quite place it.

'Who . . .' I start, but I'm almost certain it comes out as an incoherent slur.

'You were travelling with someone. What happened?' she asks.

'We . . .' I take a deep breath. 'We were attacked.'

That's all I can manage. The dimness is starting to return.

Shade?

His body's at its limit. He needs time.

Two voices. One of them belongs to the girl, the other . . . I look down, and I realize that there's a shadow moving beneath me, and it's not mine.

We'll have to take him to Seidre.

Seidre . . . Yes, this girl does remind me a little of Seidre, but that's not it. The alien memory is still far too fresh. The man with rage burning in his eyes and the Shadow stretched out beneath him. That's who she reminds me of. And that is not a comforting thought to lose consciousness at.

The Lands of Kali

Alice

Wake up screaming—huh, I thought I'd already done that.

'Calm down. It's all right.' I can feel someone grabbing my shoulders firmly, but it takes a few moments for my sight to focus enough to see my least favourite fox in all of existence. 'You're all right,' she says.

I could swear I pulled my fist back to punch her, so I really have no idea why a couple of seconds later, I'm crying against her shoulder.

I'm not a crying sort of person. At least not in a loud, emotional sort of way. If I do have to cry, I really prefer to do it quietly so that there's at least that little bit of dignity to being completely and totally torn up on the inside. So why am I bawling like a baby while the person responsible for everything I've been through pats my head in a comforting fashion? I really, *really* wish I knew.

My reasoning mind waits it out (while making a mental note to repress this entire incident later), and eventually I'm pulling away, sheepishly taking an offered handkerchief. It's only after blowing my nose that I realize that despite the presence of a hard bed and a gentle rocking motion . . . this is not the ship.

'Where . . . where are we?' I ask her in between sniffs, dreading all the possible answers.

'On a train,' says Kit calmly, using another handkerchief to primly dry off her shoulder.

'Right, of course. Where else would we be?' I stop for a moment, backtracking through my recently turbulent existence. Blowing up stuff in Hong Kong. Terminally seasick on a freighter. Trapped in the weirdest dream I've ever had. Yep. No trains anywhere in sight.

I try a different approach. 'Why are we on a train?'

'Because ships don't travel on land.'

I can feel a very familiar glare forming around my eyes. 'You really enjoy this, don't you?'

She looks at me and smiles, and for a moment there's something so weirdly sad and distant about that smile. And when she says, 'Yes,' it's almost a whisper.

'You've been out for almost three days,' she says. 'After the whales calmed down, the rest of the journey was pretty smooth. We're now headed towards Sikkim.' She sees my frown, which betrays my happy ignorance of all things geographical. 'We're headed north, towards the Himalayas.'

Well, those I've heard of. 'Wait,' I say with a bit of confusion, 'I've been asleep all this while, and you managed to not only get me into a foreign country but aboard a train as well?' I have disturbing visions of me sleepwalking through the streets.

'I didn't say it was easy,' she says with a straight face. 'If anyone asks, you're my sickly younger sister.'

'And the fact that we don't look anything alike isn't going to ruin this brilliant cover story?' I ask.

She shrugs. 'You look Chinese. I look Japanese. This is India. To them, we all look the same.'

I take stock of my surroundings. It's a small cubicle-like space with bunks on either side. By the sound of it, there don't seem to be too many people around. 'How long till we reach?'

'We've only been on board a few hours. We should be there by tomorrow morning.'

I think that spells out all the immediate necessities for the present. 'All right,' I say slowly. 'So . . . what . . . um . . . what in the world did you do to me back on the ship?' I raise a finger angrily, feeling some of the pent-up rage escaping. 'And don't tell me it wasn't you, because while I'm not certain about a whole bunch of things, the one thing I'm totally sure of is that it *was* you!'

With a sigh, she reaches into a pocket hidden in the folds of her dress, pulling out a small vial-like container. 'The venom of the Dreamsnake. Rare, extremely unstable and the snake does not part with it easily. In most people, it can induce a lifelong coma; in people like, well, me, it acts as a powerful sensory enhancer. In people like *you*, though . . . I'll be honest, I was going completely by rumour and hearsay. But then the whales backed off, so I figured it had worked.'

'*What* had worked?!' I can't help the slight note of desperation. 'What was that place? Who was that . . . that *person*?'

'You saw someone?' There's an eager light in her eyes that makes me very uneasy. 'What did they look like?'

'You answer my questions, I'll answer yours.'

She raises her eyebrow approvingly. 'That place is as much a mystery to most spirits and demons as it is to humans. Most don't even have a name for it. Others have called it many things—the Aether, Ginnungagap, Limbo, the Void. It is essentially the layer that connects the material world with all the realms surrounding it. And, insofar as legend goes, only a few can enter it. What did you see?'

In a few stumbling sentences, I spell out the surreal experience as best as I can, including everything about my . . . guide.

'I see,' she says. 'Legend does say that those who enter that realm can see the constructs that link one reality with another and can undo even the most powerful "spells", as you might call them.'

'So I basically undid whatever magic was causing those whales to attack?'

She nods.

'That's a lot of effort for undoing one magic spell,' I mutter observationally.

'Technically, you're supposed to be able to slip in and out of there even while conscious, without someone poisoning you.'

'So it's my fault you had to poison me?'

'Exactly.'

I manage to push myself off the bunk. Looking out the window, there's all kinds of agricultural nothingness.

'What about that boy, or whatever it was?' I ask.

She looks worried. 'There are things in this world that are too powerful to fully manifest in reality, but in a place like the Void . . .' She shakes her head. 'Just be careful. How do your "wounds" feel?'

'Fine, I guess.' Truthfully, I still feel like I've been squeezed through a pasta machine, but there's no real pain. Just a kind of numbness. 'What you were talking about earlier—those "children" . . . That was a long time ago, right? That story of yours about that war. It doesn't . . .' My voice breaks because I don't know how to complete the sentence. 'I didn't make any pacts with the great forces of nature, I am not the descendant of some ancient line of sorcerers—at least I hope I'm not. I did *not* choose this!'

She doesn't say anything, which is really unfair, because it's very hard to argue irrationally with silence.

'Fine,' I say with only a small amount of sulkiness. 'I'm here. I'm doing my best. What happens now?'

'We're going to be moving pretty fast when we hit Sikkim, so ordinarily I'd suggest you get some rest.' Reflectively, she taps a long fingernail against her lower lip. 'But then, you have been sleeping for three days, so . . .' She reaches into another pocket, and I immediately dart away from the window, prepared for any of a hundred possible kinds of danger.

She pulls out a pack of cards with a grin. 'Do you know how to play rummy?'

❧

It turns out I really don't know how to play rummy.

After losing a dozen games, all while trying to pry information about these Elementals and the whole stolen book thing and the possible end of the world, or whatever, I feel exhausted but still nowhere near sleepy.

It may be the three days of being blissfully unconscious, but I think I'm starting to develop insomnia.

Kit's taken the top bunk, and the sheer volume of silence makes me inclined to think she's snuck off to another dimension. Truthfully, I'd kill for a distraction right now. Or a phone. I would definitely kill for a phone.

With a sigh, I stretch one hand upwards. Since waking up, and Kit's little explanation, I've tried to ignore it; but whatever this power is, it feels way closer to the skin than before. Before, it was all instinct and desperation, but now it feels like the power's right there, waiting for me to use it. More than that. It's like it *wants* me to use it, whispering little hints as to how I can do that.

It's dark enough now that I can't see the colours, but there's a sort of *shifting* along the length of my arm. Power over matter.

Power over mind. Power over magic. That's what he . . . what *it* had said.

A part of me is terrified. I don't want to learn more. I don't want to be good at being . . . whatever I am. But then I also feel really angry at Kit and at whatever that phantom was for treating me like some kind of novice to be bullied and manipulated! I need to know more, and I need to be capable of more.

So I set aside all the terror, and the insecurity (which takes more effort than the terror), and I try and break down this whole power business. I can feel the link between mind and action. The first step is extension—reaching out all around me.

What Kit said about the Elementals makes me think of what people considered as the basic elements in all those stories— earth, air, water, fire . . . Or was it fire, earth, water, metal, wood . . .? I think I remember movies with both. But maybe the connection has to be something so basic that even a person who isn't some hyper-genius walking supercomputer can make sense of what they're doing. Maybe it's not some mystical preordained set (collect them all and save the universe!), but rather just a kind of lie so that I can *say* that I understand what I'm doing.

I can somehow *sense* the air around me—all the tiny molecules as they gather and move in streams—and I can somehow nudge them in the right direction. So let's call this move the Manipulation of the Air around Me . . . *Ugh*, now all I need is someone to tattoo an arrow on my forehead.

Anyway, second is gathering—redirecting the currents and flows so that the weird impossibility of air rushing towards a single point from all directions suddenly becomes very real. If I can control the flow, I should be able to do more than just produce shock waves. Like deflecting that metal piece back on the ship. It's like . . . thickening the air, or making some of those molecules just stand completely still. But this time, I just have to make the air move towards one point. So I focus it on my hand, like it's a kind of vacuum cleaner, slowly drawing all the air flows inward into a kind of circling sphere. Done.

Third step: compression. This is where effort hits, and I can see the back of my hand starting to glow. Power from . . . somewhere—perhaps the core of the atoms, or other dimensions, or distant stars maybe—is gathering and binding the flows together, somehow making that ball of swirling air feel like a little battery or something.

Last step: release. Now the energy's in usable form, so I just have to use it. Simply letting it go probably creates those weird shock waves, but maybe if I really try . . . What was that science lesson? Energy cannot be created or destroyed, but it can change from one form to another. Okay, so if I'm in control of the energy, then maybe I can direct which way that conversion goes.

I imagine a barrier around the compressed point and slowly reverse the flow. I focus on when it hits the barrier, and . . . I giggle softly at the resulting sphere of light. It's blue, feeble and flickering like crazy, but I can't help but think it's way cool.

'How very impressive,' says a voice from the opposite bunk, which should be completely and totally empty. Amazingly, even between sitting up abruptly, bumping my head and finally facing the bunk, the light in my hand doesn't go out.

It's not Kit. It's a woman dressed in what I can only describe as Indian clothes—all flowing silks and stuff, with a scarf type thing covering the head. Her face is hidden behind a mask. It's a really impressive face-like mask that makes me want to use the word 'exquisite'. It's jet black, almost drinking in the light, but you can still make out each aspect of the perfectly beautiful face carved on it. Behind the narrow oval eyeholes, there's just this faint . . . glimmer, which I'm almost certain isn't the reflection of my faintly glowing ball.

'Kit!' Before I can complete the short shout, I've already got my other hand up. If I'm right, I'm totally prepared to throw a wall of air forward with enough force to pin whoever this is to the back of the bunk. If I'm not . . . well, there's no real end to the possibilities of what might happen.

'The fox will not disturb us, child,' she says with this calmness that sets my teeth on edge. I am *so* sick of people around me being comfortable with complete weirdness.

All right, I think. I've been in this situation before. I think I'm getting the hang of how this goes. 'Are you also going to try and kill me?' I ask, almost totally sure that I don't want to know the answer.

The apparition (whatever she is) tilts her head to the side slightly, and, in this really freaky way, the curves of the mask seem to realign until I swear I can make out a small smile. 'No one is trying to kill you,' she says, as if the entire thing is just completely ridiculous.

'Uh . . . you could have fooled me.'

She leans forward. 'You have just entered a world filled with legends and powers that stretch back for aeons. You have seen but the barest tip of a world that defies your very notion of reality. Do you not believe that if any one of the millions of terrible things in *this* world wanted you dead, then it would be no challenge to accomplish?'

The blast of air hits the back of her bunk like a thunderclap. I don't even remember thinking about it. And for a moment I freak, thinking about accidentally killing people (or apparitions) for nothing more than the crime of being really disturbingly creepy.

But I shouldn't worry so much. I don't think those folds of silk stirred even by a centimetre.

154

'Enough,' she says quietly, and the mask is expressionless again. 'I have not tested and tried you so that you may flail around ignorant of all that is.'

Tested and tried? I think back to that evening in Hong Kong. The hooded figure in the alleyway . . .

'*You* sent those hellhounds?! *Who are you?* What do you want?'

A long silence follows, which just reinforces my fervent belief that no one anywhere has any desire at all to answer any of my questions.

She breaks the silence. 'I am the closest thing to an impartial observer you will find. The world changes under the schemes of others, and I am the one who sees the consequences. There are others like you, manipulated here by events beyond your control.'

'Yeah?' I say with as much of a bite as I can manage. 'Are they as confused and scared as I am?'

'Possibly,' she says, 'though I daresay not as sarcastic. And as far as pawns go, there are none as dangerous as you. The pathways between our worlds are opening faster than ever, and what *you* are speaks volumes as to why the world has changed.'

Elemental. I don't even want to think the word.

'The problem with times of change is that it divides the world into those who want to survive and those who want power. Ordinarily, I would have waited for you to explore and learn more and make your own choices, but there are urgent matters that the fox will not have told you about. If you cannot recover the Arcanus in time, it may be too late.'

'Too late for what?' I ask sharply. 'And please don't say the world, because, honestly, that's way more drama than I signed up for!'

She doesn't say a word.

'*Who* are you, exactly?'

The apparition shifts, and for a moment it feels like she's standing, looming rather.

'This is Bengal, child. Here, the name Kali is feared and worshipped. But that isn't important. I have as many names as the stars, and as many faces; and in this place, in this time, I am remembered.'

I can't help but frown at the words. I've heard them before. I slowly close my right hand, and the light in it winks out.

The voice of the Limbo phantom echoes in my mind for a moment. *You must remember.*

'I've seen your face . . .' I say slowly. 'But I don't remember what you look like.' I shake my head. 'No, this isn't right. I don't . . .'

And then this *feeling* just floods my senses. Like a memory, or . . .

In this place, in this time, you changed. You drowned. You died. And yet you lived. A choice was offered, and a choice was made. A covenant was sworn. The world was changed. The world was the same. You were changed. And you were the same.

And a memory was taken.

I want to say that crystal-clear understanding washed over me just now and that, suddenly, I'm free of all doubts, but I just feel . . . shaky. Is this what a suppressed memory is? Did I actually . . .

No, I don't want to think about this. I'm *not* going to think about this. I don't care about what just happened. That's for years later, when I'm in therapy.

In the darkness, her voice is so much like a ghost's that it makes my skin crawl.

'Be careful, child. I may be impartial, but that does not mean I do not care. Follow the Trickster, and find the others. Alone, you are each pawns of creatures ancient, cruel and cunning.

Together, you have a chance to write your own story. And that is more than most can ask for . . .'

Her voice fades towards the end, and I know that this particular apparition has gone. First Kit. Then the boy-demon with the weird eyes. Now this. That makes three.

I can now say with total certainty that I know how Ebenezer Scrooge felt.

The Woods and the Wilds

A day and a half later, Alice was still thinking of that conversation. It kept rattling around inside her mind as Kit scouted the way through the bowels of the Khangchendzonga National Park. That, combined with the heavy backpack, helped keep Alice's mind off the cold. By her estimation, the wind had reached biting point a good hour ago, and was now approaching icy. The exercise, though, seemed to be keeping the chill at bay.

It wasn't snowing yet, though the sky did look suspiciously grey as the sun started to set. Given the fact that they were not carrying a tent (something that Alice had mixed feelings about since she would have been the one carrying it) and that there was a distinct lack of convenient caves in the vicinity, she wholly expected to sleep under the starry sky and then wake up buried under fifteen feet of snow.

Having Kit scout ahead in fox form was turning out to be a good idea, given the frequency with which the landscape bounced up and down from unscalable cliffs to death-trap ravines. Even getting past a standard clump of trees was something of a chore and made her long for one of her old family vacations. At least in broken-down forts you knew where you stood, and it almost always wasn't knee-deep in a thorn bush.

'How much longer are we going to keep going?' she asked the world in general. It was hard to keep track of where exactly

Kit was in the forest. There was always the possibility that she'd just vanish around the next corner (or be eaten by a leopard), but Alice was doing her best not to think of that.

So far, her optimism had been paying off. Kit's head popped up (thankfully followed by the rest of her) from behind a particularly mossy rock. 'Getting tired?' she asked.

'No,' Alice said, actually a bit surprised at that. Her legs were starting to ache a little, but there was no breathlessness or fatigue or anything that she might have expected from a long trek at this altitude. She was trying not to think of the fact that there was the very real possibility that she was unconsciously concentrating the air around her to make it easier to breathe. 'But it's going to be dark soon, and I'd just as soon *not* break a leg by accident.'

Kit looked at her for a second, before turning to perch on top of a gnarly tree root. 'I wouldn't worry about that. I'm sure you can think of a trick or two for lighting the way.'

That stopped Alice in her tracks, the memory of her experimental sphere of light dragging up other unpleasant thoughts with it.

'So, what?' she said sharply. 'Were you just pretending to be asleep in your bunk the whole time? Or did you and the creepy lady arrange everything beforehand, because you thought this girl doesn't seem to have enough drama in her life already, so let's just freak her out a bit more?'

'I didn't know that she would show up,' said Kit without turning around. 'And I didn't interfere because if I had so much as stirred in *her* presence, I would have been destroyed. This is not a nice world you have entered, Alice. There is no rule of law. At least not in the way that you might envision it.'

'You mean that all you supernatural bullies can do what you like because there's no one that can stop you?' Alice sniffed. 'That's kinda exactly how I envision it, so I'm just trying to figure out why you lot don't rule the world. Or maybe you actually do, and it's all some giant conspiracy and we've all been replaced by the alien shape-shifters from dimension hell, or whatever you want to call it.'

'Getting a bit paranoid, aren't you?'

'I wonder whose fault that is,' muttered Alice. 'Who was she?'

Kit still didn't turn around. A light wind had started, and it brushed through her reddish fur, giving the impression of a shiver.

'Kali,' she said after a long moment. 'That's the face she wears in this part of the world. You've heard of her, of course. Almost everyone has, though you might have recognized her better if she'd appeared bonier, with a scythe slung over her shoulder.'

Alice stared at her, momentarily speechless. 'So . . .' she finally ventured, 'does Santa Claus exist?'

At this, Kit turned around, looking as bewildered as it is possible for a talking fox to be. And while reading the expression of a fox is a lost art indeed, every twitching whisker seemed to scream, 'Um . . . what? I just told you that you met the personification of death itself, and you're asking me about *Santa Claus*?'

Instead she said in a slightly strangled voice, 'Never met him.'

'Right, I forgot,' said Alice without emotion. 'You only hang around the creepy sort of spirits. Why is that, though? I mean, the way you talk, you've been around for thousands of years or whatever; but if it's all like this, don't you just get tired of it?'

Kit seemed to consider this seriously before answering, 'Something which has thought my thoughts, worn my face and lived my legends has been alive for a thousand years. But for me, I have changed with the flow of the ages and lived as many different lives as I've ever needed to. Sometimes it does get tiring, but that's the thing about living your life like a story. The moment you sit still, you die. Every moment has to be lived on the ragged edge of chaos, and, yes, the struggle is exhausting, and the price is sometimes so high . . . But there's so much to see, so much to do. So many wonderful, and sometimes horrible, surprises waiting around every corner.'

She turned her nose to the air, taking in the scent of the endless woodland. 'Maybe I'm just an addict—but I can't get enough of it.'

'Uh-huh,' grunted Alice sceptically. 'And what part of the "ragged edge of chaos" is hiking through miles and miles of wilderness?'

It was in the following moments that Alice most clearly understood that fate had an unusual sense of humour, and *extremely* good hearing.

There was a low rumble from behind her, which went on for an interminable three seconds. Just enough time for the rumbling quality to take on all the characteristics of a low growl.

Kit craned her neck to look past Alice and then said calmly, 'I think it's the part where we meet a snow leopard.'

Abominable Myths

Alice

Hellhounds and baleen whales and snow leopards, oh my!

I think if I get through all of this in one piece, I'm going to become a vegetarian as a kind of gesture of peace towards the whole animal kingdom.

'I thought you scouting ahead was supposed to prevent stuff like this,' I hiss out of the corner of my mouth while trying to back away slowly from the leopard's steady glare.

'You're the one who decided to stop and chat,' says Kit. 'Now just stay calm and don't make any sudden movements. He won't attack unless he feels threatened.'

Oh, right. He's the one twice my size, with sharp claws and teeth, and *I'm* the one who's being threatening. If I was in a less terrified state of mind, I'd calmly reflect on the centuries of hunting and the persecution of wildlife by tool-using humans— but as it currently stands, I just feel that animals in general need to stop being so sensitive.

I keep up my great strategy of stepping back slowly, but, in hindsight, moving backwards in an overgrown forest while carrying a heavy backpack is not the brightest of ideas.

'Look out!' Kit calls just a moment too late as I fall over backwards, having tripped on a stone.

The leopard, obviously seeing my clumsiness as part of a massive conspiracy to get it to lower its guard, snarls and leaps forward.

Let me just say that stopping a full-grown leopard in mid-leap is a whole different ball game from deflecting a tiny piece of scrap metal.

Flinging out one arm just as I land with a loud thump, I can feel the air in front of me thicken, and suddenly the leopard seems to be almost swimming in mid-air, looking very weirded out as it does so.

And I know there's a massive amount of effort that's gone into this, because I'm suddenly struck with a headache that feels like someone just hammered a nail into my skull. The colours on the back of my hand also seem to have gone haywire. Earlier it was all flows and gentle shifts, but now it's a kaleidoscope in fast motion.

It's not enough, though. It might be swimming in slow motion, but it's still moving forward and, from this angle, I can see its set of sharp teeth with a level of detail that even the best National Geographic special would be hard-pressed to capture.

'Kit!' I call in desperation, hoping that she has an idea of what to do next.

'Release it and roll to the side,' she says in an irritatingly calm voice.

I do my best, what with the backpack intent on pinning me to the ground permanently, but it seems to work. I manage to dodge out of the way as the leopard lands awkwardly. Before it can decide to attack me in panicky frustration, I attack it in panicky frustration, scrambling up and trying that whole wall-of-air trick from the train.

It's not as powerful as it might have been, but thankfully leopards seem a bit more vulnerable than the . . . ahem . . . Grim Reaper. It stumbles over sideways, yowling like crazy. I wince as the headache gets worse. I don't think I can focus enough for a repeat performance.

163

Fortunately, the leopard gets the message, and it scurries to its feet and runs off in the opposite direction with a speed that makes me very glad it didn't decide on a surprise attack.

'Important lesson to be learnt,' says Kit, who's somehow managed to get safely behind me. 'Philosophical discussions should *not* be held in the middle of a forest.'

With my head splitting from all that power use, I can't really think of any suitable retort. So I just glare. Along with boats, talking foxes and creepy, mysterious people, forests are starting to feature prominently on the list of things I'm coming to positively loathe.

We get back to walking and, surprisingly, my little ball-of-light trick seems to be helping with the headache. Maybe it's just the equivalent of a lengthy cool-down after strenuous exercise, but I can feel the pain ebb with each passing minute. It's still a bit of an effort, of course—the light has to be strong and steady for it to make any difference to the surroundings. Any moonlight or starlight seems to get swallowed up by tree branches, and the little patches here and there just look like creepy silver pools, filled with all sorts of lurking dangers, I'm sure. I think my paranoia reached a critical point a while back.

Kit is staying within range of the light; it's only good for a few metres in each direction and just enough to make out any perilous ditches or unannounced rocks. She's keeping quiet and I'm following suit; the headache has vanished and I try and figure out just where we're supposed to be going.

As far as I can tell, our destination is somewhere on the other side of the nearest range of mountains, and while that should induce a gibbering panic over the weeks it would take to find a way across, I can somehow feel that the way there is actually a lot closer. It's like somewhere further into the forest, everything just sort of . . . *twists*. Like the airflow is being sucked into some kind of portal, vanishing somewhere . . . else. Somewhere far away, but still sort of close by.

I tried asking Kit about it, but she was very helpfully cryptic. 'I know how to get to our destination by a very different route, but we can't use that, so I'm trusting your instincts to get us there from this side of reality.'

So if my instincts tell me that we're headed into that portal or whatever, then I guess that's where we're headed. It's weird, but ever since the train, the whole world seems a lot more, well . . . I don't want to say *alive*, because that's just really disturbing, but maybe more responsive . . . almost *aware*, if that makes any sense. I remember Lin talking about Shinto once (she always did like odd religions), and she said that according to those beliefs, everything that exists—rocks, trees, water—has a soul. It's kind of like that, but not quite.

It's like everything around me *remembers*, and I can almost hear these echoes in the back of my mind—like really old, washed-out memories, all vintage black and white. The endless cycles of life and death. Of fire and lightning and chaos. And painted on top of all that is something very human. Fragments of emotion and memory imprinted there by the will of . . . what's the word . . . oh, right—*sentient* beings. For example, I can tell that some kind of battle took place in this forest. Not a big war or anything, but almost like one group of people was being hunted through these trees by another group.

It's not a nice feeling.

Kit comes to a halt in a small clearing dominated by one large tree.

'We'll stop here for the night,' she says.

I don't argue, letting the backpack slide to the ground with a loud thump. 'I suppose now you want me to go around picking up firewood, or something like that,' I say dully.

'Perish the thought. Do you have any idea just how dangerous an open fire is in the middle of a forest?' Kit sniffs—and let me tell you, when a fox deliberately sniffs, it's a very loud sound. 'What do they teach children in school these days?'

'Uh . . . that when you fall asleep in the woods in the middle of winter without any kind of shelter or warmth, you're going to freeze to death . . .?'

'Haven't you noticed yet?'

'Noticed what?' I ask with increasing dread.

She pauses (for dramatic reasons, I'm sure). 'The air around you is about twenty degrees warmer than it should be. I really don't think you need to worry much about freezing to death, especially since you seem to be doing it unconsciously.'

There is a part of me that's very psyched about being able to carry my own portable climate with me, but then there's also the part that's just a little tired of strange things and phenomena that I'm somehow responsible for. I mean, there was this documentary on chaos theory and butterflies flapping thunderstorms into existence and whatnot . . . And I think I'm going to seriously blame myself the next time I read about a tsunami.

'Can I keep myself dry in the rain as well?' I ask, only half-jokingly.

Kit's tail waves lazily in a shrug-like motion. 'I suppose we'll find out when that happens. For now, though, we have enough problems besides the weather. Look around in the backpack—there'll be a small packet of white sticks. Almost like candles?'

After a moment of scrounging, I find it right next to the tightly packed bread cakes. I take it out gingerly, earnestly hoping that it doesn't explode or turn everything around me into pumpkins or anything of the sort.

'What are these?' I ask, not really sure if I want an answer.

'Magical charms.'

166

'No, seriously.'

Kit starts walking in a circle around the central tree. 'Well, maybe not exactly charms, and maybe not exactly magical, but it should help if you just think of them like that. Just take them out and place them on the ground wherever I'm marking.' She makes a point of elaborately scratching a line into the dirt with her front paw.

With a sigh, I do as she says. She marks six lines at even intervals around the tree and I place one stick on each of them. I fully expect a complete catastrophe the moment I'm done, so when the sixth stick is placed and all they do is start glowing slightly, I have to admit I'm slightly disappointed.

'What exactly are these for?' I ask.

'Listen carefully and tell me what you hear.'

'A forest? Trees, birds, winds, creepy crawly things in the bushes and . . .' That's when I actually try and listen. 'I don't actually hear any of those.' I take a deep breath. 'Y'know, I remember reading somewhere that when a forest goes all silent and still, it's generally because there's something very dangerous in the area.'

Kit nods solemnly.

'And we're not talking more leopards, are we?' I ask.

She shakes her head. 'In the direction we're headed,' she says, 'there are likely to be things there that are not entirely of this world. They've been spotted in increasing numbers these days.'

'More hellhounds?'

'Probably worse. The animals around here seem to sense it—they're all staying well away.' She gestures towards one of the sticks. 'This is a warding system. It should help conceal us from any creatures that are not . . . well, you know. It should also give us a warning if such creatures are around, and lastly—worst comes to worst—it'll gives us about ten seconds of protection if anything should attack.'

'*Ten seconds?* What . . . um . . . are we supposed to do with ten seconds?'

The tail moves in that shrugging motion again. 'If something has managed to get that close without us being alerted, it'll probably be the last ten seconds of your life anyway. You can do whatever you want.'

'Aren't you just a great big ball of optimism,' I say as acidly as I can manage. 'Isn't it time you told me what our destination is? Is the shocked expression on my face really going to be worth the effort of ignoring me the next two dozen times I ask this question?'

'If you must know, we are about to enter the lair of the Snowman.'

'The Snowman?'

'Of the abominable kind.'

I give her my most level stare. 'Are you sure you've never met Santa Claus?'

Practical Magic
Alice

It's a real miracle, but it was a whole four hours before mortal danger reared its increasingly familiar head. And while I might be my own personal radiator, waking up in the middle of the night in a forest in winter still feels probably as cold as it's possible to get without bits and pieces of me turning blue and falling off.

Of course, the fact that my prediction about it snowing is spot on does help with the chill factor, and makes me wonder . . . If the snow starts melting around me, isn't it just going to soak into my clothes, and isn't that even worse, and am I going to get pneumonia, and does the abominable Snowman happen to have a decent supply of antibiotics?

Oh, right. Mortal danger. Have to focus.

Ducking behind what is probably a bush (but also possibly a thorny beast from the sulphur pits of an infernal realm), I try and follow Kit in the darkness. What with my convenient glowing ball of light now reclassified as the 'Here I am, eat me!' beacon, it's back to navigating by moonlight, and since it's more than a little cloudy, it's actually just navigating by luck.

Something tugs at my trouser leg, which, under ordinary circumstances, would cause me to leap and yelp, if not scream; but I've become used to Kit guiding me along like this (which is not to say that I didn't leap and yelp the first time she did it), and I start moving in the appropriate direction.

And then I realize that snow makes forests very slippery.

'Could you make a little less noise?' Kit hisses in my ear, and the reason that her fox form is level with my ear is because I've just skidded down a trail of damp stones and leaves with the grace of a broken-legged zebra.

'Sorry!' I hiss back, scrabbling to a half-crouch position that I'd like to think makes me look all stealthy and invisible, and nothing at all like an arthritic crab.

'This way.'

I follow as best as I can, trying to keep from repeating the Slip 'N Slide method of travel. The hardest part is making as little noise as possible. With the rest of the population of the forest having fled in terror, the silence left behind is not a good place to pass unnoticed. On the positive side, this does make those things stalking the forest in the distance easy to hear.

All in all, it could be a lot worse.

Kit's little warding system worked perfectly, giving us enough warning to be up and away before . . . whatever these things are . . . closed on our camping spot. According to her, the circle she set up would basically act as a decoy, so it was just a matter of finding a side route to sneak on to, which, I have to say, a fox is really good at.

'Kit?' I call quietly.

'Yes?'

'So, I can feel we're getting close to that . . . that portal . . . that door-slash-reality-twisting-entrance thingy. It's like all the forest paths are leading there. Any ideas on how to get through without causing a huge fuss?'

Kit raises her nose upward, as if to test the air. 'A few ideas. The wyr aren't terribly bright. Easy to distract. Easy to intimidate. If it weren't for the single-minded ferocity, preternatural animal senses and sheer blood-thirstiness, they'd really just be pushovers.'

I don't even bother commenting on how much of a comfort she is. Sarcasm just doesn't seem to get through to her. 'Wyr?'

'Generic term for lower-order supernatural nasties. Think of them as the zombie horde in all those movies, which the hero has to kill first, before reaching the "Big Bad".'

'What movies do you watch?' I mutter glumly while lamenting the fact that I remember way too many titles that seem to fit that exact description, and that while I in no way fulfil the qualifications of a hero, I think I come remarkably close to the sidekick who dies senselessly in order to inspire said hero to win—which does kinda make me feel somewhat relieved that there is no actual hero around (there is no power in this world that will make me fit Kit into that particular role).

She tilts her head towards a tightly packed clump of trees. 'This way.'

When we reach the trees, she shifts form again, and it's weird how she seems to fit in completely with the forest even when her dress might be more suited to a high-class restaurant or something. She holds out her hand. 'Matches.'

I fumble in the backpack for the requisite item, stopping only when my brain catches up with the implications. 'Um . . . tell me you're not planning what I think you're planning.'

'Possibly.'

'We're going to cut down branches, make flaming torches and fight our way past these wyr creatures?'

She frowns slightly. 'No . . . I can't say I was planning that.'

'Then you're going to set the forest on fire and hope to slip through in the confusion?' I ask worriedly.

'That's the one. The wards at the camp have already drawn their attention there. Create a wildfire around here, and they'll investigate. The wyr are bright enough to suspect it's a distraction when they don't find anyone; so when some surreptitious intruder tries to sneak past in the opposite direction, chances are they'll catch on and go racing off that way . . . Which leaves you free to slip past.'

'*Me?*'

'In this little drama, I get to play the part of surreptitious intruder.' She grins confidently. 'Don't worry about it. I can manage to give them the slip if it's just me.'

'Okay . . .' It's embarrassing to admit, but I was actually a bit concerned on that point. 'Can we get back to the part where you cause a forest fire? I'm given to understand that they're kinda hard to control and, before you know it, there'll be whole square miles burning up, and massive ecological damage. And you want me to be hiding near all of this while it's happening?'

'Yes,' she says quite bluntly. 'After all, I expect you to put the damn thing out.'

It's weird, but between shivering from the cold, or fear, or whatever, and trying to keep from just running away into the deep, dark wilderness, I have this moment where I'm caught between wanting to be safe home and feeling really guilty about the fact that I'm not.

I'm sure they're still looking for me. It's not like any sane parents would ever just accept some teary goodbye note at face value and think, 'Oh, well, it's her choice.' Part of me wishes that they did just think that and weren't worrying. On the other hand, I'm also secretly hoping that they've contracted the best anti-supernatural superheroes in the world (assuming they exist) and that I'm about to be rescued, returned home and then grounded until I'm sixty.

A small sputtering from Kit's matchbox time bomb brings me back to more immediate problems. Watching from the oh-too-close distance of fifty feet, I can barely make out the sudden flaring as the sparks spread to the small twigs and leaves that we'd gathered together in one dry, snow-free part of the forest floor. It only takes a few moments, but those sparks burn hot and fly high, catching the dry lower branches and slowly wrapping themselves around the tree trunks.

Arson is a terrifying business if you're not a pyromaniac, and I'm really not a pyromaniac.

The fire starts spreading from tree to tree. The snow is slowing things down, but it's still way too wild for my liking. I'd start backing away, but unfortunately the plan needs me to be close. As the fifth or sixth tree starts to smoulder, I get my first glimpse of tonight's special guest-monsters, and I think I liked it better when it was whales and leopards trying to kill me.

They don't look stomach-turningly scary, like those hellhounds did. They're about the same size, but where those were all teeth, spine and sulphur, these look seriously . . . um . . . *dangerous*. Their snouts are short, like big cats', and in the firelight, their fur, or whatever it is, seems to flow— orange and black streams on a silver mirror. The legs seem just a hair too long for the sleek bodies, lending a spidery air to their movements, and their tails (two apiece) move ceaselessly in swordlike swishes.

Three of them close in on the fire, circling carefully around the trees. They don't seem the least bit scared of the flames. In fact, I can swear that one of them just inhaled some of it. Or maybe ate it.

They don't make any sounds. No growling or snarling— nothing that I can make out above the low roar of the fire—but the way they glance in each other's directions before splitting off and widening their search makes me very certain that there's some kind of communication going on there.

It takes me a second to realize that the reason I'm getting slightly light-headed is not because of the fire and the vast amounts of poisonous carbon-based gases being produced, but it's rather that I'm simply holding my breath. So I inhale . . . and get a nice lungful of poisonous carbon-based gases accompanied by a smoky cocktail of burning forest.

Stifling a cough is not the easiest thing in the world, and the sight of one of those wyr suddenly freezing in the distance and looking in my general direction doesn't help matters.

I blink from the smoke, and it's gone. Which would normally be a good thing, if not for realizing a bare heartbeat later that the place it's gone to is about ten feet from me, and it's staring into the smoke with glaring crystal-blue eyes that make me wish that I wasn't hidden behind some rocks, but rather that I had a proper invisibility cloak or whatnot.

I keep my breath held, certain that in this particular case, breathing will lead to coughing, which will lead to death. On the other hand, I've never had great lung capacity, so . . .

With a sudden start, the creature whips its head around, looking off into the distance. Just above the sound of the fire, there's this thin keening noise, like a very large mosquito. Kit's little breakthrough attempt must have caught some of the attention.

Sure enough, I blink again and it's gone, the smoke trailing in the direction of the sound.

I count to a slow twenty before trying to breathe/cough/choke/gasp again. Okay . . . immediate death threat gone. Now I just have to worry about being burnt alive in the middle of a forest.

Part of me is tempted to just leave it be and run for this entrance point or whatever—I mean, in the scale of things, is one little forest fire really going to make a lot of ecological difference? All the animals seem to have evacuated anyway. But then, the wyr creatures aren't going to be as confused as they could be, and the chances of both me and Kit making it through in one piece go way down. Also, I do kinda want to at least try and pull this off.

The fire's only spread a little beyond its immediate clump of trees, though sparks are starting to catch around the perimeter. The snow continues to slow it down, contributing to a thick blanket of smoke.

Focus.

I can see the origin point of the fire from where I am. If I just stick with what I know, I can change the point where the air gathers from my hand to where I'm looking. Have to do it fast, though.

I make sure I'm ready, that I know exactly what it's going to feel like to make this happen, and then, just like taking that one small step off a cliff . . .

The headache hits as the wind rushes in from all sides. From every direction, it rushes in towards the starting point of the fire, and starts to swirl, sucking in more air with each rotation. The fire follows, burning embers and crackling leaves swept into the path, leaving blackened wilderness behind. Even the smoke pours in—until it's one great big ball of shadow and flame.

I grit my teeth. This time around, the headache doesn't last. If anything, it seems to flow into the effort of maintaining that spiralling whirlwind and *melts* into the flame. A second at a time, I try and narrow the focus, shrinking everything into a smaller point. My vision's slightly blurry from the effort, but from what I can see, the flame's intensity has grown in proportion, until it's a single blinding point of light in the middle of a smoky sphere.

Just when I'm worrying about what to do with it now, the flame flares once and then vanishes, having burnt itself out.

Taking slow, even breaths, I wipe the sweat from my forehead, and then turn and start running before the wyr pack can circle back here.

It's hard to keep from smiling as I stumble through the forest. Now, that was just really, really cool.

The Snowman's Welcome

The structure of the Edge realms that most closely bordered the physical world had always fascinated Tao, insomuch as fascination could be said to affect him. Here were the connecting points that reached out to different parts of reality and yet were not part of any of them. There was always that hint of instability in the air, like when a string stretched to the point of breaking is released and emits a small, almost musical, sound.

In the wilds—the forests, deserts and other untamed parts of the world—the gateways were always isolated. People, animals—everyone stayed away from them without realizing, and yet almost every old city in the world also had its unreal counterpart hidden somewhere within its depths. Patches of unreality born of the history and sorrow of any place that humans chose to gather en masse.

Stories shape this world. That had been one of the first lessons. Every human life, every thread in the mortal tapestry was shaped by the stories of those who had come before, of legends and fairy tales, and of histories carved in stone. For every other realm, though, stories could be said to have a far more direct influence, cutting into their realities with the blood-soaked subtlety of a sweeping sword.

As he sensed the girl and her vulpine companion cross the boundary of the Snowman's forest, he wondered if she knew just which stories had led her down this path.

His thoughts were interrupted by the approach of a large bird. Its shape, to his mind, was that of a wind knife, cutting cleanly before stalling just above a low-hanging branch. Its soft call was higher than a trill but not yet a screech, the varying intonation delivering the Snowman's message. Gently reaching out, he brushed the buzzard's wing in response and then started down the path towards where the new arrivals were.

<hr>

The forest worried Alice.

With her recent experience fresh in her mind, she firmly believed that snowy evergreen forests were nowhere near as scenic as they appeared in movies. Instead they were just slippery, muddy, thorny deathtraps painted in dull shades of brown, green and white. That was what real forests were.

This was a movie set. Clear paths with powdery white snow. No thorn bushes or squelchy rotting leaves underfoot. Even the trees were placed a respectable distance away, where the likeliness of walking into a low branch was almost zero. As for the trees themselves—they looked suspicious. Perfectly overgrown Christmas trees with patches of white snow placed at decorative intervals. The pine needles were a deep, healthy-looking green, and the unbroken tree bark seemed to delight in its smoothness. And in the distance, Alice could hear the gentle babbling of a stream trying very hard to be musical. All in all, it was a very suspicious forest.

Not to mention Kit was looking at her strangely.

'What? What is it now?' she asked the currently fox-shaped fox.

The strange look remained. 'Are you sure you feel all right? Feeling any dizziness? Nausea? A slight out-of-body feeling?'

Alice stared back, suddenly worried if she should be feeling some of those things. 'Um . . . no. Not really. Why?'

'Hmm.'

'Just tell me,' said Alice, tired and sulky in equal measure.

'It's interesting, that's all,' said Kit, finally looking away. 'Most humans need severe adjustment after passing through that passage.'

'What? That narrowing clump of trees? I mean, sure—it was a little weird at first how everything seemed to bend in, but, personally, I think being chased by unearthly monsters requires way more by way of adjustment.'

'I'm sure you'll get used to it in no time.'

'I don't want to—' Alice bit off the retort, preferring instead to glare around at the suspiciously perfect forest. She frowned at some movement down the path. 'Say, haven't I seen that guy before?'

Kit was already looking in that direction. 'Your mystery guide from your little dream-walk?'

'Yeah.'

'That's not him.'

'Well, yeah. I figured, what with that being my personal hallucination,' said Alice in a patient voice. 'But is this the guy we're looking for?'

Seeing no response forthcoming, Alice let out a strangled sound of frustration and then crossed her arms in front of her and did her best to stare down the approaching figure. A feat that became disturbingly difficult as he approached.

The basic features and dimensions were about the same, but where her earlier visitation's most eerie aspect had been those full-black eyes, this one seemed a little less eerie and a bit more stomach-turning when it became apparent that the wounds from eyebrow to cheekbone did not take a break around the ocular area, preferring instead to carve a nasty brown-red path right across both eyes.

'Okay,' she said carefully, 'that is just totally creepy.'

Kit padded forward a bit, and sat in what might almost be called a formal posture for a fox. '*Kr'Snithikaam*,' she said, 'I ask leave of passage into this realm.'

The boy bent low in an equally formal bow. 'The Snowman sends his greeting, and bids you and your companion welcome to the forest, Trickster.'

'Hey,' interjected Alice, slightly taken aback by the pomp and circumstance. 'I'm Alice the Eternally Confused. Real nice place you've got here. Who does your gardening?'

Kit looked back at her with a tired expression. 'She does that a lot,' she said to the boy. 'It's better you just ignore her.'

The boy gave Alice a small smile in return and inclined his head in her direction. 'My Lady Elemental, it is an honour. You may call me Tao.'

'I'll do that, then,' said Alice, still unsure how to react around someone clearly part of this whole supernatural mess who wasn't trying to actively kill her or creep her out (simply looking creepy didn't count for all that much).

'If you will follow me,' said Tao, 'the Snowman is waiting to the north.'

'He's watching glaciers again?' asked Kit.

'I believe so.'

'He should really find a better hobby.'

They followed a little way behind Tao, walking along that clear, all-too-perfect forest trail.

Alice opened her mouth to whisper a question, but then thought twice about it. Suppositions of blind people having extra keen senses aside, the confidence with which Tao moved through the forest seemed to imply senses way beyond extra keen, and somewhere past the superhero standard as well.

So she just asked normally, 'What was that you called him— Kur-something?'

'A title—Hand of Judgement. Normally, there's a lot of protocol that goes along with visiting realms, though I will admit the earthward side of things has always been more relaxed. Too many humans tend to wander in, looking for lost kingdoms, and they just have no real idea of how to behave.'

'Really? Normal humans come here?'

'The ones that don't get eaten, anyway. Some end up staying here until they just can't go back, others die along the way and the few that do return either wisely keep their mouths shut and go about their lives or become crazy people. Mind you, there are a couple of great fantasy writers whose works aren't as . . . fictional . . . as most might believe, and I think one Hollywood director too.'

'Uh-huh.' It's odd how comforting it is to think of people managing to make a living based on this weird reality. 'Anyway, so that Hand of Justice thing . . . Is he someone like you—you know, a spirit—or did he just wake up one day and find himself whisked away by someone like you?'

'You make me sound like a kidnapper.'

Alice gave her a look that clearly said, 'If the shoe fits.'

'Why don't you just ask him directly?' said Kit, doing her best to look wounded.

Looking forward, Alice raised her voice slightly. 'Well?' she asked.

'I am human, my Lady Elemental,' said Tao without turning around. 'Though not, perhaps, as human as I once might have been. Around a decade ago, I was approached on the verge of death by a god who has some influence in this region. After that, I was effectively remade into what I am today.'

Alice frowned. 'How old are you?'

'Fourteen years, two months and three days have passed since my birth.'

The story tickled something familiar in Alice's memory. The same something that had been bouncing around in her head ever since she'd met Kali, even as she'd tried to avoid the thought.

She was almost certain that she'd met Kali when she was younger. Sometime earlier, and she still couldn't remember when, she had also been at that point—'the verge of death' . . . and then *something* had intervened. She shuddered and pushed the memory aside again.

'So are those cuts and things, like, part of your . . . remaking?' she asked, not entirely sure if it was polite to.

'No,' said Tao quietly. 'This happened before. They remain visible by my choice.'

Alice stared at his back and, without really thinking, asked, 'What happened?'

The voice was the same—calm, quiet and completely oblivious to Alice's complete and total horror. 'When I was four, my parents were tortured and murdered in front of me, after which I was blinded and left to die in the snow.'

She opened her mouth to frame 'I'm sorry', but the sheer insufficiency of the words stilled her voice.

Tao turned his head to show her that same small smile. 'Don't let it bother you,' he said. 'I certainly don't.'

~

The walls of the ice caverns were a perfect blue-white, lit by streams of morning sunlight that entered through a dozen different apertures before bouncing around to fill the massive space. At the very edges of vision, though, the cold light gave way to lingering shadows as the imperceptibly flowing ice ventured deeper underground. From the ceilings, stalactites stared down, but given the height of the caverns, they just lent to the grandeur rather than looking like deathtraps in waiting.

Alice didn't pay the impressive sight much mind, too occupied by what Tao had told her. Was that what Kit had meant? The blood-drenched mantle of the reluctant hero?

She shuddered inwardly and tried to focus on the situation at hand. The ground, though icy, was sprinkled with enough gravel and dirt to provide a firm footing, and the path wound downwards into the cave before stopping at a large semicircular ledge, overlooking a steep glacial incline.

Looking out over the drop was a creature that could only be the Snowman.

She swallowed nervously. She'd been expecting something out of a 'Lost Creatures of the World' album—large, very hairy, probably white or brown and with outsize feet. But this . . . was not Bigfoot. Not some white-furred ape-man, Sasquatch or beast.

To be fair, though, he *was* large—maybe twice her height and as broad as a car—and white did feature predominantly.

At first glance, it was almost like looking at an ice sculpture through smoked glass. Shadowy outlines framed broad, inhuman shoulders, and the slow shift of each limb was exactly the motion of a shifting glacier sped up a million times over. The body was definitely humanoid—that is to say, equipped with the prerequisite two arms, two legs, a torso and a head. But Alice got the impression that her own perceptions were adding to the image. And that his clothes were part of the image, rather than the reality—an icy greatcoat enveloped the Snowman from shoulders to ankles, but it was a cloak, a robe and a suit of armour all at the same time.

My eyes are lying to me, Alice thought. Maybe they just couldn't make out the entirety of something that wasn't completely . . . physical . . . in nature, something that wasn't as familiar a sight as a woman or a fox, or a creepy person in a mask even.

The Snowman turned. The way the light reflected made it hard to make out the face. It was like looking at a diamond with a blue laser shot through it. Slowly, though, it came into focus— all crags, angles and icy planes. But, as with the rest of him, there was so much more than just what was visible. Alice's gaze saw age—the age of stones, and mountains, and endless undying forests. The stern slant of the brow looked as if it could support a crown, and the eyes underneath it were a blue so bright and clear . . . and old.

She remembered a fairy tale she'd once read, in which the grand old villain had been the majestic, implacable Winter King. The Snowman looked every bit as she'd imagined that king to be, which again led her to the point of wondering just how much of what she saw was her own perception.

She glanced to either side, expecting either Kit or Tao to make the introduction. They didn't. Tao stood to one side patiently, his head slightly bowed. And Kit . . . Kit was watching.

The Snowman stepped forward, the caverns trembling perceptibly as that great foot touched down. He looked down on Alice from his vast height, and then he knelt, dropping to one knee in front of her. His voice was the thunder of an avalanche.

'I bid you welcome, my liege.'

And though Alice still couldn't really read a fox's expression, there were three things that she could detect in Kit's eyes. Grim satisfaction, an almost melancholic resignation and, more disturbing than the sight of a giant ice-man bowing before her, the barest traces of fear.

Memory of a Nightmare

Three lamps had been gathered around the table where Seidre worked. Slowly, she kept up the delicate task of sifting seeds from fibres. She glanced towards Violetta, who was sitting next to the bed where Kharsan lay.

The convulsions had stopped after they'd managed to administer the mixture of mulberry sap and crushed sour nettles. He still hadn't regained consciousness, though, and his body temperature was swaying wildly between icy and burning.

She could see Shade stretched out underneath him, a pool of darkness that shimmered slightly around the edges. According to Violetta, Shade was the only thing keeping him from falling into a permanent coma, but it was still unnerving. She trusted her sister, but that shadow was a different matter altogether. It could be lying to Violetta, it could be manipulating her at every turn, it could . . .

She turned back to the work at hand, trying to dismiss those thoughts. She'd spent so much time over the last decade trying to figure out a way to protect her sister, but in the end, there seemed little choice than to let matters take their course and hope for the best.

With a sigh, she scraped another small teaspoon of seeds into the mortar. Aurin was distilling bark oil in the kitchen. Once that was done, they'd combine the two to form the base of a stabilizing agent. The recipe was centuries old, but no living person had ever needed to mix it before.

'It's because he wasn't born here, isn't it?' she asked Violetta.

She got a nod in return. 'Shade says that this whole valley is not entirely part of the rest of the world. Unless it's during specific times, people who aren't from the valley need to adapt.' Violetta frowned. 'It wasn't supposed to be like this, though. If he had been with the other one, he should have been protected.'

'His brother?'

'I think so. Shade says he's . . . special.'

Seidre wondered about that. Santor and Eden shared a connection. When she'd accompanied the delegation there, she'd tried to find answers but had only managed to uncover more mysteries.

'You said that they were attacked before entering?' she asked. 'Do you think . . .'

'Yes,' said Violetta. 'Shade saw the imprints in his mind. The soldiers belong to the same group that attacked Santor eleven years ago.'

'I see.'

The door creaked open and Aurin stepped in, holding a small earthenware bowl filled with a glistening amber liquid. Tall and thin, he wore a worried expression on his face that made him look more than a bit awkward to anyone who didn't know him, but in Seidre's eyes, there was something reassuringly solemn in that slightly furrowed brow.

'This is all I could get for now,' he said. 'I've asked Javen to help collect some more scrapings from the forest.'

She gave him a grateful smile. 'This should be more than enough. Thank you.'

He placed the bowl on the table. 'How is he?'

'About the same. As long as he's kept stable, he should be fine until I've finished preparing the antidote. Is the distillery still set up?'

'Yes.'

'I'll need to use it as soon as I've finished gathering the ingredients. Could you make sure it's clean?'

'All right.' He took a look around the small room. 'I'll wait outside. Just give me a shout if you need anything else.'

'I will.'

She watched the door close behind him. Even if she did find his presence reassuring, in this particular situation, it left her with a rather strained sense of confusion. She'd known this day was coming, though between all her mixed feelings, she could no longer be certain if she'd been looking forward to it or dreading it, but to have it happen now, of all times . . .

Pulling one of the lamps closer, she bent over the table again. Seeds to sort, leaves to shred, roots to crush and pollen to sift. Why was it that all ancient quasi-alchemical recipes had to be this complicated?

With a tired groan, Vi dragged herself into bed with the full intention of passing out the instant her head touched the pillow. It was a particularly comfortable home-made pillow, even if it tended to roll off the bed and hide itself in some forgotten nook or cranny when left unattended.

After they'd managed to force the antidote down the throat of their unconscious visitor, his vital signs had settled to those of one in normal deep sleep. Only then had Vi called Shade away.

She'd never used him for that long before. Towards the end, the strain had been incredible; she'd felt as if her very bones were trying to shake themselves apart.

Just as she realized that the pillow was, in fact, missing, Shade spoke.

Violetta . . .

'Not now,' she muttered.

It can't wait. You know you can't afford to sleep like this.

'Ten minutes,' she said sleepily. 'Then you can wake me up and we can go through all of this . . .'

It will be too late.

She teetered on the brink of ignoring him but, as much as it annoyed her, he was right. Memory sorting was the first thing he'd taught her. The first thing she'd ever learnt. Before she could speak. Before she could walk. Because if she didn't do this, the risk was so high . . . Especially on a day like today, when she'd worked with Shade for so long.

Keeping her eyes closed, she pushed herself up to a sitting position. 'All right,' she grumbled.

It was a simple enough trick, just a matter of making sure that all her memories lined up in the right places without anything suspicious popping into view. Most times, there were at least a couple of those unrecognizable memories. Shade had taught her not to dwell on them and to just shuffle them outside her own personal experiences. It didn't stop glimpses from breaking through, but thankfully most of those glimpses were just mundane everyday memories. And for the ones that weren't—well, there were things that needed to be learnt, and faced.

Less than a second into the process, she realized that today was different.

Shade! she thought desperately, gritting her teeth against the whirlwind onslaught of alien images.

Stay focused. Pick a single memory that you know to be yours. Use that as the basis for reconstruction.

Lives spread out before her, connected by blood. Moments of idleness and of flurried activity. A man sitting on a chair as the full moon emerges from behind a cloud. A woman staring at her own blood-covered hands, but with alert curiosity dancing in her eyes. The view from a window as people gather, united in anger. The memory from moments later, as they flee for their lives.

Doing her best to keep from being swept away, she picked out herself walking beside Seidre on the way to their mother's house. From there she searched forward and back for the right memories, placing them in the appropriate positions as they appeared. And when a particular sequence or time frame was as complete as possible, she stitched them together as a larger part of the whole.

It didn't take long—maybe less than ten minutes—but by the end she was sweating from the effort.

'That was . . . difficult,' she said tiredly. Her desire for sleep had been somewhat drained by the exercise, but the exhaustion seemed to have trebled.

Consider it another lesson. Do not push yourself too hard, or a moment may come when you will no longer be able to tell the flow of your own memories from those who came before.

Moving slowly, she flopped over the edge of the bed and groped around for the missing pillow. 'You've never answered that question, you know.'

Suddenly Shade went silent, and she could feel his evasiveness, but she was too tired to care.

'How much of what they did was because they remembered the wrong memories at the wrong time?' Her father. Her grandmother. Every ancestor once bonded to the Shadow—they had kept Santor safe. But they had done such terrible things too . . .

His presence shrank even further.

Please, she thought. *I'm going to have nightmares as it is. It's better if I know . . .*

Only one person has lost themselves in that fashion, said Shade finally. *Most of the others were bound to me when they had reached adulthood and were less likely to be affected.*

That wasn't the answer she'd been hoping for. That kind of insanity was terrifying, to be sure—but at least it would have been an excuse.

They lived as they chose, Violetta, said Shade as her fingers finally located the wandering pillow.

Did they? That was her own thought, kept tucked away from Shade. How much of a choice did they really have, here, in this Valley of Shadow? How much of a choice did she have? She hadn't done anything or made any decisions, but that didn't seem to matter. She was already being forced to leave her home and walk on a path that had been laid by others before her. All she could do was swim along the flow of events and hope that she didn't drown.

Punching the pillow once, she rested her head on it and tried to recapture that urge to collapse completely. It wasn't that hard. Soon sleep enveloped her, softening all troubled thoughts. There were nightmares waiting, of course, but that was all right. They weren't hers.

Surprises

Kharsan

Surprises have always been one of my least favourite things in all of existence. That is not to say that I don't believe 'pleasant' surprises exist. I'm sure they do, and that they make some people very happy when they occur, but no surprise I have ever encountered has in any way made my day even the remotest bit better.

This time around, waking up is a painful process, like being dragged backwards through a field of thorny nightmares.

The unfamiliar surroundings were to be expected. Ever since leaving Eden, familiarity has been a rare creature. It's a small room; not in terms of size, but in that it's filled to the brim with all sorts of things—so much so that it's hard to imagine the room could have ever been empty. Tables line the walls, with rickety wooden chairs and stools in front of them. Large carpet-like tapestries are hung on the walls and a rough curtain covers a narrow window next to the bed.

The tables are littered with ageing leather-bound books, assorted oddly shaped stones and a collection of what looks like dried plants and herbs. All in all, it's a very . . . distinctive room, which seems to be trying very hard to appear cosy.

I sit up as best as I can, slightly discomfited by the fact that I seem to be wearing clothes that are far too large for me. Judging by the light, it's mid-morning; though for all I know, I

191

may have been asleep for weeks. It certainly feels like that. I try searching my memory for clues. I remember the chase across the plains, those machines, Adam and then the shadows . . . and that girl.

This must be Santor.

For a moment, I consider getting up and finding out exactly where in Santor I am, but the effort of even sitting up is quite draining.

The door opens with a slight creak, and Seidre steps in—and it takes all of three seconds for the 'surprise' part of the morning to set in with the subtlety of a gunshot to the head.

'You're awake?' she asks. 'How're you feeling?'

'Uh . . .'

I think she's guessed the reason, having seen my state of monosyllabic shock, because there's a passing wince on her face, after which she just stands quietly, waiting for my train of thought to chug past each station. They are as follows:

She's . . .

Wait, but she was in Eden two years ago . . .

And we never actually . . .

Oh, right . . .

I should shut my mouth.

I should say something.

'So . . . you're, uh . . .'

'Yes.'

'Congratulations?' I try with a sort of half-smile that I'm certain looks like it belongs on a cretinous zombie.

'Thank you,' she says, her smile still slightly worried.

For anyone still in the dark, let me just say that there are few surprises as unsettling as finding out that the person who is the closest thing you've ever had to a girlfriend is pregnant.

I look down at the overlarge clothes again, the second realization sinking in. 'I take it these belong to your . . . uh . . .'

'Husband.'

It's odd that that's an even bigger shock. I mean, that's a positive thing, right? Well, for her anyway. *I* still feel like I took a right turn into a brick wall. Inwardly I sigh. I don't have the time to dwell on all of this and get upset, or depressed, or whatever it is that people get at a time like this. Adam's still in the hands of those bloody commandos and their oversized toasters.

'How long have I been out?'

'Two days. Santor . . . is not like many places.' She looks me over with concern. 'It can give outsiders a real shock. How do you feel now?'

'Fine,' I lie. 'Thanks for taking care of me. That girl at the valley entrance . . . she's related to you?'

'My sister.'

'And the shadow?'

She keeps silent. I would guess that this is something she has trouble talking about, but since I'm having enough trouble thinking about the journey through the valley, what with its shadows that grow, move and speak on their own, I'm not particularly inclined to be sensitive about it.

'Please,' I ask quietly. 'Adam was captured just before we reached the valley entrance. The shadows are the reason my father told us to come here, isn't it?'

She swallows and then nods. 'One shadow in particular,' she says softly. 'Violetta calls him Shade.'

She explains, and my head hurts. Part of this is because of my mind trying to think in directions that human minds are not supposed to, but mostly it's because I'm trying to keep from being sheerly incredulous about this whole thing.

I look at her, keeping my face as blank as possible. It's hard. Those dark eyes are just so very earnest, and though she's only two years older, now it feels like there's a lifetime separating us. I wonder if pregnancy does that to all women.

'Just to make sure I understand,' I say, trying a reasonable voice, 'your family founded, and has ruled, this little valley kingdom for centuries, all with the aid of some kind of shadow-demon that is inherited upon death by the youngest in the bloodline?'

'That is about the gist of it,' she says.

'Right. And the current possessor of said shadow-demon is a twelve-year-old girl—your little sister, Violet?'

'Violetta. You can just call her Vi if you want.'

I stare at her, and I know this time my exhaustion shows through. 'So if I had managed to get Adam safely here, we would have been safe?'

She shakes her head sadly. 'Only for a while. Santor is vulnerable during certain times. About eleven years ago, an armed group—I think they may have been the same people who are targeting you—infiltrated the valley during an eclipse. They stole a very valuable book, and managed to kill the last . . . ruler.' She hesitates for a moment, before going on. 'My father.'

I open my mouth to offer sympathy but stop. Maybe I don't know Seidre as well as I believed I did, but I know enough. This is probably what most would call a sensitive subject. 'But this Shade . . . it already warned you that we were coming?'

'Yes. I think it could sense Adam. Violetta had planned to leave with you two.'

I nod slowly. 'That makes sense. My father said I should come here to hide and then go look for him once Adam was ready. He warned of an impending conflict. One which Adam has been created for.' I look down glumly. It's hard not to think of him as a weapon, but I have to keep trying.

Seidre looks worried. 'There was an Arcanus in Eden as well,' she said.

'What?'

'An ancient book of magical knowledge?'

My memory stirs. 'Yes, though no one liked to talk about it. It was one of the things my parents had brought to Eden. These soldiers probably have it now.'

'And shortly after that . . .' begins Seidre with a touch of dread.

'They came after us with giant metal golems,' I finish with just as much dread. That's a dangerous book.

'All right,' I say, 'I suppose I had better talk to this shadow-demon directly.'

She nods.

One thing is still bothering me, though. 'I don't suppose I could get my own clothes back?'

Clean clothes feel strange.

One of the side effects of not being able to stop to do laundry while running for your life through a dusty wasteland and only having two changes of clothing.

'Will you stop sniffing it?' says Seidre.

'I wasn't . . . It just smells a little unusual. You said you make your own detergent here, but I didn't expect it to be so . . .' I give up. 'Floral.'

'We have a good variety of flowers near the foothills. If this place were a more stable location, I bet we could have made great perfumes for export.'

I stare at her. It's getting to be a habit.

She looks back with a dry smile. 'What? You think anyone here actually enjoys being in the supernatural shadow-valley town?'

The smile slips. 'A generation ago it was fine, because no one knew any better and it wasn't as if we had much choice, but now . . .'

'You have a niche in the world of capitalism?'

Her eyebrows arch. 'Something like that. Violetta's waiting in the living room. I've told her everything about you . . .'

'What? *Everything?*'

She blushes slightly. 'No. I've told her who you are, and she already knew about Eden, and I think she, or at least Shade, knows more about Adam than either of us.' She opens the door, and then stops. 'The visit to Eden was meant to answer questions that my father left behind . . . but, unfortunately, all we got were more questions.'

'And now we've come full circle. You know, I've thought about this before—parents might really be more trouble than they're worth.'

Walking out, it's hard to keep my eyes off the floor. Seidre's advice is still fresh: talk to the girl, not the shadow. It's very disconcerting just how calm and in control she appears. It's a bit like Adam's irritating sense of confidence. Like a little power can make up for the surrounding uncertainty while growing up; and maybe it does. But he still got captured.

'Hello,' I start out harmlessly, sitting across from her, 'I'm Kharsan.'

'Violetta.'

Seidre waits at the door for a moment before leaving. She said it might go smoother if she didn't get involved. Of course, that still leaves me wondering about the best way to ask a twelve-year-old girl if her personal shadow-demon might help answer some of my questions.

'So . . . what's your sister's husband like?'

I can tell from her expression that this is not the question she expected, and that makes two of us, since I'm almost certain I hadn't even thought of that question and that if I had, I wouldn't have asked it.

'Aurin?' she responds hesitantly. 'He's . . . nice? Tall.'

'Oh. Right. Uh . . . so this Shade of yours—it knew that Adam and I were coming here?'

'*He* did.'

'Right. Sorry. He.' This conversation is not going well. 'Look, what exactly does *he* know, and not to be too blunt about it—but can any of this knowledge be used to liberate my brother from a paramilitary group that happens to use giant metal robots?'

She stares at me for a long second. On the table between us is a small bowl filled with multicoloured pebbles. She reaches into the bowl to take out a number of pebbles, which she then places on the table.

'Shade can't explain it exactly.' She moves one pebble to the centre. 'The table is the world. The cloth is that part of the world leading us down this road.' She frowns. 'He says that someone created the cloth—all the events, all the small connections. Someone laid the groundwork.'

'Who?'

'He doesn't know.' She touches the pebble again. 'Your brother. He's acting as a sort of anchor, or weight, drawing all of us in.' She lays out the other pebbles. 'Me. The Dreamer. The Hand. You. Others. All part of this—part of the story—coming together at one point.'

I fully expect to see tarot cards being pulled out any second now.

'This all sounds very . . . mystical. I don't suppose you can be a little more specific?'

She looks thoughtful, and then nods shortly. 'Yes. He's captured. You want to rescue him. So we're going to do that.'

I blink. 'I know that I just asked for that,' I try saying, 'but I think we skipped over a few important steps there. Not that I'm complaining, but why would you even want to help?'

'My sister says you're a good person.'

'Does she?' For some reason, that makes me . . . uncomfortable. Or pleased. It's complicated.

'Yes. Also, Shade says it's the only way to protect the valley. If these soldiers remain unchecked, they will come back here to finish what they started.'

And don't I just want to completely trust a shadow-demon that has probably killed many people over the centuries and held this entire community in what can be best described as its 'protective grasp'? Which is not so bad, unless you think of the worse ways in which it can be described, including 'indentured servitude' and 'enslavement'.

Then again, I don't think I have a whole lot of choice right now.

'Okay. But before we get into fully fledged rescue plans . . .' I point at the central pebble. 'Does this mean you know where Adam is being held, and how we can get there?'

'Yes. Shade knows.'

That's a starting point anyway. Maybe if I can just get the location, I can . . . get myself shot in three seconds. Shadow-demon or not, I just can't help but have reservations about putting this girl in danger by having her help out. And the fact that she's Seidre's little sister does not improve matters.

'All right, maybe you can tell me a little bit more about what Shade knows.' I guess being reasonable and non-committal is a decent stalling strategy for now. 'Though, honestly, even if everyone in this valley helped out, I don't think we're going to get far without a proper plan.'

She looks at me in confusion. 'Didn't I just say?' She touches a couple of the other pebbles. 'We're not going to be alone in this.'

The Dark Roads

Alice

Another day. Another mystical journey down weird roads filled with mortal danger. You'd think a girl would get used to it, or even bored, but no—mortal danger just always manages to find ways to be fresh and new. I think I'm in Hell. Literally.

'No. This is not Hell,' says Kit in exasperation as I bring up that observation for the hundredth time. 'This is not even *a* hell. Or for that matter any place in particular. It's just . . . a shortcut.'

I look around with a sceptical eye. 'Do all shortcuts have veins of fire pulsing along jet-black walls with thorny rock projections that I can completely swear move when I look away *and* whispering creatures at the edge of my hearing who seem to have made it their life's mission to creep me out even more than I already am?'

'Yes. Now stop avoiding the subject. You wanted some answers—go talk to him!'

I glance ahead, where the lumbering form of the Snowman is meticulously studying a fork in the road. He offered to act as our guide through these so-called Dark Roads and lead us to some weird shadow-valley to find Kit's missing library book. Fantasy scavenger hunts can be very complicated. Tao is also tagging along. I don't want to ask too much, because I overheard part of a conversation he had with Kit, and I'm pretty sure he's looking for someone to murder. Fun!

So I steel myself, and move forward. 'Um . . . Mr Snowman, sir?' What? Politeness never hurt anyone.

He turns slowly. Of course, with someone who looks like a blizzard and sounds like a thunderstorm, it doesn't matter how polite you are; you always get the feeling that they're very, very annoyed with you.

'Just Snowman is fine,' he rumbles.

I search for the right question. It's a variation of the very impolite 'What are you?', a possible relation of the confused 'What am I?' and somewhere in the vicinity of the annoyed 'What the heck is wrong with this world?'.

'What were the Children of Destruction?' I finally ask.

The impassive face seems to break into a frosty smile. 'Old friends,' he whispers. 'Old allies. They made those like me—the ice giants. We fought by their side during the war.' The smile turns sad. 'Those days are gone now.'

'But who were they?'

He looks up and gestures for us all to follow down one fork. He starts to talk slowly. 'The Elementals had many names and faces. Most are forgotten now. They were once human. They were once family. Three brothers. One sister. They were born at a time when the gods ruled as tyrants. Their people were being enslaved and slaughtered.'

His words stumble out awkwardly. It's like he's seeing all those fragments of memory again. I swallow nervously. He was *there*.

'The gods had chased the Primordials into dormancy. To prevent their power from being consumed, they reverted to the natural universe, bound by its immutable laws. But the Children bargained for another way. They offered themselves as human vessels for the lesser elements.'

'They fought the Pantheons across the world. Different names. Different battles. The Greeks remembered them best. They remembered the tragedies and the defeat of each clash. First, the eldest, Epimetheus—the Dreamer, the Storm-Bringer—betrayed by love and killed. Then Atlas—the Stalwart, the Earth-Shaker—captured and bound in the prisons beneath Olympus, the weight of the world resting on his shoulders. Third, Prometheus—the Far-Seer, the Flame-Heart—who sacrificed his freedom for his people, chained in the depths of the underworld. And lastly . . .'

He stops, his icy complexion clouding over.

'She ended the war. She sacrificed herself and her twin, Atlas, destroying Olympus along with half the world and ending the rule of the Pantheons,' he says sadly. 'Her name was Atlantis.'

He starts walking again. I try to shake off the inevitable chills. A part of me wants to make some pithy comment about the sister succeeding where all the brothers failed and history somehow forgetting that she was even a person, but I kind of feel like the point would be lost on an ancient ice-giant.

'Like the island?' I ask instead.

'Yes. She and her brother built fortresses in the oceans in those days. Beacons of hope for those who defied the gods, and bastions of fear for those who served them. Those, too, were lost in the final flood.' His eyes dim further. 'Those who fought paid the highest price. The humans taken captive during the war were enslaved in the underworld. Those like my kind have slowly perished. In war there is no such thing as victory.'

I don't know why, but I put out a hand, touching this old and sad ice-giant on the arm. I think I wanted to just say something optimistic or comforting. I don't know if it's my imagination, but his face does seem to brighten a bit.

'This . . . flood,' I ask softly, 'do you mean, like, the whole Noah story—with, like, the ark?'

He stares down at me with bewilderment. 'Who?'

'Like in the, um . . . Bible?' The bewilderment continues. 'Um . . . the book?'

He shrugs with the grace of an avalanche. 'I don't read modern fiction,' he says, and then goes on. 'The last act of Atlantis was meant to destroy all magic, and all the realms that were built with it. I understand why she did it, but I am also grateful that she failed, even if I don't know why. There is a place for us in this world.' He says the last line with a kind of cold, clear hope that almost makes me tear up. Supernatural creature or otherwise, I think that's kind of what everyone really wants to believe.

'Is that why they're called the Children of Destruction?' I ask uncertainly. 'Because of all the terrible stuff?'

'Fear and propaganda are useful tools in war,' he says thoughtfully, 'but there is a different truth as well. The Children were less than the Primordials, but their source of power was the same. They were vessels for power tied directly to the building blocks of both worlds. They were the wind, the water, the fire and the earth, and they were the story of each. Their legends and deeds are part of our understanding of the world of magic and power.' The icy brows knit together for a second. 'To live in a world where imagination reigns supreme, we are all beholden to the nature of the story. Our entire existences are shaped around a definite purpose, which we can no more deny than an ordinary human can live without breathing.

'In their time, the title was given to those four because they were not bound to that path. They should not have been able to fight, and yet they did. They should not have won, and yet they did. They were of both worlds, and yet of neither. The destroyers of fate and the unmakers of destiny.

'That, my liege, is the lineage of your power. And, as magic returns, an Elemental may be all that can save us from destruction or tyranny.'

I blink for a very long and scared moment before turning to glare at Kit. I just *knew* this whole thing was going to end with her asking me to save the world!

The Snowman stops at another fork in the road. The mystical not-Hell tunnels feel like they're closing in all around us. I've never been a victim of claustrophobia, but I can't help but think that claustrophobia's got to take root somewhere.

He raises a giant arm to point down one tunnel. 'Santor can be found this way, Trickster, and, while the Dark Roads are not as reliable as they once were, the paths to portal sites and the Edge realms should be simple to find.'

'You're not coming with?' I ask, surprisingly disappointed. It's weird, but there's something very comforting about a great big ice-giant who moves like a glacier and actually answers questions.

'This is as far from my home as I can be. My war is done.' He looks down at Kit. 'For now, you are in good hands.'

Kit tries not to look smug.

~

After leaving the Snowman there, we continued on our journey, with me trying to keep up as Kit talks with Tao.

'I met Chun in Kolkata. He crossed the border about a month after you killed the Paschid. None of his contacts had heard anything about Jhakri, but I had a few sources. Jhakri was last seen a decade ago in the Hindu Kush. I don't know what he was doing there, but it's safe to assume it had something to do with Santor. There are also rumours that the valley came under attack shortly after that.'

'The Kush?' Tao looks thoughtful. 'I have heard that Sheol has been dealing with humans there.'

Kit stops dead and, from the blank expression on her face, I can tell she's worried. 'Sheol?' she asks. 'Are you sure?'

'Moderately. He is rumoured to be growing impatient with his search. I don't suppose—'

'Don't ask,' Kit cuts him off. 'You think Jhakri is being held by these humans?'

'The laws of the story would not have it any other way,' says Tao grimly.

I think Kit really likes having Tao around. It's like she finally has someone she can talk to in her whole doom-and-gloom code—and they can understand each other perfectly.

'You two want to fill me in on what all those proper nouns mean?'

Kit doesn't even look over her shoulder before replying, 'In order: an inconsequential mortal, the city that you slept through, a mercenary group, former leader of said mercenary group, mountain range that forms the border between Afghanistan and Pakistan, the Valley of Shadow—our current destination—and a demon lord.'

Don't you ever wish you had a perfect memory?

'Oh, right,' I say in what can only be called a very lame fashion. I try sorting things out. 'Demon lord?'

'Yes,' says Kit smugly.

A further thought occurs. 'Wait, mercenary group?' I round on Tao. 'You killed an entire mercenary group?'

'The ones responsible for the deaths of my parents,' he says calmly. 'One hundred and seventeen people were actively involved in their work and, though it was hardly just, their lives were . . . promised to me.'

So not only is he creepy, he's also a mass murderer. Great— I miss just creepy already.

'I was surprised you spared Chun,' says Kit conversationally, because obviously mass murder is a topic for easy conversation now.

Tao shakes his head. 'I didn't. With the Paschid gone, he has nothing left, save my last gifts of fear and despair. His path is all too clear, Trickster. He will be dead before the year comes round once more.'

There's got to be a handbook on how to participate in conversations like these. I bet it starts with 'Back away slowly, and head for the nearest police station.'

We continue on in silence.

Creatures of Emptiness

The boy sat in the centre of the holding chamber. The pale clothes they'd provided him were in vivid contrast to the metal of the restraints locked around both wrists and ankles.

From the other side of the observation wall, Roth was doing his best to keep from frowning. Given the limitations, the good doctor had done her best, and they had collected significant data, but it just wasn't enough. 'Take me through it again,' he said.

Dr Lain didn't bother referring to the notes this time around. She'd already briefed Roth twice over the last two days.

'Starting with the basic observations—height, weight, bone structure, brain size—they all appear average for a boy of about eleven years. X-rays indicate normal bone density, and a full bio-scan reveals no abnormalities in any of his internal organs or systems. And yet the field report indicates he survived and somehow redirected a taser shock with enough amperage to take down an elephant, and subsequently took two bullets—one to the left leg and the second to the abdomen—without being physically handicapped by either. By the time he was brought in, his body had ejected the shells and repaired a large amount of the damage. On the surface, the wounds appeared as if they had already been treated and were more than a week old.' She paused, hesitating.

'The main laboratories near HQ should be able to build a better profile. Moving on to blood, marrow and tissue tests—any samples taken break down into composite proteins almost immediately after extraction. My personal theory is that the boy's entire genetic structure is continuously regulated by his will, which explains why we get normal readings sometimes and why he appears to possess certain superhuman attributes at others.'

Roth listened closely. The description sounded eerily familiar. The doctor wasn't privy to some of the other projects that were underway. Even Roth had only read one top-secret briefing about a certain *other* subject—one that related to the Kharsans' work before they had left for Eden. He'd have to request clearance for the full story. Damn bureaucracy.

Lain continued. 'If you weren't planning to transfer him to HQ, I'd recommend starting a series of stress tests.'

'Stress tests?' asked Roth absently, before realizing half a second later what she meant. He let her answer anyway.

'Responses to external stimuli, particularly of the extreme kind.' Lain shrugged, never really one for scientific euphemisms. 'Basically we torture him and see how his body adapts to it. Oh, don't bother pretending to be shocked. If I'm right, he could just turn off or suppress his pain receptors with a thought. He wouldn't feel a thing unless he wanted to.'

'I'll pass on your recommendation for testing,' said Roth blandly, and then frowned as the lights in the lab flickered. 'Is that normal?'

'I'm afraid so,' she said. 'Ever since the sentries were activated, the generators have been acting up. As much as I'd like to say it's a coincidence ...'

'Yes, these are unusual times.' Roth peered closely at the cell. Strange—the boy seemed oddly ... still.

❧

Adam opened his eyes to look up at the creature standing before him.

He had never seen anything quite like it. The superficial shape was human enough—a soldier wearing a beret—but the mannerisms were anything but. The eyes didn't blink and the micro-expressions were non-existent.

It was the other shapes, though, that truly held Adam's interest. They appeared as after-images, shadowing the creature's every movement. Each one conveyed its own sense of scale and history. A great armoured behemoth, larger than a building. A man without skin laughing amid a field of flames. A warrior wearing a helm in the shape of an insect, riding a horse that was not a horse. And others, so many others. But they all had one thing in common. There was not a single trace of humanity in any of them.

He also noticed that the creature kept its distance.

'You are the one who created those abominations,' said Adam finally.

'Abominations?' The creature shrugged. 'The bodies that once gave them form are beyond help. Now they are simply energy, to be used or destroyed.'

Adam wondered why he felt such rage at this. Much of what he'd learnt made him sad, but anger . . . no, he had never felt that before. 'They deserve an end,' he said.

'They will have it . . . eventually. But this is nothing new, boy. Golems powered by souls have been a part of our worlds since the first Pantheons. That will not change. And I am not one to sympathize. You understand what I am, do you not?'

Adam did. There were words. There were actions, and stories, and legends written into those images that surrounded the creature, but they all paled before that gnawing vortex that seemed to exist at the very core of this creature's existence.

'The Empty One,' Adam said, finding the only words that seemed fit. 'Why are you here?'

He tested his bonds again. It was too much to hope that he could break free and reach the creature before it had time to dodge, but maybe if he simply leapt towards it. Contact was essential. He knew that with instinctive certainty. He wasn't sure if he was strong enough yet to destroy the creature, but he could try.

As if reading his mind, the creature stepped back further. 'I am here to ask a single question.'

Adam glanced briefly at the observation wall. From this side it looked like a smooth, almost plastic surface, but he could hear the voices of those who watched from behind it. Or, at least, he had been able to hear them.

'This is a private conversation,' said the creature, following Adam's gaze. 'They were sensible to build this facility here, given that it allowed them some rudimentary control over powers that the mortal realm has not fully seen in millennia. But they have yet to realize that this place also allows others, far more practiced in the use of power, to exercise their will.'

'You are *using* them! They don't know the consequences of your foothold in this world!'

The creature only smiled thinly. 'Sooner or later, child, the emptiness finds us all. Who am I to stop these humans from hastening the end of their world?'

'What is your question?' asked Adam.

'For what purpose do you exist?'

Adam tilted his head quizzically. 'My existence *is* my purpose.'

The creature stood for a second longer, its hands clenching into fists. Adam could see it making the same calculation as he was. Was it worth trying to destroy one another?

Finally, it nodded. 'Fair enough. For now, let's see how this plays out.'

And then it was gone.

The boy moved, but there didn't seem to be any other abnormality. Roth tried not to think about it.

The door to the medical centre opened quietly. Madeline entered, glancing over at the holding chamber.

'I see you haven't begun your "stress tests" yet,' she said, her voice dripping with acid disapproval.

'Don't start,' said Roth with a sigh. 'What's wrong now?'

'You make it sound as if all I ever bring you is bad news.' She feigned a slightly hurt expression. 'Sarah, could you give us a couple of minutes?'

'Of course.' The doctor started towards the far section of the room. 'I'll be in my office if you need me.'

Madeline waited for Dr Lain to leave before turning to Roth. 'Two matters to discuss: One, I'm being transferred back in preparation for this project's expansion. And the current project in Toronto with the *Voca Arcanus* requires . . . attention.'

'I guess we'll have to manage without you,' he said, not quite sarcastically. She had been useful in her own way. 'What's the second matter?'

'It's about the Hong Kong flare—the "dragon", or whatever it is. Ever since the incident with Marcus, we've kept clear of direct contact; but we've still managed to pick up subsequent energy readings. First in the South China Sea, then in India and most recently in Sikkim.'

'I saw the reports. Beryl was going to try establishing a more precise way of tracking the source?'

'Yes. She succeeded about two hours ago. There's a clear line indicating that the source travelled from Hong Kong to Kolkata and then up north, finally hitting Khangchendzonga National Park. The trail ends there.'

'If they're in the wilderness, it will be easier to send a covert team. I'll see if the good captain—'

'No,' interrupted Madeline. 'The trail *vanishes* there. Either the source is dead—in which case, we should send a team to see if we can at least retrieve the corpse—or they've entered a masked area.'

'Khangchendzonga.' Roth frowned, summoning a mental map of the region. 'The Paschid incident?'

'There could be a connection.'

Roth grimaced. Too many coincidences. The Arcanus, Jhakri, the boy—there were too many pieces placed at Deacon's Hill. It made him feel vulnerable.

'Have we managed to verify who we're dealing with?'

Madeline shook her head. 'No. There are a few candidates. One missing girl, Sun Alice, seems the most likely. We're investigating her family.'

Roth looked over at the boy again. Was there any chance that there might be some further connection to Eden, or Santor? And if so . . .

If there was anything worse than having to deal with one supernaturally powered child, it would have to be dealing with a group of them, with all their actions orchestrated by God knows what.

They would have to increase security.

Shadows of the Dead

Kharsan

Portals to other realms built into a cliff-side cave is another kind of surprise I could have lived without.

Seidre is standing near me with her husband, a man who manages to make me incredibly uncomfortable by simply standing there and smiling politely. I am trying my best not to have any ill will towards him, and the fact that he's an intimidating foot taller than I am makes it depressingly easy to behave in a civil manner. I didn't really have the nerve to ask Seidre, but I get the feeling he just thinks that we're old friends, rather than old *friends*.

Violetta is at the cave entrance, staring back at the town with a forlorn expression.

'Are you sure about this?' I ask Seidre worriedly.

'Not even a little,' she says flatly, 'but it is her decision.'

'But . . .' I break off under her stare, which seems to be daring me to point out the obvious fact that the girl is only twelve years old. I understand, though. After spending a few weeks with Adam, I'm ready to believe that age has absolutely nothing to do with ability.

'Besides,' says Seidre, 'this is also about Shade. And as much as I don't trust him . . .' She pauses, the bitter twist of her mouth indicating that distrust is the least of her issues with the demon. 'He does not lie to Violetta. If he says that she must go, then there is a reason.'

'Yes,' I say, summoning my best counterargument, 'but you don't know what the reason is. For all you know, he might be planning to lead your sister down a path that leads to world domination.' I say it lightly enough but, quite frankly, anyone who thinks a child ruling the world is a joke does not know how scary children can really be.

Aurin's worried expression is testament to that, though he hides it quickly. While he appears nice enough, there is a distinct undercurrent of fear in him when around the demon, which both the sisters seem to be deliberately ignoring.

'I can't stop her.' Seidre's voice is almost inaudible as she says that. 'So I have to . . .'

She breaks off as Violetta approaches. She's looking about as depressed as her big sister. There is almost none of the early eagerness she showed while detailing this plan. Starting out always makes it a lot more real.

'It's time,' she says.

I move to the side to let them get their farewells out of the way. Hugs and tears have never been particularly welcome in my comfort zone. By the looks of it, though, I shouldn't have worried. They stand at arm's length from each other and talk quietly. Seidre does move forward for a quick hug at the end, but it's all very dignified.

As this happens, I notice some movement near the edge of the fields, where the outskirts of the town are. Multiple movements actually. I get the feeling that people are gathering just at the edge of town to see if their personal shadow is really departing. The girl is right—it's time that we were on our way.

Before that, though, comes the part that I am dreading. I walk up to Seidre and her husband and shake his hand, before turning to her and saying, 'I will do everything in my power to keep her safe.'

I hate making promises. I have this annoying flaw of wanting to keep them. She smiles before taking my hands in hers.

'Thank you,' she says honestly, and I am eternally grateful that she doesn't point out the fact that I, frail shadow-demon-less mortal, am probably the one needing protection.

~

Perhaps it is simply the dismal state of mind that I've found myself in since leaving Eden, but the rough obsidian walls with veins of fire seem almost comforting.

What doesn't inspire comfort is the fact that Violetta seems to have been in deep conversation with the demon ever since we entered the place. Shadow-demons, mystical tunnels. Barring my fondness for taking my god's name in vain, I am extremely glad that I view theology with suspicion; otherwise, I imagine, this would be a lot harder than it already is.

It is a few minutes later that I add a new rule to my own personal book. Right under 'Don't look down when climbing perilous cliffs' we now have 'Don't look back when travelling in mysterious dark tunnels'. After that little sojourn while entering Santor, I tell myself that I've grown quite used to distinguishing between different shades of darkness and that the creeping black wall of shadow following us is *not* of the regular harmless kind.

'Don't fall behind,' says Violetta sharply, and I realize that I've actually stopped to look at the oncoming wall of terror. Not the brightest of moves.

'Do you know what it is?' I ask, resuming the steady march forward.

'You've met them,' she says quietly. 'The ones that guard the entrance to Santor. Shade keeps them under control, so now they have to come with us or they might turn on the valley in his absence.'

'They're . . . ghosts?' I ask with an unfortunate lack of scepticism.

She shakes her head. 'No. They're just imprints of the last memories. Death-shadows.'

Which I'm sure is a whole different species than ghosts.

'Are they dangerous?'

'Yes,' she says bluntly. 'But they're not really very angry, or violent . . . They're just lost.'

Well, that's something anyway. When I get killed by the shadows following us, at least I'll know that they didn't really mean to do it.

'How far are we taking them?'

She tilts her head back slightly, as if listening. 'Not far,' she says. 'We're almost at the crossroads.'

The Joining of the Paths

'Look,' said Kit through teeth gritted in exasperation, 'have you ever been to, say, Somalia?'

'Saw a documentary. Don't want to go,' said Alice.

'Well, Hell is like that. More fire, less guns.' She relented. 'Well, at least the bad parts are. There are some underworld spots that are breathtakingly scenic. Still very dangerous, of course, but really very scenic.'

'But you're admitting there is a Hell, right? Filled with eternal torment and dead souls and stuff . . .'

'Eternal torment is really overstated,' said Kit, thinking that even the most sadistic demons she knew generally got bored of torment after a couple of centuries. 'And last time I was there, the denizens looked pretty lively to me. Barring Necropolis, of course, but they've always thought the bony look was very fashionable. Haven't you been listening to anything I've been saying, Alice? This isn't about whatever happens after death. These things were once part of your reality, and they're shaped and sculpted by the stories and legends and folklore. But this isn't about judgement and good and evil; at least no more than regular existence is. I've met spirits of the so-called dead—in that they didn't have physical bodies any more—but to those like me, that just means the definition of death is a lot more flexible than most humans imagine it to be.' She shrugged.

216

'So is the definition of life, if you want to look at it from that perspective.'

'I really don't,' said Alice glumly.

Kit sighed and looked towards the next fork in the road. Travelling the Dark Roads was starting to get a little monotonous, even with all the potential dangers of getting lost, encountering strange reality-breaking anomalies, or falling though a gateway into any one of a dozen potentially lethal realms.

'The Trickster is correct,' said Tao. 'The Kingdom of Avici, for one, is host to some spectacular architecture. Lord Yama has a particular fondness for spires of the neo-Gothic variety.'

Both Alice and Kit glared at him. The former because he was making an annoying habit of supporting the latter, and the latter because if he felt so obliged to support her truths, he might similarly decide to point out the falsehoods as well.

He sightlessly stared back without any appearance of noticing the glares, which stopped as soon as their wearers realized they were both doing it.

'Yeah, great,' said Alice. 'I should make a note about the next family vacation there. My mom just loves weird architecture.' She winced immediately, probably at the thought of her family in the underworld.

Kit smiled inwardly at the girl's worries. They'd keep her sharp, focused. Besides, Kit had already made sure that the family would be safe. Though, of course, she hadn't told Alice that. The girl would not have approved of her methods.

She turned back to the guiding stones.

Vi stopped at the crossroads. The fourfold path split at near-right angles, with each cavernous road disappearing into darkness.

Kharsan stood with his arms held behind his back, looking around with a worried frown.

Now what?

Wait, said Shade, his unheard voice heavy with strain. The death-shadows had always been his burden rather than that of the host, and bringing them this far from Santor was taking its toll.

Move to the centre. Stand perfectly still.

She followed the instruction, gesturing for Kharsan to do the same.

Brace yourself.

In an instant the shadows rushed in. Within seconds, they had swirled all around, blocking all the roads and surrounding them in a pool of whirling darkness. Next to her, she could feel Kharsan shiver, obviously remembering his earlier encounter with the death-shadows.

Vi kept calm. Shade was already shielding her from the worst of it, and, in any case, the shadows were probably more scared of her than the other way around. She felt Shade stretching out until he was woven into the darkness as he slowly guided them towards the next step.

Then Shade let go, and the shadows rushed outwards in every direction, whispering like the wind. Through Shade, she could feel them travelling at enormous speeds down the Dark Roads, moving further and growing weaker with each moment. And then they were gone, dissipated forever into the eternal darkness of these roads.

It's over? she asked cautiously.

Yes. And I think I sense the Trickster and her companions ahead.

She tugged on Kharsan's sleeve, directing him to the road on the left.

'That's it?' he asked, following after her. 'All those . . . imprints—they just get banished into nothingness?'

She shrugged. 'They're just memories.' Memories that could hurt, that could kill, that could almost be alive . . . She shook off the twinge of guilt evoked by those thoughts. 'Memories fade,' she said.

~

Alice looked around wildly for shelter as the wall of darkness swept towards them. Unfortunately, this particular section of the road seemed all too bereft of convenient rock outcrops or small boulders. Thinking fast, she raised her right hand, hoping that her wall-of-air trick would have some effect.

Before she could do anything, though, Kit grabbed her forearm and hissed, 'Wait!'

In the next second, the darkness washed over them. For Alice, it felt like drowning in a flood—a sensation that seemed all too familiar for her liking—except the flood was made of a thousand different voices, all whispering madly and incoherently, leaving behind pinpricks of frosted pain. It was over in less time than it had taken to panic about it.

Alice turned shakily to look at the retreating darkness, but it was already lost in the far shadows. 'What was that?' she asked, trying hard to keep her voice level.

'Death-shadows. Imprints of those that died violent deaths, usually at the hand of mystical creatures. Never before have I seen that many of them in one place outside of the underworld, but they seemed to be fading into the pathways.'

'There are many rumours regarding the demon of Santor,' said Tao. 'Though I have not heard of a single first-hand encounter. Perhaps it is responsible for this.'

'Looks like it,' said Kit before Alice could frame the obvious question of 'Huh?'

'Then it knows where we are, and is likely to be approaching soon,' said Tao in a matter-of-fact tone. 'That does make things simpler. Though I do wonder if the creature in question will be civil.'

As Alice stared at him, she was aware of Kit shifting back into her fox shape and trotting forward, sniffing the air.

'Enough chatter,' said Kit. 'They're close.'

❧

'What's wrong?' asked Kharsan. In the dim light, Violetta's face seemed to be turning pale and strained as they moved forward. She ignored him at first, or maybe she just didn't hear him. Her entire attention seemed to be forced inwards.

With concern, Kharsan moved closer. As he did so, the beam of his flashlight stumbled upon the edge of her shadow. With a soft gasp, he took a step back.

The Shadow was writhing beneath her, a twisted mass that stretched and shifted with each movement.

'Violetta!' he called, raising his voice.

She started, looking around wildly for a second before calming down. 'Sorry,' she said. 'Shade is . . . restless.'

Kharsan hesitated, uneasy at the thought of what might make a shadow-demon restless. 'Anything in particular?' he asked. 'Or is he just feeling homesick?'

'He keeps . . .' She frowned. 'No one usually asks me about Shade.'

Kharsan reflected that it was probably because most people were terrified of the demon. Not that he wasn't terrified; but he'd just grown so used to a consistent amount of terror that it no longer really affected his actions. He shrugged. 'I guess I'm just suicidally curious. What's bothering him?'

'The Dreamer, the one he mentioned. This close, he can sense what it is, and he says it's . . . wrong.'

'Wrong?' He hadn't given much thought to the vague descriptions the Shadow had given their would-be allies.

'I don't know.' She sounded genuinely puzzled. 'It's like being this close is triggering some memory of his—but he doesn't have any memories.'

'He has amnesia?'

'No! It's not like that.' She struggled for a moment to find the words, but then gave up. 'Never mind. Let's just keep moving.'

They were close now, and Shade still hadn't settled down. He wasn't speaking either. Vi had tried everything she could think of, but she couldn't get him to respond properly. All she managed to get were flashes of near-violent emotion.

Shade had never shown emotion before. It wasn't in his nature. It was the reason she trusted him in spite of every one of those memories. All the decisions of the past had been made based on the emotions of the host, and the earliest ones had even had noble intentions . . .

Now it felt as if she wasn't in control, and that scared her.

What is it? she asked again. It was as if the closer they were getting, some dormant instinctive part of Shade was waking up, and even Shade—at least the Shade that she knew—wasn't fully aware of what he wanted.

She was almost inclined to turn back, but she couldn't seem to find the willpower to do so. It was like they were tumbling down a slope, and now there was no choice but to wait and see if they'd survive the descent.

'We need to slow down!' called Kharsan from behind her. It was only then that she realized that she'd almost been running.

Gritting her teeth, she deliberately dug in her heels, forcing herself to a halt. Shade stretched out in front of her, expanding as far as she'd ever seen him go. The stretched Shadow trembled.

Shade! Stop! she yelled, giving it all the force of a mental scream. The Shadow finally stopped.

She'd never had to command him before. The necessity of doing so fanned that spark of fear. But more than that, it made her angry.

Concentrating fiercely, she drew Shade back towards her. He didn't struggle, nor did he acquiesce. Directing him based on her will alone was another thing she'd never done before, and the strain was unbelievable.

She rested halfway through, holding the Shadow in place while she tried communicating again. This time there was a tiny spark of response.

I . . .

It started to fade.

Answer me. What's happening?

Shade's awareness flickered again but before he could answer, a faint light appeared in the distance. There, where the tunnel turned sharply, three figures emerged. Vi frowned, trying to make them out. One seemed small—an animal of some sort. She couldn't make out much of the other two, except that one of them held in its hand a glowing sphere of light, its brightness almost blinding in the dim passage.

Vi heard a harsh, wordless snarl, and it took her a whole second to realize that it was Shade.

'No!' she shouted out loud, but it was already too late.

The Shadow rushed forward, straight at the figure holding the light.

Kindred Spirits
Alice

I should have really seen the attack from the shadow-monster coming. It's been almost two whole days since I was randomly attacked by anything.

I mean, here I am thinking that we're finally one step closer to being done with all of Kit's plans and plots and whatnots, and I'm even glad to turn the corner and see that they at least look relatively normal, when this inky patch of darkness that I could have sworn was the girl's shadow just lunges at me before I can even scream out what I can guarantee was going to be a really long, shrill scream of terror.

The shadow hits before I can do that, and one moment of intense psychic pain later, I'm stuck in a very familiar out-of-body experience. Like I'm in the same Limbo that Kit's Dreamsnake venom had tossed me into. But it's not quite the same misty experience it was before, where all the immediate surroundings just turned all ghostly and insubstantial. If anything, now it feels like the world's been thrown into sharp relief, the visual illusion melted away to show the reality underneath. The faint veins of fire from before now pulse in shades of bright gold, and the dark rocks fill the space in between, except they're not really rocks any more, but like . . . bundles of black thread with the consistency of steel. And just for a brief moment, I get this feeling of knowing where the threads lead, and I see all these roads like some kind of giant spiderweb, knitting together realities.

It'd be really awe-inspiring if I wasn't trying to get my bearings and wasn't being confronted by a weird apparition made out of torn black rags snarling and slashing towards me. The memory of the thorns from the last time is enough to get me to dodge. Thankfully, it's a lot easier to move in this disembodied state, because, honestly, I've never really been gymnast material. Even so, it still feels like I'm pulling muscles jerking back from its slicing movements.

'Can we talk about this?' I yell in the vain hope that this will be the one creature who will listen to my sincere plea for pacifism.

It isn't.

The last time I was here, towards the end I'd managed to destroy the thorns by doing . . . something. Kinda like the real-world shock waves, except over here it's not piggybacking on air molecules. Here, it's pure power. I try and focus but then have to dodge to one side as the creature lunges forward.

It's hard to concentrate when being threatened with disembowelment. It crashes against the wall, causing a sudden blinding flare, forcing me to look away. Bad mistake.

I can feel the movement behind me—way too quick for me to do anything about it.

'You know,' says a cold voice as I try and figure out why I haven't been cut into ribbons yet, 'one of these years you'll need to learn to survive without help.'

I whirl around and see the black-rag fiend a bare foot away from me, one claw-like limb outstretched but otherwise completely immobilized by thin white threads. And behind it . . . my own personal Limbo phantom.

Except, different. It's now a woman, but I can see familiar features in her face and build, reminding me of Mom, of Kit, Lin . . . others . . . even myself. It's the thundering full-black eyes that give it away.

At this point, I have about a thousand questions, but I know how to prioritize.

Backing away slowly, I point towards the attacker. 'You know what that is?'

She moves in until she's only inches away from the rags, studying it with intent curiosity. 'Something incomplete,' she says. 'It's like a broken piece struggling to remember what it was to be whole.'

'That's nice. Can you tell me why it wants to kill me?'

'It's not really interested in killing you. You just happened to be inconveniently in the way.'

'In the way of what?' Have to admit, it's oddly satisfying to be told you're inconveniencing someone when the last few weeks of your life have been spent being inconvenienced by the entire universe.

There's a ghost of a smile on her face. 'Me.'

I open my mouth to wearily try for a more complete explanation, but she waves me into silence.

'First things first.' She places a hand on the apparition, right where the head might be.

The moment she does that, my own awareness of it becomes a lot clearer, in a weird, possibly psychic way. The appearance matches the feeling—a shadow as black as the rags, and just as torn, yanked around by this ancient sense of anger and hatred.

'Well, aren't you an old soldier,' she mutters. 'Broken, corroded and without memory, but still clinging to old instincts and orders.' She smiles, and it's chilling to see something that might be your face wearing that kind of a cold, humourless smile. 'Let's see if we can do something about that.'

Two heartbeats. It doesn't take longer than that, but I can still follow what's happened. It's like that trick with the ball of light, except a lot quicker. The power is gathered and shaped

225

in the first step, and when released, it crashes into the friendly shadow-monster with implosive force.

The white threads binding it fall away and, before my eyes, the torn edges of the rags seem to soften. It still leaves a vague ink-like figure with no real definition, but it's a lot less scary than when it was trying to be all slasher wannabe.

'Better now?'

Yes.

It doesn't sound like a voice. Or words, really. There's just this faint scraping sensation as the meaning is imparted directly to the person listening.

'Who are you?'

I am called Shade.

'Your real name!'

The force of the command makes me take a step back. I'd feel sorry for the thing if it hadn't tried to kill me moments ago.

It still doesn't answer, though, and after a moment she steps away. 'I see. You don't even have that left to you.' She looks towards me. 'Meet a remnant from wars long past, stripped of most of its memory and thought, leaving behind the little pieces used to create its most basic form—which includes a violent hatred for a certain category of enemy.'

Elemental . . .

'Straight from the shadow's mouth,' she says dryly. 'Let's hope this little trick holds, otherwise we're just going to be back here again.' She shakes her head pityingly, turning back to the creature. 'You had better leave then. It sounds like someone's calling you.'

I can barely make it out myself. It sounds like a young girl. Maybe the same one to whom the shadow belonged. I open my mouth to ask it a few questions of my own, but it's already too late. It vanishes like smoke, leaving me alone with . . . *her.*

I look at her warily. 'Thanks,' I say grudgingly.

'You don't need to thank me,' she says, 'After all, you know what I am.'

'The reason I'm a freak!' It comes out a lot angrier than I wanted it to. I guess I've got a lot of bottled rage at my life being turned upside down.

'I'm the reason you're alive,' she says calmly. 'But that's not the right answer. Care to try again?'

I keep glaring at her, but I slowly tamp down the rage. 'Lineage of power—that's what the Snowman said. So there's a link between now and then. That's what you are.'

'Warmer,' she says with that creepy, chilly smile, 'but you're still not quite there yet.'

'And you're also me,' I say with all the glumness I can manage. It's not a nice thought. 'Like something plugged into my subconscious, giving it shape and thought because of the power. Like last time, Kit had me all focused on finding where Tao was, and now I'm kind of focused on this idea that you're some part of me—so, basically, I'm schizophrenic.'

'Except that I'm real.'

'Yeah. I bet all schizophrenic hallucinations say that.' I know she's right, though. Whatever this thing is, some ancient fragment of power, some weird element-like energy—it *is* part of me now. And it's real. More real than anything else.

I think about everything the Snowman said. 'You were there? You were one of the Elementals?'

Her expression clouds over. 'Epimetheus. Yes, I remember those times.'

I narrow my eyes. 'But you're not him. Not the human part anyway. Look—do you have a name?'

She shivers and, for a second, the form seems to waver. 'Once, I had many names. The Creator of Storms. The Father of Monsters. The Black Death.' She shakes her head. 'But you and I have no need for names. And I think it's time you were back in your own head.'

And here we were having such a heart-warming conversation. 'I'd love to, but . . .'

~

'How do I . . . Oh.'

That was sudden.

Kit's human face is looking over me curiously from an angle indicating that I'm lying down. 'Awake?' she asks.

I nod slowly. 'Tell me it hasn't been another three days.'

'Two minutes, actually.'

Strange. It felt a whole lot longer than that, but then, I guess time going all wonky while you're talking to your monstrous subconscious is just one of those things that happen.

I sit up gingerly. Looking around, the first thing I notice is the girl standing next to Kit. She looks about eleven or twelve, and is wearing a very anxious expression on her skinny face.

'Shade says he's sorry,' she says in a small voice.

I look down and, sure enough, even in the dim light I can tell that's *not* the shape of a regular shadow.

'Uh . . .'

'He didn't mean to. He couldn't control himself. And then you helped him.' She seems quite confused about the whole thing, which is actually quite a relief because I'm honestly tired of being the only one confused about stuff like this.

'It's okay,' I manage. 'No permanent damage done. Just . . . um . . .' I look at the shadow again 'Try to keep him on a tighter leash?'

She nods solemnly. With a shaky but reassuring grin, I slowly complete my journey to verticality. It's then that I notice the other new arrival standing next to Tao. Slightly tall, vaguely Indian or Arabian or whatever, and kinda good-looking, and probably around the same age as me. He's ignoring me completely (which, since I was just regaining consciousness, I take some offence at) and staring straight at Kit instead, with his mouth slightly open and his eyes wide with shock. That has got to be the single most comforting expression I've ever seen. Finally! It's on someone else's face.

'Something the matter?' I call out to him.

He turns in a slow, robotic fashion towards me. He closes his mouth, swallows and blinks uncertainly. 'She . . . is a fox.'

Kit hides a smile.

'Well, if you like that kind of obvious beauty,' I say, having way more fun with this than I thought was possible.

He doesn't seem to notice. 'And she just turned into a woman!'

'She does that,' I say in a knowledgeable, everyday sort of tone.

He stares at me for a few seconds and then leans heavily against the tunnel wall.

'Welcome to my world,' I say with undisguised satisfaction. 'I'm Alice.'

'Kharsan,' he says, and slowly sinks to the floor while shaking his head in utter disbelief. 'It's nice to meet you.'

Destruction's Eve

The campfire set up near the three-way intersection seemed appropriate to Tao. While it was warm enough on the Dark Roads, there was nothing like a small, controlled fire to set a balanced atmosphere between tension and relaxation, even if the scales were tipping towards the former. Especially after Kharsan had finished telling his story. The Elemental, in particular, was not taking it well.

'Military? As in people with guns?' she was asking in a panic-stricken voice.

'They had guns,' confirmed Kharsan with reluctance. The changing heartbeat and small movements that Tao could discern were likely signs of guilt. For leaving his brother behind, certainly, but also for involving others. A problem accented by the fact that most of the others were younger than him. Tao could have pointed out the foolishness of such thoughts, but he didn't. It was not his place.

'Look,' said Alice reasonably, 'I'm sorry about your brother and all—but I'm really just trying to stay alive right now, and invading a military base does not sound like the best way to do that. Weird supernatural powers or not, I do *not* remember signing up to join the X-Men!'

'They have the Arcanus and, unfortunately, they're after you as well,' said Kit conversationally. The Trickster had a way of redirecting Alice's emotions, letting them bubble to the point of explosion and then striking the moment they had boiled over.

'What? Why? And isn't that even more reason not to go there?'

'After my work eliminating the Paschid,' said Tao, 'I was made aware of patrols that came after, intent on finding the cause of their destruction. By the sound of it, they appear to be assessing potential threats all over the world and containing them.'

'Great! So now I'm a potential threat. Has anyone considered just talking to these guys, explaining that it's all one big misunderstanding and that we all really just want to get along?'

'Shade says that won't work,' said the other girl—Violetta. Tao was having a hard time with this . . . Shade creature. It was unlike any demon or spirit he'd encountered. The symbiotic bond with the girl was disturbingly unique. 'They stole another Arcanus from the valley eleven years ago. With the combined knowledge they now have and their new weapons, it's only a matter of time before they come back to Santor. They'll kill everyone in the valley. I . . . *we* have to stop them!'

'They do not act in a manner open to discussion,' said Kharsan hesitantly. 'I understand why they may have attacked Eden without warning but, subsequently, they made no effort towards peaceable contact. They do not wish to talk and they will not negotiate, because we do not have anything that they cannot take by force.'

'Fine,' said Alice, exasperated. 'So we can't talk to them. But that's no reason to waltz right in and volunteer for dissection.'

Tao felt Kharsan wince and nod heavily.

'You're right,' said Kharsan. 'You shouldn't have to come with us.' Tao noted the short turn of the head towards himself.

'I have business of my own with these soldiers,' he said, before turning to Violetta. 'Your . . . Shade—he knows the way to their encampment?'

She nodded. 'Yes. He says they can be reached along these roads.'

Kit shrugged. 'It makes sense. If they're dealing with Sheol, they've likely set up their base at a portal site so that he can visit freely. For now, that's a limited number of places, and most would be connected by these roads.'

Scratching his head, Kharsan sat forward. 'Getting there is all well and good, but there's no way to know what to expect. They have giant metal robots, of all things, so I don't think anything can be ruled out. For all I know, they could have magical anti-personnel death-rays that automatically wipe out anyone who isn't on their official visitors list.'

Alice nodded approvingly at this stretch of imagination.

Tao, while acknowledging that automatic death-rays were possible, thought them highly unlikely and suggested as much. 'However,' he went on, 'once we leave the Dark Roads, whether we're inside their perimeter or not, there are a few things I can help with.' He laid out the various options, stopping only when Violetta chimed in with a few suggestions of her own.

It wasn't a master plan, certainly, and even had a few glaring holes in it that might see all of them dead, but Tao had to admit to a small sense of satisfaction in knowing that the things he'd learnt while hunting the Paschid could be put to use. In a private corner of his mind, the small part that was still almost entirely human, he could hear the imagined argument that this gave their deaths a greater meaning.

The thought vanished a moment later, though. He could, at least, control the foolishness of his own thoughts.

❧

The tea tasted terrible, but Alice barely noticed. Every minute or so, she touched the rim of the cup to her lips while staring at the ground blankly. After some time, she noticed with some surprise that the cup was empty. She looked up for the first time in a while and got the further surprise that the little committee meeting she'd been trying to ignore was over.

Violetta was repacking her bag, muttering to herself (or perhaps to her shadow). Tao was staring sightlessly into the campfire, which had started to die down. The dark threads of lichen and moss they'd used in place of firewood were smouldering to ash, leaving smooth pebbles underneath. Alice was almost certain that moss-covered stones weren't supposed to burn like that, but there were plenty of other things to worry about.

Kharsan had moved away from the centre and was lying down with his head against his rucksack, staring blankly up at the ceiling. Alice was tempted to go over and try to start a *normal* conversation, but before she could make up her mind, Kit tapped her on the shoulder and gestured for her to follow.

She trudged along reluctantly until they were well away from the circle of light cast from the fire.

'Look,' said Alice, trying to pre-empt the conversation that she knew was coming, 'I get that all this is important, and that saving that kid is a good thing to do—assuming he isn't another mass-murdering sociopath—but I'd probably just be in the way, and . . .'

Kit raised both hands to stop her just as her line of argument was starting to head towards mindless babbling. 'At the bottom of your backpack,' she said calmly, 'there's a package wrapped in white plastic. In there you will find three things.' She held up three fingers. 'One: five different passports and accompanying credit cards. Different nationalities, different ages—averaging around sixteen—and genuine enough to fool most governments.' She saw Alice's wide-eyed expression. 'It's not any kind of "magic". I have a friend in Kolkata who's remarkably good at forgery and hacking diplomatic databases. Two: a small amount of assorted currency. Not much, but enough for emergencies. Lastly, there's a black book in there. Eighty-four names and contact details distributed around the world. Useful people who owe me favours, and will help you out if you need it.'

'What . . .' Alice finally managed.

Kit didn't let her get the words out. 'I don't know how far this military base is from here. Honestly, I'm terrible at directions, but with the help of that shadow I should be able to find you another exit point somewhere. You can't go home; you already know that. But the world's a big place. You know how to handle your powers well enough to defend yourself, and as for getting by . . . well, I hope you've managed to learn *something* watching me deal with people.'

She looked at Alice for a moment longer, her expression unreadable. 'I can't go with you. The Arcanus in human hands was bad enough; but if Sheol gains a foothold in this part of the world, there will be many more victims than just Santor. I still have a job to do but, trust me, you will be fine.'

With that, Kit moved to walk away. She hadn't taken more than two steps, when the confusion in Alice reached a sort of breaking point and emerged as uncontrollable anger. 'You complete *bitch*!' she hissed, shocking herself by the ferocity of her tone. 'Do you think I don't know what you're trying?'

Kit didn't turn around. When she spoke, her voice was harder and colder than Alice had thought possible. 'What I'm trying to do is provide you with an escape hatch in the hope that it will guilt you into coming along on this crazy adventure. This is what I am "trying". But at the end of the day, it's up to you.'

'*Up to me?*' said Alice bitterly. 'What part of any of this was up to me? You said it when we met—I'm not the chosen one. I'm the unlucky one. The person who just *happened* to get into some kind of accident at around the same time as this air Elemental was looking for a human vessel.'

'Yes,' said Kit, 'and you decided to live.' She looked over her shoulder and, for a second, smiled warmly. 'Being chosen is easy, Alice. What you have to do is a lot more difficult. Get some sleep. Decide tomorrow what you really want.' She walked off.

It wasn't till a while afterwards—the moss-fire had turned fully black, the tunnels now lit only by the faint glowing veins— that Alice finally moved from the spot. She lay down next to her backpack. Her hands wouldn't stop shaking.

When the captain entered the room, Roth gave him a perfunctory nod and gestured for him to take a look at the screen.

'Earlier today, there was a report from surveillance team sixteen.'

The captain frowned. 'Erwitz's team? They were the ones still deployed in Santor. Someone came out?'

'No.' Roth pointed at one image on the screen. It showed the great cliff wall that hid the Valley of Shadow from the world, and there, towards the centre, was a long thick black line. 'The valley entrance appeared some time this afternoon and, unlike previous times, is not going away. Add to that, the static interference around the valley has dropped quite heavily.'

'Has anyone emerged?'

'No.'

'Then it could be a trap,' suggested the captain.

'Yes,' agreed Roth. 'Which is why we're not moving yet. You had put together a plan for invading Santor using the sentries and the knowledge from the Arcanus?'

The captain nodded.

'Adapt it to the current scenario and make sure that we have a strike team fully briefed. We'll wait until the boy is transferred, and then we can go ahead with the attack.'

'Yes, sir,' said the captain glumly, certain that his sleepless night doing paperwork was now going to be a sleepless night doing actual work. 'Do the parameters for the mission still stand?'

Roth did not miss the strain showing on the man's face. 'Is that a problem?'

The captain took a deep breath. 'Eden was one thing, sir—but from the previous incursion into the valley, we know that the majority are non-combatants. Leaving no survivors is . . .'

'We left people alive eleven years ago, and the Shadow survived,' said Roth coolly. 'We will not make the same mistake again.'

'Yes, sir,' said the captain with something of a sigh. While the Rangers were notoriously flexible in such matters, he knew that missions like this had a cost much higher than simple casualties.

'And, Captain, the other orders still stand. Anyone who enjoys this mission too much does *not* come back.'

'Understood.'

Roth studied the captain closely. Besides Madeline, and those that she reported to, no one else knew the extent of the information Sheol had shared. He supposed it did make sense to have at least one more person in the loop.

'We need to be on alert as well,' he said. 'There are other paths out of Santor, and if the boy has allied himself with the Shadow, there may be a rescue attempt.'

'We'll be ready, sir. How would you like the sentries deployed?'

'Hmm . . . prep one scout-class sentry and the assault-class sentries for the mission to Santor. Other than that, put a few on perimeter duty, but keep the rest deployed near the medical wing—where our subject is—and also . . .' He pulled up a schematic of the base on the screen and pointed to where the summoning chamber was. 'Around there.'

The captain nodded as Roth stared at the screen, almost willing them to come. He didn't like loose ends.

～

For Adam, it was easier to study Deacon's Hill during the night.

He'd known almost from the start that the facility had been built into the warren of caves that were remnants of long-dried streams. Caverns had been hollowed out into large chambers, tunnels reinforced into corridors and the largest connected plateau had been converted to a camouflaged hangar bay. It wasn't just some military base. This was a fortress.

It had taken him a while to get his senses acclimatized. So far he could pick out conversations within a ten-metre radius, including levels above and below him. He'd also managed to decipher the numerical passcodes for all the surrounding security doors from the sound of the entries throughout the day. He would still have to do something for the palm and retinal scanners, but those were only installed at a handful of checkpoints.

Touch was a less reliable source of information—there were too many disturbances—but the scope was larger. Footsteps, sliding doors, elevators—all of them were connected; and after three days of pinpointing the source of each vibration, he could roughly map the layout of the base along with patrol duties and shift changes.

Freeing himself from the restraints and breaking out of the chamber wouldn't be a problem. If direct flight was his objective, he could probably manage that too. Unfortunately, that was out of the question.

Regardless of distance, he could feel the sentries. Some were patrolling the area surrounding his chambers; more were deeper in the facility, where he suspected the demon's gateway was; a few were scattered around the perimeter; and a group was in one of the larger hangar bays, awaiting deployment.

Whatever it was that bound those pieces of metal to unnatural life—a web of torn emotions and pain, enslaved in eternal turmoil—it had to be destroyed. Every step those abominations took left a scar on the world. And the commander, Roth, was the key.

It would have to be dealt with. Adam took a deep breath and began mapping the facility in his mind again. The command centre, Roth's personal quarters and office, the detention areas and the main barracks. It would soon be time.

Still, he couldn't help but feel a small twinge of guilt.

It looked like he would have to break rule number one.

Morning Tea
Kharsan

My body clock wakes me up to what it believes is morning. It feels like the wretched sort of morning when you've spent half the night worrying and the other half having nightmares about your worries and you've finally woken up to the fact that the worries are still there—only a lot closer than they were the previous night. I hate mornings. And worries, for that matter, but mostly mornings.

It takes a minute or so to adjust to the gloom. The lack of movement in the surroundings is quite marked, and while I am glad not to have been shaken awake by a cheerful 'Time to leap into the jaws of death!' the stillness is disconcerting.

The boy, Tao, is still sitting meditatively where he was last night. Violetta is still curled up against a wall, occasionally stirring and muttering, as if stricken by nightmares. Next to her is the fox-woman, lying with her snout between her paws, but her green eyes are alert and glittering in the dark. As I watch, she lifts her head and looks backward with what might be an exasperated expression. Squinting closely, I can make out that this is probably because Violetta, in the midst of her nightmares, has seen fit to grab her tail.

And, finally, there's the Chinese girl—Alice. Sitting up against her backpack, she is sporting dark circles under her reddish half-closed eyes that make it all too evident that I am not the only one lacking for a good night's rest.

After washing my face and hands with a pitifully small cup of water, I reluctantly consume some of the cold tea left over from yesterday. Violetta had brought along the leaves, recommended by Seidre. Despite the awful taste, I have to admit it is somewhat effective at washing away fatigue. Or perhaps it is simply the shock to the taste buds that acts as a stimulant.

Hoping it won't be misconstrued as attempted poisoning, I offer Alice a cup. She certainly looks like she needs it.

'Thanks,' she mutters, before taking a sip and making a face. 'I think.'

'I'd light a fire to heat it, but I'm afraid I'm not that comfortable around combustible lichen.'

'Really?' she says. 'I kinda think it's nice and soothing and normal. Compared to everything else anyway.'

I don't respond. I don't quite understand how this girl got involved in all this, but I am guessing that it is a sensitive subject. She swallows the tea in one gulp and sets the cup down. 'Hey, do you mind if I ask you a question?' she asks.

'If you like,' I say warily.

'I know it's a really stupid question and that it probably has a really obvious answer and all . . . but I kinda just want to hear it, so playing along would be really great. So, okay?'

I nod uncertainly.

'Why do you want to save your brother?'

I hesitate a bit before answering. It's a question that deserves thought.

'Three reasons,' I say, sitting down across from her. 'The obvious one: he is my family. Honestly, I'm not even sure if he is human, but he is my brother, and I'd like to think that means something.' She nods slowly. I did tell everyone enough about Adam's history so they know he's different, though, hopefully, not enough that they might be terrified of him. 'Also, I was asked to protect him, and since there's no one else volunteering to do that, it will have to be me—even if I have no idea *how* to protect him.'

'What's the last reason?' she asks after I don't go on.

'Mostly that if I wasn't trying to rescue Adam right now,' I say, half-sighing as I do so, 'I'd have no idea what else to do.'

She frowns. 'What do you mean?'

'I mean that I'm sixteen years old, with little in the way of formal education—though a lot in the way of informal education—and have spent the majority of my life growing up in what would be accurately classified by most human beings as a fanatical nuthouse for highly intelligent terrorists. Quite frankly, other than rescuing my brother and then proceeding with the original plan of finding my ersatz father and killing him for getting us into this mess, I have absolutely no idea what I should be doing with my life.'

Ah . . . so *that* is what happens when you suppress your emotions for too long. I clamp my jaws shut and go for an expression of 'Please pretend you did not hear any of that.'

'You've got some serious unresolved issues, you know,' she says.

'I know,' I say, shifting to deep glumness.

A short silence follows, during which Alice idly brings her hands close together, palms facing each other. I notice a slight stirring in the air. Wind, perhaps?

'So . . . um . . .' I start, wondering how to broach the subject. 'What is it that brings you here?'

'You mean what's a nice, normal girl like me doing in a place like this?' she asks facetiously.

I keep my silence. That type of question tends to have a rather large hook in it.

She shrugs after a second. 'Standard sort of story. Woke up one day, got chased by hellhounds, got abducted by a crazy fox-lady spirit, met creepy people, nearly got killed, met even more creepy people, nearly got killed again, drank terrible tea. That's about it.'

She sighs, and I suddenly realize that the airflow is somehow centred on her. Or rather, towards a point in between her palms. From the tired way in which she looks around the campsite, I would guess that she's not even entirely aware that she's doing it.

She goes on. 'You know what I miss? I miss normal. Just waking up normal. Not wanting to go to school. That's what I miss—the perfectly clichéd normal life, or whatever it's called. And more than all that, I miss normal people. The regular sort of people who aren't mysterious or weird or mass murderers—or at least they're unlikely to admit it—and just . . . I miss my best friend. I miss my parents. I miss people like me.'

It's some comfort to know that I'm not the only one suppressing things.

A spark flares between her palms, growing into a perfect sphere of blue-white light. The surprise on her face would have been comical if it didn't slip to despair a moment later.

She sees me looking at the light, and sighs before folding her hands together and extinguishing it. 'Well, maybe not *exactly* like me. But you know what I mean. Or at least I hope you know what I mean, because otherwise I'm just randomly talking to someone who doesn't get it, and that's just . . .' She trails off and shoots me a defiant glare. 'And on top of all this, I've got to decide whether or not to help with this stupid suicide mission. I'm fifteen! I haven't even been on a date, and suddenly I have to face off against people who have guns! And while I've had plenty of time to get used to creepy supernatural spirits, hellhounds, wyr and snow leopards, I have no idea how to deal with people with guns—and, honestly, they scare me a whole lot more than the rest.'

I open my mouth to reiterate my position that it is probably best she *not* come along on this venture, but it turns out she isn't finished.

'And do you have any idea why that Violet girl keeps looking at me funny?'

I blink. 'Sorry, what?'

'The girl with the shadow-monster? I get that the shadow-monster just instinctively wants to kill me—though, hopefully, that's been taken care of for the moment—but she keeps looking at me as if I'm some kind of strange specimen. What is that about?'

I think back. I noticed something similar, but I figured it was just Violetta getting used to meeting new people . . . Though, come to think of it, the odd looks had been restricted to Alice and the fox-lady.

I frown. 'I'm not entirely sure, but I don't think she's ever met anyone from, um . . . East Asia before.'

'Really?' She sniffs in an almost offended fashion. 'What rock has she been living under?'

'Santor—the Valley of Shadow. They haven't had much contact with the outside world for a few centuries.'

'Oh,' she says blankly. 'That's a big rock.'

I nod in agreement. It's oddly comforting to have someone around who's evidently even more ill at ease than me in this situation. Of course, none of this takes away from the fact that there's a very real possibility that I'm going to be dead within the next twenty-four hours.

I really do hate mornings.

Choices

Alice

Everyone's finally awake. Kharsan and Tao are packing away the few odds and ends scattered around. From what I can tell, Kit finally bit the shadow-girl to get her up, and I try not to smile as Kit stalks around with an air of wounded dignity and a slightly stiff tail. What this means, though, is that I can't really put it off any longer.

Ha! 'Decide tomorrow.' That's got to be the worst advice in history. All sleep does at times like this is give you nightmares, and now I've got to make a life-changing decision while desperately sleep-deprived and traumatized by my own subconscious. Not the best frame of mind.

Still, I do manage a half-mocking smile as Kit approaches. 'How's your tail?' I ask.

'I don't know what you're talking about,' she says calmly. 'Made up your mind yet?'

'Kind of,' I say, though I totally haven't, 'but before we get into that, I want to ask a favour.'

She tilts her head curiously, inviting me to continue.

'I want some answers. Honestly, right now I don't care if you're lying, telling the truth or whatever. I just . . . need to know some things. Or at least I need to *think* I know some things.'

'All right,' she says simply.

Well, that was easier than I'd thought.

'Yesterday, in Limbo, I got this glimpse of what these tunnels really are.' She listens patiently, so I go on. 'Like cracks, or not really . . . Like, say, a . . . a marmalade sandwich—and then someone pulls the two pieces of bread slightly apart so that in between you have these sticky threads joining the two pieces together. That's what these tunnels are.'

'Sticky marmalade threads?'

'I like marmalade sandwiches,' I say defensively. 'But you know what I mean. This is just like that passage in the forest that took us to Tao and his Snowman friend. A link bridging a part of reality that's torn in two.'

'Your point?' she asks patiently.

'These tunnels are growing. Not quickly, sure, but they're stretching out a little more with each moment.' She doesn't deny it, which leads me to think I'm on the right track. 'You said magic started to return to the world fifty years ago. Is that when your books went missing?'

She nods slowly.

'But the rate at which these tunnels are growing . . . the connections are now stronger. Which, I think, has something to do with me.' I take a deep breath. 'An Elemental is a source of magic. That's kind of what the Snowman was hinting at. That's why someone manipulated my . . . powers . . . into being. Right?'

She fixes me with a stare. 'I don't know the whole story but, yes, all that fits.'

'And I think you know who this someone is.'

She shakes her head. 'I can only suspect. Finding you all and recovering the Arcanus—it's repayment of a debt I owe to a very ancient and very evil creature. I don't know if he's the one who set things in motion, but the fact remains that now it's pretty much everyone for themselves.'

I bite my lower lip. 'And what does this ancient evil creature want?'

'Believe it or not, I think he wants to save his people. He wants to save his corner of the underworld from destruction.'

I think about that for a second. The Snowman said that magic should have died at the end of the war. That all the other realms should have been destroyed. And Kit talked about the slow destruction of the other realms. Maybe they just figured out a way to slow things down. And maybe the only way to stop the destruction was to reconnect all these mystical realms to this world . . .

'What happens in the end?' I ask, because it beats the big and uncomfortable question 'Can it be stopped?'

She grins. 'What do you think is going to happen? Old gods resurrected from who knows where leading heavenly armies to restore order to a chaotic world? Demonic forces on the other side seeking to destroy everything and bring about an eternal dark age? That shouldn't worry you. I've seen a few of the movies— you humans always win in the end.'

'Very funny,' I say sarcastically, hoping like mad that she's joking. Movies are all well and good, but I, personally, can't trust my own species to restrict CO_2 emissions, much less fight a supernatural war. They'd probably just end up nuking the entire planet.

'It isn't like that,' she says. 'Yes, there are dangers out there that are very real. But there will always be people and things who want to control or end the world. '

'And what's your plan for me?' I look over at the others. With the exception of Tao and his greater-than-Daredevil senses, they're not really within hearing range of our conversation. 'Or for any of us? This whole meeting up here and having a sort of common goal—there's no way that's a coincidence.'

'True enough,' she says, and she seems positively proud that I was suspicious enough to pick up on that. 'But beyond getting you all to this point, there is no larger plan here, Alice. Everyone walks their own path and makes their own choices. My favour is done with. And you, at least, are ready to face whatever you need to.'

'What does that mean?'

She smiles, and it's a weird, nice, not-at-all-malicious smile. 'It means you're no longer entirely ignorant or incompetent. And that you've learnt enough to survive. Now, in addition to making sure the Arcanus is out of the wrong hands, I think this mission could help answer a lot more of your questions. But the real reason why I'm trying to get you to come along on this rescue attempt is that it will give you an edge.'

'And what edge is that?'

She looks over at the others before speaking. 'Knowing that you're not alone.'

I have to admit that it's a strong selling point.

I sigh. I know I'm going to say yes. Not because I feel obligated to help or because Kit is some kind of master at mind control (though she might be), but because it feels a lot like what Kharsan was talking about. If I don't do this, I have to stop and think about what happens next. And, in some ways, that's a whole lot scarier than being possibly shot to death.

'What do you want me to do?' I ask, almost pleading. 'I come along and do what? Try and stay out of the way? I can barely control my powers, and I'm telling you right now—I'm not going to randomly wave people away and hope that they survive. I'm not going to kill anyone. You want to talk about wrong hands and ancient demons getting too much power? Fine, but this is not that. This is the start of a very stupid war!'

'I'm not saying it isn't,' she says sadly. 'So, yes. Come along, stay out of the way and try not to kill or get killed. That's a better plan than most. But understand something—everything has a price. And if you want to really take control of your life, then maybe this is what you're going to have to pay for it.'

I glare at her again, but I can't really find the anger this time. So instead I just nod and start packing while muttering to myself, 'You are a very powerful elemental creature, and you probably have a lot of self-defence magic that you just haven't tried out yet, so you're going to be just fine.' I get weird looks from the others, but that's also fine. Embrace the weird. That's my new philosophy.

You know, I've always wondered why heroes in movies and stuff don't have better plans. They just seem to flail about in accordance with the villainous plan of the day and randomly pull it off in the end by sheer luck and determination—and all the other fine qualities of righteous idiots. But I'm coming to realize that they're not the stupid ones. The stupid ones actually have time to think things through, weigh the consequences, have partial emotional breakdowns and then still decide to flail about in accordance with the villainous plan of the day.

Kit's little emergency packet is stuffed up my shirt. According to the girl speaking for the shadow-demon, we're only an hour away from the exit.

Time to find out if stopping bullets is any easier than snow leopards.

Inside the Walls

The transfer was due to take place in one hour.

Adam had figured that they'd start in the evening. By all indications, a long-distance craft couldn't land anywhere near Deacon's Hill, so they'd use a helicopter to transfer him to a nearby airfield and then fly him out under the cover of darkness.

Just before they began the transfer would be the best opportunity. They were busy right now, securing the exit routes and preparing for any possible breakout attempts as they escorted him to the hangar.

The doctor in charge of studying him, Lain, spent the majority of her time in the office to the rear of the larger room. Outside the chamber's heavy door, two guards kept watch, with shifts rotating every four hours. Alongside them stood one of the smaller versions of the abominations. In a further part of the wing was a long row of beds. Adam had recognized the occupant of one of them. E'Cha. While he currently seemed medicated beyond all reasonable limits, there was still a use for him.

It was a pity that he could find little compassion for the man. In some ways, Eden had been remarkably similar to Deacon's Hill. Both had seen evidence of a rising new power, and sought to harness it in different ways, trying to meld science with legend. In Eden they had talked of their hopes for him, for the world.

Adam did not judge them for what they had tried to do, but he did not sympathize either.

He took a deep breath and began a slow count to a hundred.

～

Roth's gaze darted continuously back and forth, checking the surveillance monitors that covered the transfer route.

'Captain,' he said into his earpiece, 'double the security at the first-level intersection. If he's going to go for a direct escape, that is a likely point. Also, make sure the systems and maintenance rooms en route are secured.'

'Affirmative' came the captain's tired reply. Judging from Roth's estimate, the man was running on three hours of sleep in the last two days. According to the base psychiatrist, the captain's insomnia had been somewhat offset by specific stimulants that improved his alertness (even if they did disqualify him from international sporting events), but Roth couldn't help but feel a little uneasy about that.

Still, the captain was the only one he could trust to take this transfer seriously. The majority of those involved tended to wonder why such a big fuss was being made over transporting an eleven-year-old boy.

Roth did admit that he might have gone a little overboard. He'd even reassigned most of the security-class sentries to guard the route and two were already in the helicopter that was going to be used for the transport.

His real worry was that the boy had some ulterior motive. In their first interview, the boy had said nothing, only demanding the immediate destruction of the sentries. Roth had no idea how he planned to accomplish such a thing, but he wasn't about to take any chances.

He looked over at the monitor for the containment cell. The boy was seated with his eyes closed. Ideally, Roth would have preferred sedating him, but none of the existing medications seemed to have any effect on his metabolism. The only alternative left was to go overboard on security and hope.

On the monitor, the boy opened his eyes and smiled.

'Captain?' said Roth, the icy lump in his throat manifesting as the merest quiver in his voice.

'Sir?'

'Get to the lab. Get everyone there! Now!'

~

From Lain's viewpoint, it was over almost as soon as it began.

She had spent most of the day stoically ignoring all the preparations for the subject's transfer and trying to cram in as many short-term tests as she could possibly think of.

Still, her request to transfer with the subject had been approved and she'd be part of the main research team in a few days. At least, after she'd managed to find a replacement for herself. Going through the personnel files, she eliminated all those that she considered incompetent, inflexible, idealistic, or those that she simply didn't like. That didn't leave too many names.

As she was delving intrusively into the personal lives of the remaining candidates, she heard a muffled crack. She rushed to her office door, and watched with an open mouth as the subject—who, by all appearances, had spent the last few days quietly meditating—escaped.

Her analytical mind automatically broke down the disparate parts of the scene. The subject had somehow managed to spring towards the rear wall of the chamber, and using the linking chain of his ankle cuffs, had prised loose a corner for one of the sensor packages. Using that corner as a kind of hook, the chain was then snapped and the covering panel popped free in the same movement.

By now the guards and the robotic sentry had started to react. Opening the door was out of the question as that would have only helped the subject, but they did activate both the alarm and the internal pacification field. Unfortunately, neither the anaesthetic gas nor the electrified floor seemed to hamper the subject in the slightest and, with a movement reminiscent of breakdancing, he used his feet to throw the removed panel towards the sealed door with unerring accuracy.

The sharp corner struck the reinforced fibre glass with enough force to create a small series of spiderweb cracks. The subject moved and, using his momentum and the arm restraints as a crude hammer, he directly pounded the panel, shattering a portion of the transparent door. A large enough hole for the subject to slip through.

Both guards backed away. Lain knew that their standing orders were to let the sentry deal with such an eventuality and, if possible, shoot to cripple if the opportunity presented itself.

Before the sentry could move in, though, the subject shouted towards the guards.

To Lain's surprise, what he shouted was 'Shoot me!' and, to her even greater surprise, the guards complied. They fired a single tightly focused burst, right at the subject's torso. The concentration of the bullets should have torn his upper internal organs out of his body, if not for the fact that he caught almost every bullet on the thick, reinforced restraints that bound his arms together.

It was a testament to their strength that the restraints survived the barrage, but as the guards stopped in shock of having obeyed, it was apparent that the damage done was already sufficient. The subject broke his arms free just as the sentry fired a restraining net towards him.

The net, Lain knew, was built of a barbed metal-cored elastic fibre and should have been unbreakable. Unfortunately, it seemed that the subject had little interest in testing its durability. He moved back, his left hand catching the edge of the net with superhuman speed, and moved towards the sentry.

Doing so presented an opportunity for the two guards to aim for his limbs, but as they took careful aim, the subject called out again. This time in what Lain vaguely recognized as a regional variation of Farsi. Focused on the action before her, she didn't even notice the supposedly comatose prisoner, E'Cha, spring from his bed until he barrelled right into the two guards.

It wasn't exactly an even struggle, since both guards were heavily armed and heavily trained, and the assailant looked like he was acting on a completely subconscious level, but it did give the subject enough time for his next move. He dodged forward under one of the sentry's arms, which now had a protruding skewer-like attachment, and managed to tangle the sentry in its own net before it could recall the device.

The subject then swiftly proceeded towards the two guards, knocking them unconscious as they fought off the other prisoner. He then placed a hand on the prisoner's shoulder, and he also fell unconscious.

In all, it probably took less than half a minute, and it was quite possible that anyone who did not have Lain's analytical abilities would have merely seen a series of blurred actions for the most part. The moment of stillness that followed was enough to shock her out of her role as open-mouthed spectator. She moved to shut the office door and sound the alarm but, in her haste to do both at the same time, accomplished neither. In the blink of an eye, the subject was in front of her.

Before she could even jump back and yell, the subject smiled politely and said in that eerily boyish voice, 'Do not worry. This will not take long.' With that, he left her quite alone, moving past her to access her computer.

She stood frozen at the open doorway, her mind racing for what to do next. After a long moment, she simply gave up and thought, with no small amount of sadness, that there probably wasn't going to be a proper research project on the boy after all.

Adam worked furiously, punching in commands as fast as the machine could take them. He wasn't particularly skilled with computers, but part of his training had been in basic cyberwarfare and, after listening to the doctor work for a few days, he felt that he knew a little bit about Deacon Hill's computer network.

He didn't have long. The sentry was almost done untangling itself from the net. By his analysis, the sentry would move from non-lethal countermeasures to crippling attacks in its next strike. He had enough to keep him occupied even without having to avoid high-intensity laser cutters and their like.

Adam now had about forty seconds before reinforcements came in. A few were already outside the section door. They couldn't have missed his actions on the security cameras. Still, their standard procedure would be to completely secure the exit and then enter with force. That gave him time.

Getting into highly secure systems was out of the question, but the doctor hadn't logged out of the network and he estimated at least another twenty seconds before they disconnected this terminal. He knew a few tricks that would work for some low-security, yet essential, systems. For example, one of the drawbacks of having an installation built into a mountain was that it was necessary to have effective ventilation.

❧

Outside the laboratory, the captain stared at the closed door with intense distaste.

He had suspected that something like this was bound to happen but had dismissed it as natural pessimism and gone on with his job. Of course, there was nothing he could have done differently, but still.

He turned to glare idly at the two sentries that had been tasked with being the first wave. While he had to admit that they were effective and probably the best way to deal with the current threat, he still couldn't get used to the way his skin crawled around them. His earpiece crackled.

'Are you in position?' asked Roth's clipped voice.

'Almost. The teams pulled from the chamber are still on their way, though.' He took a second to glance at the security camera feed displayed on his personal tactical monitor. 'Any indication of what he's trying on the terminal, sir?'

'He deployed a low-level encrypted sequence to keep us from locking him out, but so far all our priority systems are secure. I'd advise you to get in there before he manages to do some real damage.'

'Acknowledged.' He turned back to his preparations. At one end of the corridor, the barricade was already in place, the guards there equipped with riot gear and supported by yet another sentry. Once they secured the other end, they'd be all set to breach the room.

The captain looked around uncomfortably. Bringing this many personnel into the narrow sections of the inner base was becoming annoyingly claustrophobic. He glanced towards the barely visible vents lining the edges of the ceiling, and then froze as something occurred to him.

'Sir,' he said, activating the earpiece, 'are the ventilation shafts big enough for the boy to use them to get past us?'

There was a brief, very busy-sounding silence, before Roth's voice came in. 'No.'

Before relief could set in, though, Roth interjected tensely, 'Captain, the guards inside weren't equipped with a full ordinance package, were they?'

The captain frowned. 'No, sir. We didn't want to risk any chance of grenades or explosives being used against us. In addition to their guns, they had a basic, non-lethal arsenal. Stun sticks, batons . . .' His voice trailed off in the horror of realization. 'Flash bangs . . . and smoke grenades.'

Cutting Roth off, he moved to the side of the door, signalling everyone to prepare to breach. He quickly reviewed the camera feed, and winced. It was already too late.

❧

For Kharsan, exiting the tunnels was every bit as disorienting as entering them had been, and nearly as bad as the entry into Santor. Low-grade dizziness and nausea threatened to envelop him with every step. He felt nearly chilled to the bone, his skin prickled with goosebumps and a sensation of tightness permeated his lungs. His vision kept blurring. His eardrums ached with a high-pitched ringing sound. None of the others seemed to be affected in the same way. Or, if they were, they were hiding it quite well.

His steps were starting to falter as well. Before he could stop, though, he felt a warm pressure on his hand. Looking to the side, his vision focused enough to see Violetta.

She blushed slightly but kept a firm grasp on his hand, urging him forward. 'Seidre said this might happen,' she said. 'It'll be all right.'

Kharsan forced himself along, wondering which was worse—the fact that the twelve-year-old girl he had promised to protect was trying to reassure him, or that it was working. His field of vision continued to narrow and the sound in his ears kept building as they moved forward, but he managed to keep pace. Finally, from up ahead he heard Kit calling for them to stop.

'We're here,' she said. 'Just wait for a second while I figure out how to open . . .'

Her voice faded as the hum in Kharsan's ears swelled to block out everything else. He felt all his senses starting to overload. It seemed to last both an eternity and a single second at once. Then the sensation passed.

He blinked. Everything was still a bit blurry, but the walls of a dimly lit room started to come into focus.

It wasn't a large room. And with the five of them crowded in it, it seemed even smaller (even if one of those five was fox-sized). Light emanated from a few lanterns. The floor was rough and stone-like, contrasting with the smooth cement of the walls. In the centre of the room was a raised stone platform that positively screamed 'altar'.

As his vision improved, Kharsan could see the floor was marked with a series of patterns and symbols that might well have been from the occult. Also, the stone altar had a suspicious stain on it that might have been either blood or, in defiance of the ambient evidence, dried ketchup.

He let go of Violetta's hand. 'Thanks,' he said as she gave him a reassuring smile.

The others (with the exception of Tao) were also looking around at the new surroundings.

Alice had turned to look back at the way they'd come in, only to see a blank expanse of wall. 'Okay . . .' she said slowly. 'That is just creepy.'

'It's a constructed gateway, different from the naturally existing ones,' said Kit. 'A deliberately established link. All the symbols, the altar—someone was playing at summoning.'

'Like spirits and demons?' asked Alice, edging away from the floor markings.

'Something like that. Most of it is just window dressing, but it gets the job done.'

'Where are we?' asked Kharsan.

'We're inside what appears to be some kind of mountain fortress,' said Tao, his head tilted back towards the ceiling. 'They seem to have built it around existing tunnels. This cavern in particular is deep in the mountain.'

'Great,' said Alice. 'Now not only are we in the heart of enemy territory, we're also in danger of being buried alive.' She frowned as she looked over at Kharsan. 'Are you all right? You look terrible.'

'I'm fine,' he said. 'Transitioning between realities does not appear to agree with mere mortals.'

Her responding expression was equal parts sympathy and envy.

Kharsan turned towards the door. So far, things were looking up in the sense that they hadn't been incinerated by automatic anti-personnel lasers and there weren't fifty armed guards waiting.

He turned to ask Tao if his eerie supernatural senses could indeed map their immediate surroundings. Before he could get the words out, though, the sound of what could only have been an alarm echoed from outside the chamber.

Alice sighed. 'Please tell me that wasn't because of us.'

Diverging Objectives

As smoke filled the screens, Roth almost gnashed his teeth in frustration. But he didn't, because it wouldn't have done any good. Over the earpiece, the only thing that could be heard was a disturbing combination of static, gunfire and strangled shouts. After a few seconds, the sounds faded to an even more disturbing silence.

Before he could call into his mic, however, a junior officer approached with a different communication device in hand.

'Sir,' said the man, bravely going on despite Roth's glare, 'it's from the psi division. They say it's urgent.'

With increasing trepidation, he took the device. 'This is Roth.'

A nervous voice that he vaguely remembered as belonging to a supervising lieutenant answered. 'Sir, we have a situation here . . .' The voice trailed off hesitatingly.

'Lieutenant,' said Roth, biting off each word, 'we have a bit of a situation here as well.'

'All our operatives are down, sir.'

'Down?' He blinked in confusion. 'What do you mean "down"?'

'About a minute ago, something seemed to hit them all like a massive migraine, and now they're all unconscious. Beryl's still awake, but I can't make much sense of anything she's saying.'

'Put her on,' he snapped.

259

After a brief pause, he heard a faint mumbling on the other end. 'Beryl?' he asked sharply. The mumbling stopped for a second and then continued. 'Beryl, this is Roth,' he said gently but firmly. 'I need you to focus. What happened to you? What happened to the team?'

Silence.

Then, finally, 'R . . . Roth? I-I . . . It's here.'

If his blood hadn't already been running cold over the subject's escape, this reply would have chilled it. 'What is?'

She burst into sobs on the other end of the line. 'Marcus. The thing that killed him . . . The dragon.'

Roth closed his eyes and handed back the device to the waiting officer. *How?* Madeline's report had last spotted the anomaly at Khangchendzonga. Did that mean the creature from Nepal was here as well?

He didn't have time to sort out his whirling thoughts. His earpiece crackled and the captain's voice came through, the tight, bitter tone telling Roth everything he needed to know.

'Sir,' said the captain, 'he's managed to escape the corridor. The remaining sentries have secured all exits but, with this much smoke pouring out of the vents, we have no idea which route he's taking.'

There was nothing for it. Knowing that it would do absolutely no good, Roth let out a wordless snarl and thumped his fist violently on the table in front of him.

❧

Adam moved slowly through the haze. The smoke he'd introduced into the ventilation system was an effective cover. Almost everyone relied on sight, and even the abominations had been confused when he'd closed with the soldiers, confusing his heat signature

260

with theirs—but it wouldn't last long. The smoke had barely been enough to blanket this level, and once they regained control of the ventilation system, that, too, would be taken care of.

He'd have to move fast soon enough. For now, though, he focused on recovery. His escape hadn't been without its toll. He'd already reduced his dislocated shoulder and stopped the bleeding, but he needed to let some of the damage repair before he was ready for the next step.

Roth would be in the command centre, a few levels up from here. Carefully, he prised a bullet out of his ribcage, suppressing the pain easily. He thought he sensed something in the lower levels. With all the chaos erupting, he didn't have time to focus his senses, yet he couldn't help but conclude that his brother had come for him, and he hadn't come alone.

Even if ending the abominations was the right thing to do, he was sure that his brother would not approve of his methods. He would have to hurry.

Steeling himself, he moved further into the smoke.

The darkness crept up the man's body like oil flowing uphill. It stained the military uniform in long streaks before reaching the face. It covered the skin with shadow, until the man might have been wearing a black mask. For a moment, the man's eyes stared out from that mask, fear and horror radiating from them, before the Shadow closed in on the eyes as well.

Vi watched Shade impassively, ignoring the shocked expression on Alice's face.

Make sure you don't kill him, she told Shade.

She felt his slow assent. Ever since his attack on Alice, he'd been quieter than normal. He didn't want to talk about the incident, so Vi didn't push but, sooner or later, there would have to be a 'discussion'.

Still wrapped in darkness, the soldier turned, his movements jerky and unnatural. One arm swung up to place a hand on the panel next to the door.

The code is 351468.

She relayed Shade's information, and Kharsan entered the code into the keypad. The door lock snapped open, and Vi called Shade back. As the darkness flowed away, the man crumpled to the ground, unconscious to the world.

'He's still alive,' said Vi when Alice moved forward to check on him.

Alice nodded uncertainly. 'That is one heck of a scary trick. Useful, but scary.'

'Three guards in this entire section,' muttered Kharsan uneasily. 'Either this is the most convoluted trap ever, or that alarm is unrelated to our entry.' He glanced over at where Tao stood, leaning against a wall. 'Do you have an idea yet?'

Vi also turned to watch. In contrast to his normal, relaxed demeanour, he looked like he was under tremendous strain. His face was expressionless except for a slight pulling back of the lips, but his complexion had paled to a sickly grey. The gashes across his eyes seemed to pulse, the dried, matt blood turning to fresh crimson. Vi couldn't help but notice that the other wounds on Tao's exposed flesh did the same. He had so many scars, though few were as obvious as the ones on his face. Through Shade, Vi could almost feel Tao's presence spread throughout the entire mountain, scouting ahead without taking a single step.

A drop of blood ran down Tao's arm. Shivering slightly, he pushed away from the wall and nodded slowly towards Kharsan.

'I think your brother has escaped. I can feel his presence four levels above us, towards where the passages open to the outside. He doesn't seem to be heading for the exits, though.'

'He never does anything in a straightforward fashion,' grumbled Kharsan.

'The majority of the guards are in pursuit of him from three levels up. This includes a number of those golem creatures that you described. They appear to be more . . . man-sized than the ones you encountered, though. Your best bet is to take the spiral staircase and go two levels up, move south past three corridors and then climb up the stairwell on the left for the remainder of the way. I've managed to sever a number of connections to their camera system so they won't be able to see you. But you don't have much time. They're starting to suspect that there are other intruders. Once you get to the right level, Shade should be able to guide you to him.'

Vi nodded slowly. Shade had always been vaguely aware of Adam's presence, and from that close . . .

I can do it, he said, reassuring her.

'Wait,' said Alice. 'Aren't you coming along?'

'No,' said Tao. 'I have other business to attend to.' With that, he started moving in the opposite direction from the door. He stopped briefly. 'Be careful,' he said towards Kit. 'The Arcanus is also kept on the same level. Much danger awaits you.'

'I—we know,' replied the fox. There was an uneasiness in Kit's posture that Vi readily identified as certain dread of what was to come.

Alice seemed to notice it too. Frowning, she opened her mouth to speak but then seemed to think better of it.

Kit moved to the now open door and lightly bounded through.

Behind them, Tao had already vanished.

The Lord of the Abyss

Alice

I'll say this about Kharsan's kid brother—he does know how to leave a trail. Two levels up, venturing into the corridors, the best word for it is chaos.

There's a lot of smoke in the air. It's starting to clear out, but for now it swims all around. Strips of red light glow on the walls, making me feel like I'm on the school stage with bad special effects all around me (my finest dramatic moment: Forest Tree #4).

There's also a lot of stuff littered around the floor—riot shields, sticks . . . guns. It's only when I trip over something and fall that I realize this assortment also includes people. I tell myself that they're only unconscious, and am eternally grateful when one of them groans to reinforce that theory. Thankfully, the more awake sort of people are nowhere to be seen.

Keeping to the right pace while moving is actually quite hard. According to Kit, rushing around is not a good idea, but when walking normally, I keep getting this urge to start tiptoeing around while furtively looking over my shoulder, which is probably the most suspicious thing I could do. Then again, if anyone's close enough to make out how weirdly we're walking, that means they're close enough to see that we don't belong here (except as prisoners).

Kit's leading the way in human form, though I'm pretty sure that if we're caught, even she won't be able to talk us out of that kind of situation. I am kinda curious to see if she could, but not curious enough to wish that someone would catch us.

Vi's next, with me following after and trying really hard not to step near her shadow. Kharsan brings up the rear, nervously holding some kind of stun stick that he took off one of the guards. I get the feeling he's really not comfortable around weapons, which does make me worry about trusting him to guard our backs but, at the same time, I'm relieved that at least someone here doesn't act like they were born on a battlefield.

At the risk of sounding clichéd, though, the one thing that is worrying me the most is that all this is just *too* easy. Combine that with Tao's warning and that weird look on Kit's face, I just know that something bad is just waiting to happen (and that's not just because something bad generally *does* happen). Still, nothing to do but keep following. Trying not to tiptoe. Trying not to run. Trying very hard not to unexpectedly get killed.

⌒

We finally reach the level Adam's supposed to be on, and then the plan—using Vi and her shadow-creature to track him—kinda falls through.

You see, there we are, through the first security door on the level, entering an area that is not blanketed by smoke and filled with assorted junk, but is still somehow bereft of armed security guards keen to shoot intruders on sight. Two metres in, the pathway forks left and right at forty-five-degree angles.

We look at Vi for guidance, and she calmly and confidently dismisses the existence of these choices, points straight ahead and says, 'He's that way.'

'So all we need to do is walk through the walls,' I say calmly.

Kit looks at me sidelong with her best 'Is this really the time?' look. Then she says, 'He's somewhere on this level, and we need to find the Arcanus as well. We can split up and try and find both, and meet back here. Our best bet for escape is back the way we came.'

Kharsan nods reluctantly, obviously not pleased with this idea any more than I am. 'We should meet back here in twenty minutes.'

And so ten minutes later, I'm alone with Kit. The corridor is still eerily deserted as we sneak into a securely locked armoury, courtesy of a stolen security card and a wonky magical-looking device of Kit's that either mimics a human eye or has a human eye stored inside it. I tell myself it's the mimicking thing.

'Should be somewhere in here,' she mutters. It takes us a minute to find a locked display cabinet and another ten seconds for Kit to jimmy it open, revealing a large leather-bound volume.

She inhales deeply, taking it out carefully and running a hand over the cover. 'The *Anima Arcanus*,' she says. 'The Book of Souls.'

Honestly, it doesn't look all that mystical. I step back as she tries to hand it to me.

'It's just a book,' she says in exasperation. 'It's not going to bite.'

'Forgive me for being paranoid,' I mutter, but I take the book, stuffing it into my already overstuffed backpack. As we make our way back out into the corridor, I desperately try not to listen to the voice in my head, which is now entering panic mode over how easy this has been.

And then I hear a cough that somehow manages to be both a polite announcement of presence and the crashing of leaden tombstones all at once.

Slowly, we turn to face a man calmly standing in the middle of the corridor.

He's dressed in one of those military camouflage-type outfits, all splotches of greens and browns, topped by one of those round

French hats that I can't seem to describe as anything but blood red. His skin seems to take on the colour of the ambient light, which makes him all sorts of pale and slightly chameleon-like. And his eyes . . . I'm not even remotely surprised that his eyes are nowhere near human.

For one, he has no eyelids, lashes or brows. Instead they're set in the face like two black gems, all the angles and facets glinting. As with the Snowman, I get the feeling that I'm only seeing one tiny part of the whole picture. Unlike with the Snowman, though, I know that I'm desperately trying to stop myself from seeing more, because I really, *really* don't want to.

'Hello, Kitsune,' he says in a cold voice that's surprisingly humanlike. 'I've been waiting for you.'

'You know him?' I try whispering to Kit, who's gone all frozen and stiff.

With a heavy sigh, she nods her head and puts on a fake cheery smile. In a low voice, she says, 'Meet Sheol. Or if you want it in ceremonial detail: Wielder of the Eighth Plague, former Horseman of War, once Battlelord of the Seraphim, Slayer of the Archangel Gabriel, Faithful of the Fallen, High Commander of the Infernal Army, third in line to the throne of Shaitan, Locust King, Lord of the Abyss—the Demon Lord Abaddon.'

As I try to sort out that little mess of titles while hoping my head doesn't explode, Kit's smile widens even more and she lifts her head towards the man . . . the demon.

'Hi, Abby,' she says brightly. 'How's tricks?'

Judging by the glare that seems to fill the entire corridor with palpable sulphurous rage, our friendly neighbourhood Demon Lord doesn't seem amused.

'Your flippancy is as tiresome as ever, vixen,' he says, and for a second his eyes land on me, and it takes everything I have to not run screaming. 'This is the Elemental, I suppose. Have their kind not done enough damage? Or have you forgotten how the war ended? Or how the Abyss was born?'

'She isn't your concern,' says Kit through gritted teeth while I try and make sense of anything, really . . .

He shakes his head in contempt. 'Perhaps. Regardless, Trickster, we have matters to discuss.'

'I suppose we do,' she says, and then whispers to me under her breath, 'When I step forward, run! Find the others. Get out of here.'

'But—' I try hissing back. Running seems like a good option, but the way she's talking . . .

'I'll hold him back,' she finishes grimly. 'No arguments. I'll be fine.'

Before I can protest further, she pushes me back and, in the same movement, steps between me and this Sheol. In that second, all my effort towards not seeing the surrounding auras and images wavers, and I get hit with a real glimpse of the demon.

It sweeps across the land like a plague. A ravening, quenching its inexhaustible hunger with the blood of all who stand before it. Black armour like an insect's carapace, smooth and indestructible against any mortal effort. The bloodthirst breaks again and again, like a hurricane brought to life for no other reason than to destroy. And always and always that terrible hunger. Never to be sated. Never to be filled. Not till all is consumed and naught remains but the barest bones of existence.

I take it as a great point of pride right then that my sanity doesn't shatter and that I don't wet myself. I do let out a feeble whimper and start scurrying away as fast as I can, but that's a decent compromise, I suppose.

I don't look back once.

Two corridors later, my legs give way, the unreasoning fear that drove them finally going past critical. I'm shivering like mad and biting my lip to keep from bursting into tears, and there's a little voice at the back of my head that won't shut up.

It keeps saying, 'Kit's still back there.'

As a punctuation point to that, I can suddenly hear her screaming.

I should go back. I should do something.

Do what? Go back and die? Against that . . . that being?

I owe her. She's kept me alive.

She's used me. She's *still* using me.

But she's my . . .

What? *My friend?* She's a liar. A manipulator. This is probably just another trick. Something to make me feel guilty about. Or maybe to scare me away. Something . . .

I can feel my mind trying to tear itself apart on this. To go back . . . or move on, keep running and stay alive.

This is the part where I'm supposed to reach into myself and find some inner reserve of strength, activate all my destiny-changing powers and just save the day. But I can't, because I'm just too scared. Still whimpering, I pull myself to my feet and start moving away. Away from Kit. Away from her screams.

I mean, I knew that this would happen. I knew from the moment that I started blowing things up randomly that this was going to happen. I'm not a hero, I'm not some—

The screams cut off with chilling suddenness.

I keep moving away.

Stories That End in Death

'Are you quite finished?' snarled the Demon Lord in annoyance.

Kit unconcernedly held up one finger, asking him to wait a moment. Clearing her throat slightly, she let out another heart-wrenching scream of agony before dramatically cutting it off in mid-stride.

She coughed theatrically and then turned back to Sheol, carefully suppressing the very real fear she felt. 'Okay, now I'm done.'

'What was that about?' he spat out.

'Oh, just giving her something to think about. Anyway, you wanted to talk?'

'I have questions, Trickster. If you do not wish for your screams to be real, then you would do well to answer them.'

Kit tried not to roll her eyes. She did so hate those like Sheol. Always so direct, relying on their own immense powers to force their way through any situation. Not that she didn't acknowledge the effectiveness of direct action, but there was such a thing as style. That was one of the reasons she'd always been fond of Ja . . .

'Where is he?' asked Sheol, interrupting her thoughts.

It looked like the time for playful banter was over.

'I can't tell you that.'

'But you do not deny that he sent you on this errand of yours.' His eyes glittered. 'We had a plan, Trickster. Or didn't he tell you? I kept my end of the bargain. I have held back the Abyss as long as possible, but the time for half-measures is done.' The anger radiated off Sheol in waves, and here, at a place where his power could touch the physical world, she felt the strain of reality stretched to the point of breaking.

'There is chaos in every corner of every realm. The Exile have laid siege to Dis. The Seraphim scheme behind our backs. I could have salvaged that. I would have broken the truce and started the war with them if it hadn't been for that jackal.' His mouth twisted, as if he were remembering something unpleasant. 'And yet he hides, sending *children* into battle before they are ready.' He raised a fist, the illusion of his glove transforming to an armoured gauntlet for a second. 'Tell me why I shouldn't just kill them all.'

Kit narrowed her eyes. 'Well, firstly, I'm not entirely sure you could.' She took a step back. 'Look, I'm just here to clear my debt. Your grand plans for war and destruction are really more of a headache than I asked for.' Surreptitiously, she palmed a thin adamant-plated dagger from her sleeve. It wouldn't do much, but it would be better than dying without a fight.

She felt Sheol's anger grow, and took a deep breath. It wasn't easy being a Trickster. Sooner or later, you had to gamble. 'And secondly,' she said, 'I have a message for you.'

Faint surprise showed on his face. 'Speak!' he barked.

She opened her mouth, but what emerged was not her voice. It was the deep calm tone that she'd last heard on the porch of a small rustic house in rural Japan. 'Your work has not gone unnoticed, old friend,' said the voice, 'but for one last time, I need your trust. Let matters take their own course. One way or another, destruction is coming.'

Kit twisted her mouth in distaste after the last of the words had left her. She'd never liked being treated as a messenger pigeon, but it did have the undeniable edge of authenticity.

The Demon Lord stood perfectly still, and then his wave of fury and darkness seemed to abate. 'One last time, then. I will keep my oath just this once.' He unclenched his fist. 'It matters little. I have given these humans enough tools. They will kill or imprison the children and recover the Arcanus. They will spread my work across this land.' Then he laughed—not an evil maniacal laugh, but a sad, almost bitter one. 'And then the Abyss will consume us all.'

With that, he stalked down the corridor. Before he was halfway, Kit felt, rather than saw, the sharp crack as reality shattered for a tiny second before the Demon Lord vanished.

She stood still for a moment or two, gathering herself. It was always such a bother dealing with these sorts of situations.

Sheol's presence had somehow managed to drive the soldiers away from this level, but they would be returning soon. And there were still a few matters to take care of.

~

'Captain,' said Roth, affecting the most reasonable tone that he could possibly manage. 'What do you mean you're "lost"?'

'I know it sounds crazy, sir, but I don't know how else to put it. We moved up in pursuit of the subject, using a standard four-team formation, and we sent a couple of teams down to check out the other alerts. But when we tried to coordinate next, we were all on different levels and we didn't even realize it. Most of the sentries have ended up on the perimeter—and it might not be a bad idea to just let them stay there for now . . . As for the rest of us, we're trying to gather on level two and then see if we can coordinate the search from there.'

'And you have no idea where the subject is right now?'

'We're almost certain he hasn't left the inner facility, sir.'

'How comforting.' Roth closed his eyes in frustration. He couldn't for the life of him reason out how the boy had managed something like this. Perhaps the other intruders were responsible in some way, but still . . .

The camera and sensor systems on the lower levels were still inoperable, so if the boy was hiding there, they'd have to manually search those areas. By the looks of it, barring securing the perimeter, the priority had to be securing the summoning chamber.

He opened his mouth to relay the orders, when something occurred to him.

'Captain, give me a breakdown of where all the teams are currently situated.'

The captain slowly checked with each one and forwarded the information. From the dormitories to the research wings, the engineering bay . . . One unfortunate pair had even ended up in the first-level toilets.

But one thing stood out.

'Can you confirm that again?' he asked with an edge to his voice. 'There are no troops anywhere on the command level?'

'No, sir,' said the captain, picking up on the implication. 'We're heading there now.'

The door to the centre slid open. Without turning, Roth winced. 'Do try and hurry,' he said in a tired voice. Only then did he turn to face the escaped subject directly.

'Your security is not very good,' said Adam disapprovingly.

Tao took particular care to avoid killing those guarding the detention areas. It wasn't too difficult. Both his lessons and his experiences with the Paschid had left him with a fairly accurate picture of human anatomy and its weaknesses. After that, it was only a matter of propelling a blunt object towards their cranial areas with just the right amount of force.

It would have been infinitely easier to kill them, but he didn't. Their lives weren't part of the arrangement. It took him ten minutes to reach his destination. The long-term holding cells. Ten sealed rooms lined either side of the area. Seven were occupied. Five men. Two women.

The question now was how to find the right man. He couldn't rely on facial recognition. Not after ten years and the fact that the way he saw the world now was fundamentally different. Sound, though . . . The man's voice was still clear in his mind. It would take too much time to speak to each of them. Stretching out as best as he could, he divided his attention between the five. His sense of self, his existence, filled each chamber until he was able to reach out and then . . .

Five short screams echoed at the same time.

He picked out Jhakri's voice in an instant. The timbre had changed, along with many of the other characteristics, but he could still tell.

He focused his mind and broke the lock gently. Stepping through, he was aware of the man feebly trying to scramble to a sitting position on the long bunk. For a brief moment, Tao wished he could see the expression on the man's face. Instead, he paid attention to other things—the trembling of the man's fingers, how the weak heart had suddenly begun pumping blood faster and the steady limpness spreading through the body as the man slowly came to terms with the current situation.

'So, you've come at last,' said Jhakri.

Tao didn't respond. He moved to the centre of the small cell, stretching his presence until he could feel every tiny atom of the chamber. Only then did he face the man.

'This will not be a long visit,' he said. There was a part of him that was almost reluctant to do this. Once Jhakri was dead, that would end this chapter of what passed for his life. Still, he had no second thoughts. This had to be finished.

'You have to understand—I had no choice! There are so many of them—the Infernal Circle, the Seraphim, the humans. They're all plotting and scheming. Everyone is trying to find a place . . . I had to serve.'

Why? Tao couldn't understand the desperate plea. Jhakri had to know where this encounter would inevitably lead. Did he really value his life? Trapped inside a cage, weakened after years of captivity. Was such a life really worth anything?

'I was bound,' said the man. 'I couldn't have stopped. Even my voice was sealed. They keep trying. Pain. Drugs. Anything. I would have told them all, but I can't.'

Tao did not respond.

'But, you . . . I can tell you. You're the exception. Help me escape! I will tell you who orchestrated your creation. I can tell you—' Jhakri's voice broke into a fit of coughing.

Even if Tao hadn't been able to tell that the man was lying, the offer did not tempt him.

'No,' he said. 'My vengeance ends with you.'

He felt Jhakri's mouth open. What would it be? A desperate plea for mercy? Or forgiveness?

It didn't matter. Tao didn't move so much as a finger but reached out nevertheless. A small chip broke away from the concrete walls, and then shot forward.

Tao felt the man die in an instant. He felt no sense of satisfaction. No closure. Nothing.

He had expected that. The price for his vengeance had long been made clear, and it had fit Yama's objectives as well. After all, if a disciple was to walk the mortal realm again, they could not be allowed any modicum of volatility. Perhaps there were other definitions of justice, and perhaps those other definitions worked in some places, but in the courts of Avici, justice had no heart, and it did not exist to salve the pain of the dead. The dead were beyond pain.

Tao turned and walked out of the cell.

❧

Before any of the security officers could draw their weapons, Adam lightly tossed a grenade forward. It bounced once before coming to a halt at Roth's feet.

Adam lifted his left hand so that everyone could clearly see the string running from his finger to the grenade pin. It had been fortuitous that he found the entire level deserted. He'd even managed to break into an armoury locker, making the situation a whole lot easier.

He spoke directly to Roth. 'No one else need die.'

The scowl on the man's face deepened, but he nodded. 'Everyone,' he said in a loud clear voice, 'lay your weapons on the floor, and then make your way to the conference room.' He pointed at an adjoining chamber. 'Barricade the door and get as far back as you can. Wait for rescue.

'Is that acceptable?' Roth directed the question at Adam.

'Yes,' he replied.

They waited in silence till the last people had entered the room and the door had been firmly shut. Only then did Adam lower his arm and move closer to a more conversational distance.

Adam shook his head in wonder. 'As your "prisoner" here, I have spent my time well. I have learnt much of you and those that serve your cause.'

'We don't have a "cause".' The man's eyes were alight with wariness, but Adam simply smiled.

'In some ways,' he said. 'You are infidels of the highest order. Unwilling to believe in anything. Not the science of one world, or the magic of another. Thus you are unfettered—free to do whatever it is you wish. Forever changing with each new piece of the grand puzzle.

'And yet, you *believe*. You ignore all rules. You stain your hands and hearts with blood and ash, and you do this willingly. Not because you delight in your own ability to do so, but because you think that there must be someone who does these things to safeguard human existence, and because you fear that no one else would be able to do so.'

'Perhaps. What would you suggest as an alternative?' Adam could tell that Roth wasn't really listening. He was just trying to buy enough time for his soldiers to come. That didn't concern him. Whatever sorcery had been woven over this level was slow to fade. But there were other reasons to hurry.

Still, the man deserved to know why he was going to die.

'Do you even know what those creatures are?' he asked.

'The sentries? The golems of legend?' Roth shifted uncomfortably but didn't back down. 'The storybooks believe that they were empowered by the word of truth on their foreheads. My lead scientist believes it to be a form of self-sustaining neurological energy. Or, if I were to put it in more colourful terms, the souls of the dead empower those shells.'

'You fool,' whispered Adam, even though he had expected this very answer. 'Not the souls of the dead. The souls of the *living!*'

Roth frowned, obviously not grasping the difference.

'I felt the traces of what was done here,' said Adam. 'You created the link. Your blood, your life. You bargained with the demon. You allowed him to create a conduit. On one end, your lifeless shells; on the other, creatures—living, breathing, intelligent beings, taken to the point of death and held there to be enslaved as your mindless, obedient machines!'

Roth swallowed, but his eyes still didn't waver. The depth of his resolve was almost admirable. 'What do you know?' he spat out harshly. 'What makes you so certain about all this? Do you really think you're what they tried to create? I read the surviving notes, the transcripts from the prisoners. Do you seriously believe that you are this world's new *saviour*? Their genetically engineered prophet?'

Adam shook his head firmly. 'I am myself,' he said. He knew that. More than anyone else in the world, he was himself, and it was that certainty, more than his genetics, that Roth should have feared. It was what the demon had been afraid of.

Adam tilted his head to listen to something, and sighed. He had taken too much time.

'I am sorry,' he said, and charged forward in a flash.

'Adam—stop!' shouted his brother from the entrance.

Another Way
Kharsan

His hand stops a bare inch from the man's chest. Just the slightest of movements, and his palm would rest directly atop the heart. I have no doubt that Adam can kill with a touch. But he listens to me. I wish to Allah I knew why, but he listens to me.

'He must die, brother,' he says and, for the first time, I can hear his voice shake as he's torn between listening to me and acting on his own superhumanly infallible instincts.

'Well, I can't really argue that point, since I have no idea who he is, or why that's the case, but before that can you please just explain?' I try not to think of the fact that we probably have no time for explanations. Even if this entire level seems eerily empty, it's only a matter of time before we start getting shot at.

Thankfully, Adam does lower his hand and back away.

Breathing a sigh of relief, I move into the large room. There are screens everywhere, arranged in stacks, rows and circular bays. One door to the side is locked shut and I can make out some movement behind it. I'm guessing that's where everyone else who was here is hiding.

Violetta comes in behind me. She looks nervously at Adam, and when her eyes wander over to the other man, there's a flash of recognition. The man, in turn, frowns at her as if trying to figure something out.

'First off,' I say, closing towards Adam and grabbing his shoulders, 'are you all right?' I doubt that there is much they could have done by way of permanent harm, but still—I feel almost obligated to ask. Besides, there are *some* visible wounds, probably a result of the mess he'd left down below.

He smiles that same irritating know-all smile. 'I am fine, brother. They have been most . . . hospitable.'

'Right . . . good.' I let go of him and turn to the other man. He does not look particularly happy, though I am surprised to see that there doesn't seem to be even a little bit of fear on his face. 'So . . . um . . . you are?' It isn't the best way to interrogate, but I'm honestly at a bit of a loss as to how this particular scenario is supposed to unfold.

The man looks around at all of us with a dry expression. 'I suppose you could say that I'm in charge here.'

'Oh . . .' I blink at that. It's not that he doesn't fit the image of being in charge, but rather that I would have expected even Adam to have a bit of difficulty getting this close to him. 'Listen,' I say with very little hope, 'I don't suppose there's a chance we could all just sit down and negotiate a truce.'

'We could try that,' he says slowly.

I look at Adam, who shakes his head. He's always been able to tell when people are lying. Even when they lie to themselves.

'I guess not,' I say glumly. I see Violetta on the side, looking like she's wondering if she should interrupt. 'Oh . . . Adam, this is Violetta.' I point to the Shadow at her feet. 'And that's Shade. Violetta, Shade—this is Adam.'

She raises a hand in greeting, forcing a smile in this awkward situation. 'You can call me Vi,' she says with a pointed look in my direction. For some reason, I can't seem to call her anything other than her full name. She turns to the man after that, 'You are Roth, yes?'

His eyes flicker towards her shadow and he nods. 'You're from Santor—the "heir" to the Shadow.'

'You two know each other?' I ask, not really sure if I want to know the answer.

'Not really,' says Violetta. 'He led an attack on Santor when I was a baby. He killed my father.'

No, I didn't want to know the answer. 'Oh . . . I suppose you want him dead as well, then.'

She frowns at that. 'No. My father wasn't a very nice man.'

'I see.' I let out a sigh. And I thought I had parental issues. 'Okay, so why do *you* want him dead?' I ask Adam.

'He created the link, brother. He allowed those abominations to be brought into this world. The only way to destroy the link, to lay those creatures to rest, is to kill him.'

As much as I hate to admit it, I find myself wondering if this is, in fact, a good idea. I know that Adam's reason behind seeing those golems destroyed is probably different, but I can't help but think that this would be a lot easier if we didn't have to fight those things. But still . . .

'Adam.' I don't quite know how to put this, but I still have to try. 'You cannot kill a defenceless man.'

It sounds even more absurd out loud. This is no place for moral rules. This is like standing on a battlefield with enemies all around and saying, 'I will not kill unless someone tries to kill me first.' This will see us dead. And shouldn't I trust him in this? I believe that he will not kill without reason. I believe that he will always try to do what is right. And I know that he is a killer. I know that he has killed before. They taught him that.

No. He may be a killer, but if I can stop him from being a murderer . . .

'There is no other way to break the link,' he says.

281

I look at Roth during this. He still seems remarkably calm for someone who's having his own death sentence discussed in front of him. I notice that his right arm is very subtly inching behind his back (probably towards some sort of concealed weapon) but it doesn't really bother me. Adam will have noticed as well.

'There must be some . . .' I frown, suddenly remembering the chamber we first emerged in. 'Wait, by link, you mean that gateway down below?'

Adam nods. 'Yes, brother. I believe you and your companions came through it.'

'Adam,' I say, almost overwhelmed by the relief that there *is* a solid reason for this moral stance, 'that is currently our only escape route.'

He blinks, and I realize that he hadn't even thought of this. Of course, he probably thought it would be easy to fight his way out of a heavily armed military installation.

'But—' he starts out.

'Look, we have to head back there. Perhaps we can figure out another way to destroy the gateway.' I look at Violetta. 'Does . . . uh . . . Shade have any ideas?'

She shakes her head worriedly. 'No, he says it would take greater power than he has to break that kind of construct.'

'I think I can help with that,' says a soft, worried voice from the doorway.

Desperate Plans
Alice

Okay, this collection of surprised, more than slightly doubtful stares is not the *best* reaction I could have hoped for.

'When did you get here?' asks Kharsan.

'About a minute ago,' I say. It's amazing the turn of speed you get when fleeing out of sheer panic, even if you do account for three guilt-ridden stops as I tried to tell myself that I was doing the right thing, or at least the smart thing. It didn't help, but anyway . . . 'This is your brother?'

The kid waves cheerfully at me.

'Yes,' says Kharsan wearily.

'Okay. Hi, I'm Alice. Who's the other guy?' I ask, pointing at the military-type fellow who looks like a thunderstorm.

'This is Roth,' says Kharsan. 'Apparently, he's in charge here.'

'Really? Hey—I don't suppose we can talk about a truce or some . . .' Wow, that's one annoyed glare. 'Okay. Never mind. We'll just go about mindlessly trying to do horrible things to one another. That works as well.'

'That does seem to be the overall consensus,' mutters Kharsan. 'Now, you said you could help? How?'

I shrug, moving closer. 'Collapsing the gateway we came through. I think I can do that.' From what Kit said earlier and whatever I managed to get from this discussion, this is just some kind of spell, or magical construction. And if an Elemental can destroy magic . . .

Of course, I'm nowhere near 100 per cent certain (or even 30 per cent, if I think about it) but I don't say that. Maybe it's a result of leaving Kit behind, but I feel so totally useless, and if I can do this, then maybe . . .

'Are you sure?' asks Kharsan.

'No. But it's better than killing this guy and then trying to break out of however many hordes of armed people they've got closing in on us.'

Vi looks up from her personal shadow-monster and nods. 'Shade says she can do it.'

'Thanks, I think.'

Both Kharsan and the kid nod slowly in sync. I guess they really are brothers.

'Then, I suppose we should really hurry up and get going before we're shot. Is it just me, or is it really weird that there are no other soldiers on this level?'

'It won't last long,' says the kid as if he knows exactly what he's talking about.

Just then, I see a flicker of movement from the guy who's supposed to be in charge. Before I can even see where he's going, the kid moves and Mr Grumpy crumples to the floor.

'Adam!' snaps Kharsan.

'He is just unconscious,' says Adam. 'In case her plan doesn't work, we may have to kill him. Please grab his legs, brother.'

Kharsan opens his mouth as if to object, but then he gives me a quick doubtful look, shrugs and moves to pick up the guy's legs.

'Your confidence is totally overwhelming,' I say, though I can't really bring myself to be offended. Heck, I'm still not sure how I'm supposed to even do what I just said I could do.

At least I'm not feeling entirely useless. Confused, worried, sick-to-the-stomach and still very guilt-stricken—yes. But not entirely useless.

Vi looks up at me as the boys carry the unconscious man out. I try and ignore her, because I'm almost certain what she's going to ask, but she tugs on my sleeve anyway.

'Yeah?'

'Where's Kit?'

I avoid her eyes. 'She's not here.' The words just sound so very, very small.

The End of Choice

Tao waited near the chamber they'd arrived at, stretching his senses outwards to keep an eye on developments.

Sheol's presence had started to fade from the upper levels and, by some miracle, it seemed that everyone was still alive. The Trickster had also vanished, though it was possible that she was simply hiding from sight. The Kitsune of Japan had always been particularly skilled in those arts.

The others were on their way back, accompanied by the one he assumed was Adam. Such a curious presence. Something that almost did not seem to exist, and yet, at the same time, it did so with such weight that it threatened to destabilize the world around it.

They were also carrying someone with them, though he couldn't tell who it was.

Which was just as well. With Sheol gone, the spell keeping the patrols away had faded from the command level. A large number of soldiers had congregated there, along with half a dozen of those metal creatures. Even as he kept track, they started to move. Within the minute, their objective was clear. Tao gave no outward sign of impatience, but silently he willed the others to hurry. They had helped him fulfil his vengeance and, for that, a small debt was owed. And a disciple of Yama always paid his debts.

The captain was doing his best to hide his unease, but inwardly he was carefully and precisely banging his head against a mental wall in sheer tired frustration. The people rescued from the conference room had confirmed that the boy did have allies inside the Hill, which made things all the more problematic. He'd been somewhat briefed by Roth on these matters, and his people had trained rigorously to combat even threats such as these, but there were still so many unknowns. And now they'd taken Roth.

'Captain,' reported one of his team commanders, a wide-faced woman named Treil. 'We've confirmed all upper-level footage and set up the appropriate perimeter guards. Wherever they are, it has to be on the lower levels. Though, we're not really sure how they slipped past the teams that were heading *up* here.'

Maybe they could all turn invisible, thought the captain sourly. Aloud, he said, 'We still have one squad stationed at the lower levels. Divide the rest into two teams to take primary and secondary stairwells down. Each team should have three of the sentries. Organize backups to sweep each level as we pass, but I want both teams to congregate on the restricted area of level three.'

That had been where Roth had initially suggested reinforcing the guard. The captain supposed the man had been right in suggesting that it was a vulnerable spot in their security. It was likely that the intruders would attempt some sort of escape from there, making it quite imperative that they hurry.

'Treil,' he said as they started walking towards the stairwells, 'get the order out as well—Roth's safety would be preferred, but if he's being used as a hostage, his own guidelines have him marked as expendable. Make sure everyone knows that taking the intruders alive is *not* a priority. Shoot to kill.'

The woman nodded without hesitation.

❧

They were almost back at the portal chamber when things went wrong.

Vi and Shade were watching their rear. Ahead, Adam had been pointing out the passages they should take, and suddenly he froze, dropping the unconscious body of the commander and shouting a warning.

'Get back!'

They barely managed to get around a corner before the bullets started flying.

Kharsan muttered something that sounded like a swear word. He turned to Adam. 'How many?'

'Three soldiers. One of the golems is approaching fast.'

Alice gritted her teeth. 'I'm not sure I can stop bullets, but I think I can get, like, a good hurricane-like wind going.'

Kharsan opened his mouth as if he had questions, but another round of suppressing fire quelled his curiosity. 'Violetta, can Shade stop them?'

She shook her head. 'He can't reach.' She looked around at the brightly lit corridor. 'There's too much light.'

The thumping of large metallic footsteps was getting closer.

Adam placed his hand on the walls, and then pointed to a small box-like protrusion on it. 'Brother, the circuits run through there.' He turned to Alice and held up five fingers, and started to count down.

With a slight panic, Alice pushed herself to the corner, taking a deep breath. As Adam counted down to one, the air in the corridors stirred and, within a moment, everything went from stillness to windswept fury. The shooting stopped and Adam rushed forward.

Vi peeked around the corner. The soldiers were bracing themselves against the wind, and Adam swept right past them to attack the golem, its onward rush also stilled by the force of the air but otherwise unaffected.

'I don't think I can keep this up for long!' shouted Alice above the howl of the wind.

Shielding himself with his forearm, Kharsan managed to pry open the panel, and found himself staring at a nest of breakers and complicated wires. For a second, he froze, and then shrugged and shoved the stun baton he'd been carrying into the circuitry, pulling the trigger.

The corridors went dark.

Shade, ordered Vi, and he shot forward.

The wind died and, with a grunt of effort, Alice summoned a small orb of faint blue light, just barely showing the scene ahead.

The three soldiers stood immobilized, with tendrils of shadow wrapped around them. The golem was swinging long blades at Adam in wild sweeps while the boy dodged around it, looking for an opening.

There didn't seem to be one. Adam tried to back-pedal and take one of the guns from the guards as they crumpled into unconsciousness, but he was a hair too slow. The golem charged forward, kicking out with a metal limb to knock the boy back. Adam crashed into the wall and then scrabbled to his feet, clutching his side.

Kharsan and Alice rushed to Adam's aid as Vi tried to direct Shade towards the golem. The Shadow didn't seem to affect it— the soul-energy within was too carefully shielded.

The golem loomed, raising a blade-like arm for an overhead strike.

There was a loud *CRACK*.

They all looked up, golem included, as part of the ceiling broke away. Propelled by a force that only a skilled telekinetic disciple could muster, a large concrete slab crashed down on the golem.

Tao stepped forward into the range of Alice's pale light. 'We had best hurry,' he said calmly. 'They will have a good idea of where we are now.'

Kharsan nodded sharply and then went back to retrieve Roth while Alice checked on Adam. Tao went with him, and the unconscious body slowly rose into the air.

'I take it there's a reason we have a hostage?' he asked politely.

'Yeah,' said Alice with an obviously forced grin. 'He's in charge here.'

'I see,' said Tao. 'He's not doing a very good job, is he?'

'No,' said Kharsan, 'but I think we can save a full performance review for after we get out of here. Oh, this is Adam.'

Tao turned to Adam, who was apparently none the worse for wear, and inclined his head in greeting. Before he could say anything, though, the large slab shook as the golem underneath began to move again.

'These are resilient creatures,' observed Tao. 'Leaving this power unchecked could have . . . consequences.'

Vi swallowed nervously. She could imagine an army of these creatures coming to Santor. They would tear her home apart.

Kharsan sighed. 'Agreed. But we sort of have a plan.' He looked doubtful.

Alice reached out to touch Kharsan's arm. 'It's all right,' she said. 'I can do this.'

Tao frowned. 'You plan to collapse the gateway?'

'Yeah,' said Alice.

Tao gestured for the others to follow him down the corridor. 'In that case, we should prepare. We will have to fight.'

The Abyss

A thunderclap sounded in the throne room as the Demon Lord Abaddon rematerialized.

He stalked forward, through the room and towards the inner chambers. There wasn't a soul in sight, but there was someone waiting. A familiar presence, one that few creatures in any world would ever welcome.

Unwelcome or not, though, it was one that could not be ignored. Abaddon turned left down the stone corridors to the doors of the transference chamber.

Inside, the room was lit with the golden glow of the containment vacuoles lining both walls in seemingly endless rows. Murky shadows moved in a few dozen of them—a far cry from the wars of centuries past when every single vacuole contained a living creature.

The visitor stood in front of one of the occupied vacuoles. In long black robes, it stood quietly and anonymously, both face and hands hidden.

'Why are you here?' he demanded.

The figure reached out towards the golden surface with one obscured arm. As if in response, the dark shapes seemed to coalesce for a second into the clearer shape of a humanoid.

First the extermination of the Ailuros, and now this . . . How much will you destroy before you are done? The words echoed inside his head.

He felt the emptiness stir within. The urge to strike out without thought of consequence, laying waste to it all . . . He had been patient for so long. Endured so much . . .

'Why are you here?' he asked again.

Here? The figure turned towards him and, for a moment, he glimpsed the hooded face. The shadows concealed much and, in the flickering light, the features seemed to flow between an ivory skull and the exquisite shape of an obsidian mask showing the face of a woman.

I am everywhere, Lord of the Abyss—even inside the great darkness that you have guarded for so many ages. But as to why I am manifest here . . . A robed hand stretched out and, for a brief second, he could make out the barest shape of skeletal fingers resting on the vacuole's surface. *It is almost time for them to rest.*

Forty-Five Lives

Kharsan

'So we can't just go through the gateway and collapse it behind us?'

I knew there had to be a catch. It's some law of the universe that nothing is ever as easy as you hope it might be.

'That is correct,' said Tao. 'The gateway must be active if the Lady Elemental is to destroy it.' He turns to Alice. 'Do you know how long it will take?'

She shakes her head nervously. In spite of her assurances, I know that she is in over her head. Given the alternatives, though, this is the best option.

'So we will have to hold them off till the last minute, and then retreat into the gateway as it collapses.' Tao makes it sound simple.

'Shade can slow down most of the soldiers,' says Violetta. 'But he can't touch the golems. They're too powerful.'

'They are limited by their physical form,' contributes Adam. 'Their movements can be hampered and their senses confused by attacking both their limbs and heads. But they are still dangerous.

'Can your . . . abilities affect them directly? Can you reach into them?' he asks Tao as I wonder the same thing. This would be a lot easier if he could just sabotage their circuits or gears, or whatever those golems have.

Tao shakes his head. 'I cannot intrude easily on bodies or objects that are controlled by the will of others. And the will of these creatures is stronger than most.' He turns towards the stone altar in the middle of the room and, as he does so, it shatters into large, jagged pieces. 'However, this should be sufficient to hold them back for some time.'

'I'd better get started, then,' says Alice doubtfully, moving to the back of the chamber.

'Good luck,' I offer, though it does little to alleviate the grey uncertainty that seems to be hanging over her. I didn't ask what happened to the fox-woman, but I'm guessing that it wasn't good.

I can hear the soldiers approaching already. Hard, regular footsteps, interspersed with dull thuds that I can only imagine belong to the golems.

Violetta and Tao move to either side of the door in preparation. They can begin the defence even before the door itself is breached, and that leaves Adam and me to take care of those who make it through.

I sigh quietly. This is going to take more than a stun baton.

I go over to where our unconscious prisoner is. Given the cold-blooded efficiency of this entire place, I somehow doubt that using him as a hostage is going to give us any advantage. I turn him over on his side. Let's see, now . . . Yes, there it is.

The gun he was reaching for when Adam struck him is still there—a 9mm pistol. I recognize the type from some of the armaments in Eden. Though I never practised, I did learn to shoot.

Further searching reveals two spare magazines. Forty-five rounds in total. In someone like Adam's hands, that's forty-five lives . . . I steel myself. They will be attacking us directly. And I promised to keep them safe. I made those stupid bloody oaths.

And now it's no longer about just Adam or Violetta. Everyone here is here because I asked them to be here. Even Alice, looking up at the ceiling and muttering to herself as she tries to figure out how to do something that I can only imagine is inconceivably complex. For them, this is the least I can do, and I suppose it's also the best way to protect my own life. After all, I've never seen myself fitting the role of a completely (or, honestly, even mostly) selfless person.

I move to the centre of the room. The remnants of the altar make for decent cover. Adam also waits there.

When I reach him . . . it's strange. He's looking over at Roth's unconscious body with an odd expression. It takes a moment to identify the emotion, as I've never seen it on Adam's face.

Doubt.

'Are you all right?' I ask.

He nods slowly, and then looks down at his hands. His small hands. I normally have no idea what is going on in that head of his, but for a second there, I understand. I quickly look around at the others, and I can feel the same thing. Everyone gathered here is . . . unique. But that does not matter. They are more than supernatural oddities in the same way that my brother is more than a weapon.

I try a reassuring smile. 'Let's get out of here in one piece, okay?'

He looks up at me, and I can see the doubt fading. He nods again, this time with determination. 'Brother,' he says decisively, 'thank you for coming to rescue me.'

I blink, having no idea how I should react to that, so I just nod back and take cover next to him.

As I take aim at the door, I look at him. 'Don't die,' I say. 'And try not to let anyone else die either.'

'Yes, brother,' he says with a grin. And then, in a movement so casual that I don't even think to react to it, he places one hand on the side of my head.

'Sleep,' he says.

Elemental

Alice

The sight of Kharsan dropping limply to the floor is enough to shatter what little concentration I managed to gather.

'What—' I splutter in full confused splutter mode. 'Why . . . You . . .' I close my eyes and take a deep breath before almost yelling, 'Will you please stop randomly knocking people out!'

Tao and Vi both look back to see what's happening, though neither of them seems to react much. In fact, they turn around almost immediately. I'm guessing there's enough going on outside to occupy their attention.

Adam carefully takes the gun from Kharsan's hand and places it atop the remains of the altar. 'He did not wish for me to be a murderer,' he says quietly. 'I do not wish for him to be a killer.'

He moves forward to stand in front of the door, leaving me with the option of either continuing to splutter and wait for us all to get captured or killed, or get back to what I'm supposed to be doing.

With one last look at Kharsan, I try and focus again.

I've been forced into that Limbo twice now—the first time courtesy of Kit and whatever that venom was, and again when Shade attacked. I try to remember what it felt like. It wasn't like being ripped out of my body, but more like being forced *into* it. Compressed so far into my own consciousness that it rebounds. And in that moment of expansion, I could see a reality that intersects with all possible realities—I try to remember that too. A space that can be used to create links from one world to another.

296

Trying to force that sensation is painful. Like using just your fingernails to climb a mountain. Maybe I should just ask Vi if she can have her shadow-monster attack me again. A brief glance forward puts that in the impossible column. Vi's kneeling down in fatigue, the Shadow stretched out under and beyond the door, and I can hear the resulting shouts and confusion. Tao stands perfectly still but, at the same time, he seems to be almost trembling. I hear louder thumps from outside.

No. I need to concentrate.

Maybe just pushing inwards isn't enough. Maybe . . .

I can feel my skin start to crawl as the colours flow across it. Slowly, I try pulling air towards myself. Not a whole lot—I can't afford to just suck this entire area dry—but enough so that it's a layer around me. And bit by bit, while focusing inwards, I start forcing power into that layer.

Because the source of that power is through the Aether that Kit was talking about—Limbo, where all-powerful phantom me resides. That's where the links that bind me, or my consciousness, or my inner power, to every atom of air in the atmosphere are. So if I can somehow channel that in the right way and just . . .

The pain blankets all other thought. It's like being torn straight down the middle by a blunt, chipped knife.

Then, like scales tipping over the balance point, there's this brief feeling of weightlessness, and then . . . I can feel my eyes squeezed shut, tears leaking from the corners. I'm not in that place. I didn't succeed. I'm still standing like a fool in the middle of an underground room and bad things are about to happen to everyone around me.

I shouldn't always be so pessimistic. I open my eyes and can't help but let out a small gasp of sheer and total wonder.

I can suddenly just . . . *see*. Everything. Every flowing thread of air. Every tiny detail. And how they all fit together on some tiny subatomic scale. Every spark of energy has its own colour. Every movement ripples.

So this is what it looks like when you can see realities intersect with one another.

I can see everyone else in the room in different ways as well. Vi, the sweat pouring down her brow with effort, the tiny blue fire-like links joining her and Shade, how the darkness of her own shadow is swallowed into him and the symbiosis between the pair. Shade himself is different. No longer just a creeping patch of darkness, but almost a visible, ghostlike apparition. Similar to what he looked like in our earlier encounter, but more powerful here in the real world. And, at the same time, he looks even more ragged, as if torn to shreds . . .

Tao—his physical image stands in the centre of a presence that fills the entire area. More than anyone here, he's linked to this world, his own body held together by the ability to make his surroundings part of himself, manipulating them.

Adam—I can barely see him. A slim, dark arrow, somehow existing almost independently of the world around him.

Even Kharsan. I can see the way his body heat flows into the air, and the barest glimmer as his unconscious mind works on the edge of dreams.

And to one side, where our precious base commander is, I can make out the link between him and the portal, sustaining its existence with a force as strong as life itself. Which does remind me that I don't really have the luxury to spend my time gawking around in wonder.

I take one sharp step back, triggering the gateway. The world around me seems to blur and twist as a physical link is created between two different planes of existence. Through the wider gate, I can see them now—the thin pulsing wires that reach through and circle outwards, outside the door and beyond. The links that keep the metal monsters powered.

298

Even as I think that, the door of the chamber bursts open with one such metal monster forcing its way in. Adam leaps to intercept it, his movements a blur as he tries to push it off balance. Tao's awareness stretches back for a second, and a small stone from the broken altar rockets forward to strike the creature's head.

I wonder if I should try and help . . . No. This is not the time to go all scatterbrained and do a dozen things at once.

Carefully, I look over the framework of the gateway. Severing the link with Roth and collapsing the framework—this is way beyond a simple forest of thorns.

Breathing evenly, I try and gather more and more power, pouring it into the layer around me. It's easier than it was a minute ago.

A couple of soldiers break in behind the golem. Shade moves like a serpent, and they crumple to the ground. Adam takes the opportunity to trip the golem over one of them. It falls into the doorway with a loud crash.

The power keeps flowing. It's almost automatic now. I can see it enveloping me . . . and more than that. It's like parts of it are leaking out. Black, vapour-like threads escaping upwards. They burn the air as they float.

Almost there. I open my mouth to call the others. To tell them to get ready to pull back. Which is why it's a moment of pure panic when I realize that I can't get the words out. The power keeps growing, and I realize with a sick feeling that I'm no longer fully in control of this. It's escaping like water from a blown reservoir—threatening to take on a form of its own.

I can feel the escaping threads starting to knit together, trying to bridge the gap and create something. A presence. Something powerful beyond all words and descriptions. Something so massive that it almost seems to warp reality. Something that can destroy anything it touches.

It's pulling me along for the ride, and I can *feel* it, like this total high . . . I could do anything. I could bring down this entire mountain on our heads, and I just know I'd be able to walk out alive. But no one else would.

Just like leaving Kit behind.

I start to panic. The others seem to have noticed that something's wrong because they start retreating to the broken altar. Tao's presence pushes forward with near-solid intensity, stopping waves of bullets.

Just as I can feel myself starting to break apart, though, I have this totally surreal moment where I can almost feel the rush of the wind outside flowing across me. I realize that the power's breached the confines of the mountain, but this feeling—it reminds me of what the Snowman had said. *'They were the wind, the water, the fire and the earth, and they were the story of each.'* And what Kit had tried to teach me right from the start. Why she told me so many stories. About the power of them, of how they can . . .

I stop fighting the flow for a second and try thinking along a different line. I look at the others—Adam, Tao, Vi, Kharsan—and think about how weirdly different we are. But we're all just trying to get through this in one piece.

I get it then. The flow stabilizes, and I reach out. I can do this. I can get them all through the gateway, and break the structure just as it happens. And no one else needs to get hurt.

I know I can do this, 'cause right in this moment, this tiny frozen second in time, I get it. This is *my* story. And I don't know much, and the stuff that I do know is all sorts of questionable, but I do know this . . .

I look around at everyone as the black threads seem to fill the entire world.

Here and now, we're all way too young to die.

What Comes After

Kharsan and Alice

I wake up on a moving stretcher. Never a good sign.

'Stay still,' mutters a voice in my ear. I look up at the medic pushing the stretcher, her face covered with a surgical mask, showing only a familiar pair of green eyes.

The fox. Kit.

'My brother, the others—' I whisper. 'What happened?'

'Alice got them out,' she says. 'A little awkwardly, but she is just getting a handle on her abilities. You should be grateful that she left you behind. You might not have survived that journey.'

'Uh-huh.' I try looking around warily.

There's a lot of dust, shouting and general confusion. There are other people also being carried on stretchers or limping along. We're outside, on some kind of helipad. I can hear the whir of helicopter blades and the whine of VTOL engines.

'What's going on?'

'Evacuation,' she says. 'Thankfully, there are a lot of unconscious people and even more confusion. Everyone's being airlifted out to the nearest military outpost, and they hope to sort things out from there.' She winks. 'I think that gives us a few opportunities to slip away.'

I stare up at her incredulously. This creature has an inordinate amount of confidence.

'I need to find Adam.'

'Eventually.' She shrugs. 'A little independence might do him some good. For the moment, your energies might be better spent elsewhere.'

We come to a stop at the end of a long line. Ahead, a man in uniform is waving people back. Kit inclines her head towards the other soldiers.

'Your parents used to be part of this organization?'

I nod. 'A long time ago. And much to their regret, I believe.'

'There are many paths to saving the world, Khadim,' she says with a touch of grimness. 'I think you might be the right person to decide which paths have too many consequences. Do you know where to find your father?'

I think about it. 'No, but I know where to start looking.' I clench my hands. Home. Sooner or later, we all go home.

Ahead, a large transport touches down, the cargo doors opening with a thump.

'I will need some help,' I say as the people ahead start to board.

She gives me a quizzical look, pushing the stretcher again.

'Citizen or not,' I mutter, 'I have a feeling that getting back to London from here is going to take something akin to magic. The tales you hear about immigration are bloody terrifying.'

As we move into the plane's cargo hold, I can't help but notice that her eyes are gleaming with mischief and that she's grinning underneath her mask. That makes me shiver.

'I think,' she says as the doors close behind us, 'that we can manage something.'

❦

When my vision clears and I finally feel like I'm no longer being torn apart by massive mystical forces, it comes with this weird kind of calm.

I have no idea where I am. I have no idea how I got here. I have no idea where anyone else is. But all that's fine. I'm optimistic that I somehow managed to not only collapse the gateway but also get everyone out safely, and everything is going to work out perfectly . . .

Okay, so that lasted two seconds. Time to panic.

'Alice, where are we?' asks someone, and I whirl around to see Vi standing there, shielding her eyes against the sun.

'Um . . . good question.'

I look around. It's somewhere outside and desert-like, judging from the sand and the bright glaring sun. There's a road up ahead. I suppose this could be some kind of supernatural hell—but then an old Toyota trundles past, making me think probably not.

There's no sign of the others. I try and remember what happened. I remember feeling the gateway start to collapse, and then reaching out to grab the others with tendrils of air. And then everything just went blinding white.

Did I get everyone? I think I did.

'Do you remember what happened?' I try asking Vi.

She shrugs. 'It was very sudden. Shade says you pulled us all into the gateway, but then it kind of went wrong. I think, instead of getting back to the Dark Roads, we got tossed out at some other exit point.'

Great. Random teleportation. I'm surprised I'm not panicking more. Maybe it's the adrenaline.

I do a quick inventory check. I still have Kit's package with all the passports and stuff. And my backpack. I look inside and pull out the Arcanus, the Book of Souls.

All this trouble over one book . . .

'We did it, didn't we?' asks Vi. 'We stopped them.'

I can't help but smile at that, but then my inner cynic kicks in. 'For now,' I mutter glumly.

303

It's strange, but I don't feel all that terrified about what comes next. We survived. Maybe what's coming next is worse; but for now, maybe surviving is enough, and we can take a moment to relax and be normal.

No. Kit's gone. Everyone I know is back in Hong Kong with no idea where I am. And I'm in the middle of nowhere with a twelve-year-old girl and her personal shadow-demon. There is no road that leads back to normal.

But maybe there is a way forward. I heft the book. I can find answers. And I have Kit's contacts and everything she taught me.

'Come on,' I say to Vi. 'We need to start walking. We can follow the road to the nearest town, and from there . . . we figure out what's next.'

She nods solemnly and picks up her own pack.

I take a deep breath. Focus on the problem. Focus on the solution. Magic is back in the world. Also, that may be causing the end of the world. And just maybe I can do something about it. I mean, I know I'm not some hero or whatever, but that doesn't mean that I don't want to be.

So, before we head out, I figure it's time to learn a little more about this weird world. Time for some real answers.

With something almost like excitement, I crack open the Arcanus.

Oh. Damn.

'Hey, Vi?' I call out. 'How's that shadow of yours with ancient, really-weird-looking languages?'

Okay, so maybe I can wait a little longer for answers.

Epilogue: Threads of a Changing World

'All passengers flying on Introspect Airlines 641 are requested to report for security check.'

The sounds of the airport filled the lounge. From the slightly tinny announcements to the soft conversations, even the subtle sound of suitcase wheels—they all swept around the area, bringing with them a reassuring sense of calm.

Madeline gently sipped her latte. She had developed a fondness for airports, and this particular lounge in Frankfurt's main terminal was a favourite of hers. The soft lighting over the orange and brown shades of the furniture, and the scent of freshly roasted coffee beans—it was almost as relaxing as visiting a school.

Between sips, she idly listened to the conversations of other passengers. She didn't bother much with the contents, preferring to read the tones instead. The low strain of bored words, spilled out to pass the time. The quiet anger of an argument, caged by the necessity of not making a scene. The sparks of flirtation flying at a chance meeting. There was a certain music to it all.

After the cup was empty, she pulled out her cell phone. It had been designed to look like a regular phone, and as far as most features went, it was, in fact, a regular phone. The one major modification that her employers had installed, though, was making it completely and absolutely untraceable and impervious to any form of electronic surveillance known to mankind.

And on her travels, she'd met a few clever people, one of whom had further modified the device so that it was selectively invisible to her employers as well.

Taking care to note that there was no one within earshot, she dialled the number from memory. It rang four times. A simple no-frills ringtone that almost caused Madeline to smile. It fit the personality.

'You're late,' said the cold, brittle voice of the woman on the other end of the line.

'I was waiting to see if any new information was going to surface. As it turns out, it didn't.' Truthfully, she hadn't expected it to, but it was always better to be cautious.

There was a pause. 'Deacon's Hill?'

'Evacuation began two days ago. With confirmation that the Shadow has indeed left Santor as well as the destruction of Eden, my "superiors" have decided that a permanent base there is not in their best interests. Not to mention the failure of that particular batch of sentries.'

'Ha! They're offered ancient and terrible power, and they decide to create bloody toys. Do you think they'll try again?'

'Yes, though they will find it challenging without the Arcanus,' she said, thinking of the secondary facility already under construction in South America. 'From their perspective, the sentries have a unique purpose. They're almost like an extension of the Black Rangers. Small, specialized units in possession of enough power to decapitate any "unstable" government. It would certainly be a lot more effective than their current methods.'

'You've certainly got that right,' said the voice dryly. 'Now, what are the other details?'

'Not much. The captain and his Rangers have been pulled into reserve for now. The psi ops team has been relocated and temporarily hospitalized—they were in pretty bad shape.

Also, Roth was found comatose after the incident. Personally, I'd have preferred that he died, but this is an acceptable alternative.'

'I thought you said he was a very useful individual.'

'Indeed,' said Madeline sincerely. 'But he's also intelligent and highly adaptable. He would have proved a hindrance sooner or later. There were no fatalities save Jhakri, but we expected that already. Regarding the children—there was no sign of them. No bodies, so we should assume that they're all still alive.'

'Good. It would have been better if we had them under control, but still . . .'

Madeline understood. Even the fact that they existed was good enough.

The voice continued. 'What about eyewitnesses? Do we have confirmation of what happened?'

'Most of the soldiers were too close to the source to make sense of it. They report black clouds and smoke, odd sensations and noises—but that's about it. There was an incoming helicopter at a sufficient distance, though. Unfortunately, only one of the crew happened to look out at the Hill. According to him, it looked like an enormous black creature had perched on top of the mountain. He avoids using the word "dragon", but I think it's safe to assume.'

'I knew it!' the voice hissed. 'I could *feel* it, even from here. Did your organization manage to find the Elemental?'

'Unfortunately, our biggest lead was a bust,' said Madeline with regret. 'Sun Alice. Her body—or what was left of it—was found in Victoria Harbour last week. But we have other possibilities.

'By the way, did you get my earlier report?'

'About Sheol? Yes. It's good to know that he, at least, seems fooled by your apparent humanity. He always was a blind fool.'

'Yes.' Madeline checked her watch. It was almost time to board. 'That's all the news I have for now. I'm returning to headquarters for a full debriefing.'

'Be careful. Your position is not as secure as it could be.'

'Speaking of, how are you enjoying English politics?'

The voice took on a tired edge. 'Not at all. I did find quite a unique assistant, however, and I tell myself I'm at least having a better time of it than dear Genevieve. Corporate America does not seem to be her favourite playfield.'

'She'll adapt,' said Madeline. 'She's good at that.'

'Of course. I'd suggest you keep in touch with her, though. We may have to act quickly in the coming months.'

Madeline frowned. 'Has something happened?'

'You know about the fire, yes?'

'I read the reports,' she confirmed.

'It may be the real thing. And there's another particularly troublesome variable that's entered the equation.'

'What is it?'

'Jack is in London.'

The name rang a faint bell, but it still took Madeline's memory a few seconds to connect it to a form. 'I see,' she said. 'Well, I'm sure you can handle *one* toothless dog.'

'I suppose that I will have to.'

The phone cut off.

Madeline folded it away, and got to her feet. The boarding call had just been announced. She hummed quietly to herself as she pulled her luggage behind her. Flying was another thing she quite enjoyed.

The human world really did have so many wonderful things to look forward to.

The man sat on a clean cloth that had been laid under the shade of the willow tree, his eyes half-closed as the wind rustled in the branches.

He cradled a small earthenware bowl in his left hand, a matching bottle standing on the cloth next to him. As a sparrow settled down in the subtly overgrown garden, he raised the bowl to his lips and took a small sip of the colourless liquid.

'You're really taking this getting-into-character thing way too far,' said a voice from behind him.

He smiled slightly before moving to refill the bowl. 'I trust you have been successful,' he said.

A vixen with two tails slunk into the garden. Even if one ignored the second tail, it did not have much of the appearance of a real animal. Her lush, sleek fur shone far too brightly, a small white leaf-like pattern on her forehead, and her narrow green eyes were lit with sparks of deep cunning. A ceremonial form almost.

She sat carefully at the foot of the tree, taking a moment to inhale the clear, fresh air of her homeland.

'Yes,' she said. 'Abby's incursion and the humans' plans have been stopped for the moment. And the children—they are now irrevocably part of each other's stories. The girl was a bit out of her depth getting them out of Deacon's Hill. They got scattered at different exit points, so we'll just have to see how well they cope on their own for a while. Though I am confident they'll land on their feet.'

'Good. It couldn't have worked out better. You did take your time coming here, though. Were there any problems?'

'Had to help someone out for a bit. Also, a small issue with a corpse. Just a few loose ends.' She yawned, her long pink tongue curling slightly at the tip. 'I'm not going to bore you with all the details.'

The man took another sip, before looking at her with a hint of wearied amusement. 'Especially if the details weren't part of the arrangement. Tell me, Trickster, do you still despise me so much?'

She tilted her head in surprise. 'Do you really need to ask?'

'No,' said the man. 'I suppose I don't. No matter—you may consider your debt cleared. Though you are, of course, free to involve yourself on your own initiative.'

'I'll have to think about that.' While she'd never been fond of a quiet existence, there was such a thing as too much excitement. 'Oh, Abby sends his love.'

'Really?' asked the man wryly.

'Well, he threatened to kill everyone and said the Abyss will consume us all, so basically, his version of love.'

The man sighed. 'Whatever am I going to do with that demon?' He set the bowl down and leaned back to look at the speckles of blue sky that broke through the tree branches. 'One last matter—did you confirm what I'd asked you to?'

She nodded hesitantly. 'As much as it could be confirmed. There's so little left of him. He doesn't remember anything. He doesn't even seem to remember what he *is*. Or used to be.'

'But he is alive,' said the man with no small amount of satisfaction. 'Tell me, what name is he known by?'

'Shade,' said Kit quietly. 'He is called Shade.'

Acknowledgments

Thank you to my family for driving me crazy enough to write, and then being supportive after realizing that was something I was actually doing.

Thanks to Jit Chowdury and Meena Rajasekeran for creating the amazing book cover.

Thanks also to everyone at Penguin Random House India for their hard work and faith in the book: publishers Hemali Sodhi and Sohini Mitra, publicists Piya Kapur and Srishti Katiyar, and especially the editors who worked on it—Nimmy Chacko, Niyati Dhuldhoya and Kankana Basu.

A special thanks to Ameya Nagarajan, whose continued interest in a still unfinished story about Theseus was the seed for the Great War and made this book possible. I'll finish writing that book one of these days, I promise.

And to my friends Aditya Vishwanath and Gaurika Kapoor—thanks for being around and showing me that even though the world is a dark, dismal place that is probably doomed to oblivion, it doesn't mean we can't laugh about it.